REVENGE

CORRUPT EMPIRE
BOOK THREE

SARAH BAILEY

Cover Art by Sarah Bailey

Published by Twisted Tree Publications
www.twistedtreepublications.com
info@twistedtreepublications.com

Paperback ISBN: 978-1-913217-02-0

This book is dedicated to Avery & Aiden
You're two imperfect souls who found each other in
the dark in the midst of tragedy & sorrow
Thank you for telling me your story

PROLOGUE

Avery

Blood.

There was so much blood everywhere.

It soaked through my clothes. I felt it on my face, in my hair, on my skin. The metallic smell made my stomach roil in protest.

What the fuck had I done?

How had it come to this?

In all my darkest moments, I never imagined I'd have to fight this hard to survive. Just to see the next day. To have a future where monsters didn't walk the halls and taunt me with their awful deeds.

My heart thumped against my chest. It didn't negate what I'd done. I had to. I was fighting for something so much bigger than this.

The door beyond opened. I clutched the knife in my hand tighter.

Who the hell was this?

I couldn't let anyone see me covered in blood. They'd know what I'd done.

I looked up, catching sight of their face. The knife clattered on the floor as it dropped from my hand. And a gut wrenching sob emitted from my lips.

I fell to my knees.

"Avery?"

ONE

Avery

The past six weeks had been the best and worst of my life. There was never a point where I considered turning back. Where I decided it wasn't worth sacrificing everything for. It could spectacularly blow up in our faces after tonight, but I'd never look back and regret the actions I took to secure the downfall of my own family, the business and everyone connected to it.

I felt like the whole room was staring at us with shock and confusion. No one had been expecting me to get up here and announce to the world I was marrying Tristan Shaw. It was the one thing I hadn't really wanted to do, make this announcement, but I had to.

Did I care I'd just lied to everyone?

Not particularly.

I'd spent the past six weeks lying to Frazier Shaw. Convincing him I was willing to marry his son. So this wasn't really any different. Aiden told me I'd become quite the actress. The only time I'd been myself was when we were alone or amongst friends. Those friends had been instrumental in making sure we achieved our goals.

This would all be over soon. And I'd finally be free to call myself by my new name.

Miss Daniels didn't exist any longer.

Mrs Lockhart had taken her place.

Six weeks prior

"And how exactly are we going to go about doing that?" I asked, staring up at Aiden with wide eyes.

He shifted on his feet, handing me back the document.

"You might not like my idea."

"Aiden…"

"Frazier wants your money, that much is clear."

I couldn't believe my father had agreed to this clause. It completely negated everything he'd said to me in the past. About how I would go on to take over the world by myself. And yet, as it stated in black and white, if I was to marry before my twenty fifth birthday, full control of my trust fund would revert to my husband. Essentially, they'd have the power to take my inheritance from me if they wanted. The wording made it very clear.

"And he can have it if I marry Tristan."

As if I didn't hate my father enough, this was the fucking icing on the cake. I wanted to tear up the paperwork. I threw it into the pile and looked at my feet. Outrage bubbled up inside me. The fact that he'd ever even think this was an acceptable thing to do to me made me sick. Fuck him.

Aiden nudged the paperwork away with his foot before kneeling in front of me and taking my hand.

"You're never marrying that cunt. You're mine."

He was right. I wouldn't marry Tristan. We'd been over this before. Nothing had changed. The only person I wanted was right in front of me. And he was already mine.

"I don't even want the money."

He stroked his thumb over my palm.

"Princess…"

"I thought this couldn't get any worse, but it has. I knew deep down it was about the money. If that's what they want, I'll give it to them. They can have it all as long as they leave me alone."

"Do you mean that?"

I shook my head. I didn't want Frazier getting his hands on my trust fund. The plans I had for it were important. If we were going to save all the girls my family had abused, then I'd need that money. There was no if about it. We were going to save those girls if it was the last fucking thing we did.

"I want to punish him. No… I want to punish both of them."

"I know."

I looked up at him. His grey eyes were full of compassion. Something I never thought I'd ever see when I first met him. I didn't know he was capable of it. Aiden had changed so much in the time we'd known each other. Changed in ways I never expected.

"What's your plan?"

He let go of my hand, rubbing the back of his neck.

"We can't let them get hold of your money. Four years is too long to wait until you have full control."

"Well yeah, Frazier isn't likely to drop this subject any time soon."

If I knew anything about the man, it was that he was like a fucking dog with a bone when he wanted something.

"Then we just need to make sure someone you trust has control of it."

His words made my skin prickle. What did he mean by that? That I should just get married?

"If you're suggesting I have a fake marriage to someone just so we can keep Frazier from getting it, then you can just stop right there."

"Not a fake marriage, no."

I raised my eyebrows. Maybe I was being completely dense, but this didn't seem like something Aiden would ever suggest in a million years. I mean, he did want me to get fake engaged to Tristan at one point, but that was in the past.

"Aiden, please don't be cryptic. I'm not in the mood for guessing games."

He reached up, cupping my face and stroking my cheek with his thumb.

"Marry me, Avery."

Did I mishear him? What the fuck did he just say to me?

"W…What?"

"Marry me."

6

I jerked away from him, falling back onto my hands. Marriage? Was he really asking me to marry him just so Frazier wouldn't get access to my trust fund?

"Are you fucking nuts?"

He smiled, shaking his head.

"No."

"Please be serious."

"I am."

He reached for me again, but I scrambled back out of his grasp. He was fucking crazy. Absolutely batshit crazy.

"No. No, we're not doing this."

I got up off the floor, putting my hands up. It's not like I didn't want to marry Aiden. Hell, I knew I wanted this man for life, but this isn't how I wanted things to be. I wanted us to be free from all the shit with my family so we could have a future together. I wanted him to propose to me because he really wanted to marry me, not just to get me out of this shitty situation with my trust fund money.

"Princess…"

"Take it back. Please, don't do this now. Not like this. I don't want it to be for this reason."

He put his hand out to me.

"Come here."

"No."

I shook my head, taking a further step back.

"Avery, come here."

"No. Not like this, Aiden. No."

He got to his feet, his grey eyes turning dark. I tried to back away further, but he caught my arm and dragged me closer. He held me in place, staring down at me intently.

"Let go of me," I whispered.

I wanted to be away from him at that moment. There were too many thoughts rushing around in my head. How could Aiden think this is how I wanted our relationship to move forward? It felt so fucking wrong. All I wanted was for us to be free. Free from all our burdens so we could be together openly.

"No, we're going to talk about this and I'm not letting you run away. Not like last time."

My stomach dropped out from under me. Last time we'd talked about engagements and marriage, I'd left him. But that hadn't been about us getting married.

"That's not fair."

"When has there ever been anything fair about us? There's no fucking fair in our relationship. There's just you and me."

I couldn't exactly deny that. Our relationship had been messy from the start, but we'd worked it out somehow.

"Aiden—"

"Do you think I'm just saying this to make sure Frazier doesn't get hold of your trust fund?"

I nodded. What was the point in denying it?

"I wasn't going to give this to you until your birthday."

He let go of my arms and dug something out of his pocket, turning my palm up and placing it in my hand. I was rendered incapable of all speech. I couldn't even move. After a long moment of silence between us, he reached over and opened the little box for me. Tears welled in my eyes at the sight of what was nestled inside.

"When did you get this?" I whispered.

"The day after Josh was born."

"And you've been carrying it around in your pocket this whole time?"

He nodded before he rubbed the back of his neck.

"I've never pretended to be anything else other than what I am. Before I met you, I never wanted any of this. I'd have gone the rest of my life alone and closed off from the world. Then I met a girl with a fiery temper and doe eyes I can never resist. You're the light of my life."

Nestled inside the box was a pair of silver angel wing earrings. He took the box from me. Brushing my hair back, he secured the earrings in my ears, smiling when he stepped back.

"I want to marry you because I love you, princess. So fucking what if we have to speed up the process to keep you safe. You must know I'd do anything for you by now."

He slipped the empty box back in his pocket before taking my hand. I didn't know what to say. What to think. Even if we did go through with this, we'd still have a world of trouble to deal with.

I needed a minute. Looking down at my hand in his, I took a breath. All my feelings were conflicted. I wanted to be Aiden's wife. Take his name as my own. I'd known that for weeks. It started before Rick took me. Despite everything, my heart was irrevocably his.

Could we really do this?

Wasn't it completely insane?

When had anything between Aiden and I been sane?

"I… I can't give you an answer right now."

That was the honest truth. Too much to process all at once. I rubbed my forehead with my free hand, trying to numb the pain starting to radiate from my temple.

Aiden dropped my hand and captured me up in his arms, cradling me close. He leant his cheek on top of my head.

"Why is everything in our lives always so complicated?"

9

He didn't answer me. I wasn't expecting him to. It was complicated because I was a Daniels and he was the man I wasn't supposed to fall in love with. Wasn't supposed to know intimately. Hell, he wasn't meant to tell me the truth about my family and set me on this path.

What if I wasn't there that night? I might well have ended up never knowing how awful they were. I shuddered at the thought. Never knowing Aiden. Never truly knowing myself. Those were not outcomes I wanted to consider.

"Can I just say this proposal is worse than Ben's?"

He laughed, pulling away slightly to look down at me.

"Should I try again?"

"No…"

He kissed my forehead.

"That means yes."

I was about to protest, but he was right. If he was serious, then he'd do it properly. I stepped away, folding my arms over my chest.

"Even if you do, that doesn't guarantee I'll answer."

He shrugged before he grabbed me by the waist and hoisted me over his shoulder like I was a ragdoll.

"What the hell are you doing?"

He walked out of the room, leaving me dangling precariously over him.

"Taking you to bed so I can fuck you."

I felt my cheeks burn and heat flooded my veins. Was it really necessary for him to carry me like this? He could've just told me he wanted to fuck me. I would've come willingly.

"So what, you're going to act like a caveman?"

He placed me down on the bed when we reached it, pulling down my pyjama shorts and underwear in the process. I hadn't bothered getting dressed since we weren't leaving the flat. He ripped off my t-shirt, leaving me naked before crawling over me.

"No, just a bad boy."

I snorted. He really was idiotic sometimes. I liked this side of him. Where he made jokes with me. His grey eyes glinted.

"Is said bad boy expecting me to just let him take advantage of me?"

He took my hands, pinning them above my head.

"Mmm, yes. I intend to take many liberties."

I squirmed beneath him. He could take all the liberties with me he liked. I was his to command.

"Tell me what you want."

"Just you. Only you. Forever."

Before I could respond, Aiden kissed me like he was drowning in me. And I forgot all about my trust fund and his sudden proposal. When Aiden and I touched it was like fire burning in my chest and heat spread between my thighs.

"I love you, princess," he whispered as he kissed down my jaw.

He pulled away, leaning over towards the bedside table. Opening the drawer, he tugged out two sets of handcuffs. He cuffed me to the headboard, smiling at me with his grey eyes glittering.

"You're so fucking beautiful."

He spread my legs wide with both hands and stared down at me. His expression was that of a hungry beast ready to devour his prey. That prey just happened to be me. I squirmed again. His gaze heated my entire body, scorching my skin.

He leant down, giving me no warning when he bit down hard on my nipple. I bucked against the handcuffs and him, moaning. His hands pressed me back down on the bed, fingertips brushing down my stomach.

"Who do you belong to?" he said, the rich timbre of his voice vibrating through me.

"You."

"That's right. Mine."

He ran his tongue down my stomach, flicking over my bellybutton before continuing his path towards my pussy. I couldn't breathe.

"I can't wait to see your skin covered in art, princess. You'll be even more stunning. My tattooed beauty."

"Does that make you my beast?" I whispered.

He glanced up at me, a wicked grin on his face.

"Only if you say yes."

He spread me open with his fingers and then his tongue lashed against my clit. I lost all sense of rationality in that moment. Aiden mastered my body. He commanded every inch of it. His tongue was magic. And I was under his spell.

He pulled away abruptly, trailing kisses up my inner thigh.

"Say yes, princess. Marry me," he whispered against my skin.

"Aiden…"

His fingers brushed over my entrance, causing me to twitch before he pressed one inside me.

"Say yes."

I moaned as he pressed another inside me. How I fucking wished it was his cock. I needed it. Hell, I really needed him to fuck me hard. His breath fluttered over my clit, rendering me completely at his mercy.

"Aiden, please."

"Marry me."

His tongue met my clit again and I swear I almost combusted on the spot. His tongue and fingers worked me until I was dangling precariously over the edge. Only then did he pull back, kissing my thigh again.

"Please, that's not fair."

"Mmm, what do you want?"

"I want you to fuck me and let me come, that's what I want."

I stared down at him. He was grinning. I wanted him to let me out of these handcuffs so I could give him a piece of my mind. Also, I wanted to pin him down on the bed and ride his cock, but that was beside the point. He was deliberately driving me crazy. I knew his game.

"Are you sure you don't want anything else?"

I glared at him. I'd already told him I wasn't giving him an answer. How could I? My mind was a mess of conflicting thoughts and emotions. And it didn't help that he had me handcuffed to the bed and was driving me to distraction with his tongue and his fingers.

"Take your clothes off and fuck me."

His eyes darkened. He withdrew his fingers from me and rose up on his knees.

"Did you forget the rules, Avery?"

The ones about him having my submission in the bedroom? Well no, but he was testing my patience. I wasn't in the mood for this. Tension radiated throughout my body, desperately seeking a release.

"No."

"I think you have."

He slipped off the bed, walking away towards his cupboard. He'd moved the stuff out of the box under his bed so we'd have easier access to it.

"Aiden—"

"I suggest you stop talking unless you want me to leave you alone, worked up and unable to touch yourself."

I snapped my mouth shut. What the hell had gotten into him? Was this because I wouldn't give him a straight answer about whether I wanted to get married to him or not? Was he punishing me?

I shifted, trying to ease the tension inside me, but failing miserably.

"Stay still, Avery."

He brought two lengths of silk rope with him. Kneeling on the bed, he grabbed one of my ankles and tied the rope to it before securing the other ankle. He shifted off the bed and secured the other ends, leaving me spread wide and immobile.

"Are you punishing me?" I whispered, knowing this would likely get me into even more trouble.

He stroked a hand down my calf. The touch electrified my skin. I desperately wanted those hands in other places. I didn't fucking care about being tied up or at his mercy. All I wanted was Aiden. His touch. His tongue. His mouth. His words. His cock.

"Do you think you deserve pleasure, princess?"

I knew the answer he wanted me to give.

"No."

He didn't react, merely trailed his fingers along the top of my foot.

"Tell me who you belong to."

"You."

"Do I have your submission?"

"Yes."

"Is it okay for you to tell me what to do?"

I shivered. His tone was cold, chilling me to the bone.

"No, it's not. I'm sorry."

His hand went to his jeans as he walked around the bed towards the headboard.

"I would've given you what you wanted, but now… now you're going to give me what I want."

When he slipped out of his clothes and knelt on the bed. I knew exactly what he was going to do. *Holy fuck.*

"Open your mouth and do not fucking close it, understood?"

I nodded. He straddled my chest, gripping my hair in one hand, holding it tight. I opened my mouth for him and he fed me his cock. This angle made it a little difficult for me to take too much of it. He fucked me with slow, shallow thrusts, staring down at my face intently.

"Do you remember the first time you sucked my cock? You were so innocent, so inexperienced. You wanted to please me. I could feel it in you. That's what you've always wanted, isn't it? I made you so reliant on me. You'd do anything for me."

The way he said those things made me shiver. He wasn't wrong. I was aware how fucked up it had all been, but he'd let me walk away and I'd come back. Come back because I loved him and I wanted everything he gave me. Isn't that the saying? Let someone go and if it's meant to be, they'll come back to you?

There'd been so little choice in the beginning of our relationship, at least for me. The day I'd left changed everything. It had forced Aiden to confront the truth of what he'd done and how he'd felt about me. And it had changed everything between us. Everything but this. When he took control of me in the bedroom. When I chose to submit.

"You drive me fucking crazy, princess. I want to be nestled between your legs, inside your heat, it's the sweetest fucking ecstasy."

He pulled out of my mouth and shifted back.

"I shouldn't give you this, but I need it. I want to make you scream."

Before I had a chance to make a sound, he was wedged between my legs and pressing inside me. His cock stretched me, making me groan.

"Fuck, so fucking hot and wet."

"Aiden…"

He captured my mouth, sealing away anything I'd wanted to say to him. His thrusts weren't gentle. He gripped my hips and fucked me, pressing deeper each time.

"Marry me."

Were we going to keep coming back to this? Him asking whilst he was brutally fucking me felt a little more appropriate given the nature of our relationship.

"I love you, princess," he whispered against my lips. "I want you forever. Take my name. Be my wife. Marry me."

His fingers drove between us, finding my clit as he stroked and fucked me. I cried out, unable to move because of how he'd tied me up and his bulk on top of me.

What was I really scared of? The fact that it was too soon? The fact that we weren't safe? Hell, I had to stop thinking like this. I was Aiden's and he was mine. We'd established that the day I left him. This was just an extension of that. Could I really think of Aiden as my husband?

"Yes."

As soon as the word left my lips, I felt myself fall right off the edge. I bucked against him, explosions going off along every inch of my skin. I didn't get to see Aiden's reaction to my answer. He didn't miss a beat, fucking me whilst I clenched and trembled around him.

I panted, opening my eyes as I stared up at him. He'd stilled, watching me with an unreadable expression.

"Say that again."

I bit my lip.

"Yes, I'll marry you."

His eyes softened. He leant down, capturing my mouth as he thrust inside me again. He fucked me hard until he grunted in my mouth, going rigid as he came too. He pulled away, resting his forehead on mine.

"Thank you."

"For what?"

"Agreeing to be my wife."

I smiled. I still had so many reservations about what we were doing, but there was one overriding factor.

I loved Aiden.

He loved me.

And that was the only reason I needed to say yes.

TWO

Aiden

Present Day

C huck stared at me for the longest time, his mouth hanging open.

"You're fucking kidding me," he said, rubbing his hand across his face.

I shrugged.

"I'm just fucking with you. I barely know your niece. Do you really think I'd keep that kind of shit from you?"

He shook his head, rolling his eyes.

"Fuck, Aiden, you scared the crap out of me for a moment there. Still, she shouldn't be marrying that little cunt. He's no good for her."

I'd just wanted to see Chuck's reaction. Avery would probably kill me for almost revealing the truth to him. My eyes flicked over to where she was still talking to the audience with Tristan beside her. I hated that she was holding his hand. The sick fuck looked so fucking smug. Too fucking bad for him. She was already my wife. My fucking wife.

"Didn't know you cared that much."

"Still my niece even if she does questionable things. We're getting off topic. You haven't explained what the fuck happened with you and Robert. Don't bullshit me."

I looked at my fingers, raising an eyebrow.

"He deserved it."

Chuck's expression darkened.

"I never said he didn't. My question is where are my girls?"

I shrugged again. They were safe with Tina. They were healing from the trauma of being stolen and sex trafficked. Raped. Beaten. Abused. They were being cared for now. No fucking thanks to Chuck and whoever The Collector was.

"Why would I know?"

"You fucking took them."

"Did I? Are you sure Robert told you the truth?"

The more I played with Chuck's paranoia, the better. I wanted him to distrust all his associates. Turn them all against each other. That's how we'd win. And I would fucking relish the day this was over. I could have a normal life with my wife when it was done. Something I desperately craved.

"What reason would he have to lie?"

"He got beaten the shit out of. His pride is bruised. Perhaps he lost them and didn't want to tell you or he wants to get back at me. Either way, why the fuck would I have touched them? Not my business. You know I don't want to be around that shit."

He stared at me for the longest moment. I could see the cogs turning in his head. Chuck trusted me. Too fucking much. Proving my loyalty to a man like Chuck was never easy, but the past four and a half years had shown him I was more than willing to get my hands dirty.

He turned from me, scanning the crowd. When his eyes met Robert, they narrowed.

"That little fuck. Trying to stir up shit."

He waved a hand at me.

"Say I believe he's lying, it still doesn't explain why your father is involved in all of this."

I'd have to give him something. Perhaps if I did, he'd let this shit go. Keeping Chuck on side was imperative. For now.

"Rick took your niece and Robert helped him."

Chuck turned back to me, his eyes widening.

"How the fuck do you know that?"

"Did you ask her what happened?"

He frowned.

"No, I didn't think it was important."

And that just proved to me how little he actually cared about Avery. He needed her to be the face of the company. That's all he cared about. Keeping face so no one would discover what kind of sick shit they did behind closed doors.

"She told John. You know Rick showed her some pretty disturbing things. Perhaps you should ask her about it."

Chuck's frown deepened.

"How does she know who he is?"

"She doesn't. She said he kept referring to her as 'darlin'."

I hated that fucking word almost as much as I hated the man himself. Even more so now I knew he'd called my fucking woman by it. She wasn't his darling. She was fucking mine. My wife. The need to have her by my side burnt through me. She'd had to take her ring off. It was sitting on the bedside table at home. Our home. No one would know she was really mine.

"Well fuck. If he's involved, the shit really has hit the fan."

He rubbed his head.

21

"This is a fucking disaster. Avery's gallivanting off to marry the Shaw cunt, Rick Morgan is in our fucking business all over again and I have two girls missing. What the fuck more can go wrong today?"

Watching Chuck's armour crack in front of my eyes gave me a smug sense of satisfaction. Now, all I had to do was use it to our advantage. I'd planted the seeds of doubt whilst proving he could still trust me. Except his biggest mistake was ever trusting me in the first place.

We were going to burn them down one by one.

And they'd never see it coming.

Five Weeks Prior

"I can't believe we're getting married in four weeks. I mean, I get why it has to be so soon, but still, you're expecting me to get everything sorted so fast," Avery said as she reached up into a cupboard above the sink.

The whole thing required careful planning, especially given the fact we had to give 28 days' notice along with it being fucking displayed in the registry office the entire time. It was just fucking lucky we'd not only got an appointment but a wedding date because they'd had a cancellation. Given London was such a big place, there was every chance they'd never find out. I didn't think Chuck or Frazier would go so far as to check registry offices on the off chance Avery had given notice she was getting married. They had absolutely no reason to.

"You're not exactly inviting the whole world to it."

We were literally having six guests, seven if you included Josh. The fewer people who knew, the better. She was adamant we couldn't just get married with some random people as witnesses. She wanted the people we cared about most there and I agreed with her. Ben would have my head if he wasn't the best man. And the reason it had to be so soon was because her birthday event was in five weeks. We wanted it sorted before then.

"You really think Frazier is going to buy it when I tell him I'm okay with marrying Tristan?"

That was the other reason. Having a fake engagement to Tristan had driven us apart before, but now, she'd made up her mind. The only way we'd take the Shaws down was by getting closer to them. And this time she'd be safe in the knowledge they could never force her to marry him when she'd got what we needed.

In a few short weeks, she'd be mine completely. It's not as if she wasn't already bound to my heart permanently but binding us together legally was the last step. I wanted the world to know I was hers and she was mine.

"It's what he wants. I doubt he'll care if you're really on board or not."

She popped two wine glasses down on the counter.

"I suppose so. He's coming in tomorrow, so I guess we'll see then."

I finished uncorking the bottle, coming around and standing behind her. I pressed into her as I poured the wine out, kissing the top of her head. Placing the bottle down, I curled a hand around her waist, turning her around gently. She stared up at me with those doe eyes I loved so much.

"You're going to do fine, princess."

"I hope so."

I cupped her face. Her guard was down, her expression showing her vulnerability, her fear. She needed me to reassure her. She told me once I knew what she needed before she did. Knew she wanted to submit and belong to me before she'd admitted it to herself.

"Even if I'm not right next to you, I'm always there."

I ran my hand down her jaw and neck before brushing my fingers across the A on the chain around her neck. The first gift I'd given her. I didn't know it at the time, but I really did love this girl back then. She'd dug her way into my soul and reminded me what it was to feel again.

"Let this remind you. I'm yours and you're mine."

"If I didn't know you any better, I'd say you're being ridiculously gooey right now."

I grinned.

"Am I not allowed?"

She shook her head.

"Nope. You're only allowed to be commanding, rough and brutal."

Her smile told me she was taking the piss. She craved not just my control, but when I was soft with her too. When I took care of her in the ways I knew how.

I wrapped a hand around her neck loosely. I'd never harm her. If I physically hurt one fucking hair on her head, it'd kill me. I wasn't like my father or hers.

"Is that so?"

She swallowed, her pulse thudding against my palm.

"Yeah, it is."

"Go sit at the table before I decide to tie you to it and fuck you."

I released her neck and stepped back. Her eyes darkened, but she didn't say anything. She picked up the wine glasses and took them over to the table, setting them down before sitting. She eyed me over the rim of one of the glasses as she brought it to her lips. I knew what she was thinking about. The brutal pounding I'd give her later.

Her phone rang. She slipped it out of her pocket, staring down at the screen for a moment before putting it to her ear.

"What's up?"

She held the phone away from her ear for a moment.

"Hey, Gert, please, stop screaming."

She rolled her eyes at me.

"So you got my text? Yeah… You can do this weekend? Good. I'll ask John if he's free… Why do I have to have him there? I've told you before, my uncle insists on me having a bodyguard… What, no, Aiden can't come. He's not allowed to see it before the day… God, you really have no shame. No, I'm not bringing him so you can spend the whole time drooling rather than looking at dresses with me."

I laughed. Avery told me Gert referred to me as 'the sex god' and that had nothing to do with my bedroom skills. She just thought I was hot. Avery didn't appreciate it in the slightest, having her best friend making eyes at me. It wasn't like it was serious. Gert had a girlfriend who she was all 'loved up' with according to Avery.

"You make me sick. No, for the last time, I'm not telling you how much we have sex so just shut up… I'm hanging up now… Oh god, seriously, Gert, get your fucking mind out of the gutter… Goodbye… No, oh god, no. Enough, I'm going."

She hung up, staring down at her phone with disgust.

"What did she say this time?"

She looked up at me, placing her phone down on the table.

"You really don't want to know."

I raised an eyebrow as I served up dinner.

"That bad?"

Her face flushed and she looked away.

"She wanted to know if you had um… piercings down there and then she asked me how… how big your cock is."

I tried not to smile. Tried and failed. Fuck she was so cute when she was embarrassed.

"And you didn't want to enlighten her?"

She looked back up at me again, a horrified expression on her face.

"No! God, I don't even know why she thinks that's appropriate. That girl is really fucking sex crazed."

"And you aren't?"

She scowled. I walked over with the plates and set them down on the table, grinning.

"I blame you entirely for that."

She picked up her fork, twirling it around in her fingers for a moment.

"And why's that?"

"Have you seen you? I defy any girl to not get instantly wet at the thought of getting fucked by you. Besides, I know how good it is."

I couldn't help laughing as I dug into my own food. Tonight was our own little engagement celebration, so I'd made steak. Something she appreciated as we didn't often have it.

"I suppose those women will just have to be jealous. My interests only involve you naked and at my mercy."

She bit her lip, cutting into her steak. I could see her face go red all over again. Sometimes she could be so shy about sex and at others, she was a little vixen who told me exactly what she wanted and where. Just yesterday, she'd begged me over and over to give it to her deep and hard whilst my cock was buried up her arse. Told me to use her like she was my plaything. Such a dirty girl when she wanted to be. I shifted in my seat, readjusting myself as thoughts of her naked played on my mind.

"So, did you get around to speaking to Ben today?"

I nodded slowly. That had been a conversation and a half. I think I rendered him speechless for the first time in his life. Never once did he think I'd ever meet a girl I'd want to marry.

"He did ask me if you'd said yes under duress."

She raised an eyebrow.

"Well… you did tie me up."

She was right. I had. Afterwards, I'd spent the rest of the day asking if she really meant it until she'd told me in no uncertain terms to 'shut up and stop asking or she'd go stay at her own flat just to get away from the inquisition'. I was worried she'd only said yes because I was being so insistent about it during sex. I hadn't meant to, but the thought of her saying no fucking killed me. I wanted her to be my wife despite all the shit with Frazier. This girl was my universe.

"You didn't want to answer."

She rolled her eyes, turning her attention back to her food.

"You just have no patience ninety per cent of the time," she muttered.

I decided to let that go considering she was only speaking the truth. When it came to her, I rarely tolerated any delays. If I told her to do something, it needed to be right then.

I reached out across the table, putting my hand out to her. She eyed it for a moment before putting her hand in mine.

"Ben is happy. He thinks you're good for me and he'd be right about that. I love you, princess."

"Love you too… I hope Skye makes Josh wear one of those faux tuxedo baby grows. That will look so cute."

I rolled my eyes, retracting my hand. Whilst I did like my nephew, I didn't find baby stuff cute at all. Avery knew that. It was a subject we weren't going to discuss any time soon. I had no idea if she wanted kids or not. In all honesty, I had no idea how I really felt about it. If you'd asked me before I met this girl, I would've said fuck no. Now, I wasn't sure of anything at all. Maybe one day.

"Oh, come on, Aiden, even you have to admit he's like the cutest little thing ever."

"I don't."

"You forget, I've seen you with him."

I didn't respond, wanting to get off this subject immediately. I'd much rather think about how I was going to tie her to the table. What knots I'd use. How hard I'd fuck her and where. I desperately wanted to bury my cock in my girlfriend who would soon be my wife. I'd wanted to pin her down this morning before she went to work, but she'd run away from me, locking me out of the bathroom whilst she had a shower.

My need for her never dampened. Maybe I was obsessed, but who fucking cared? She was mine. I'd told her after the first time I fucked her, I'd want her daily. And that was still true now.

I shoved my empty plate away, watching her finish her own. I sipped at the wine she'd poured. I was patient, but once we were done and the table cleared, she wasn't getting any mercy at all. I'd fuck her until she begged me for a release.

That girl across from me was going to be my wife.

And I wasn't fucking letting anyone else near her again.

THREE

Avery

Present Day

My hand felt clammy in Tristan's. I hated being anywhere near him. He made my skin crawl. The arrogant prick was looking like he'd won the fucking lottery. I'd long since finished my impromptu speech and we were busy being congratulated by various people. I'd forgotten who half of them were. I didn't really care in all honesty. I just wanted this night to be over already.

Tristan leant towards me as the people we'd been speaking to left. His hot breath against my ear made me shudder and not in a good way.

"I know what you agreed with my father, but make no fucking mistake, Avery, I'm going to have you naked," he whispered. "I'm going to fuck that tight little cunt of yours and you're going to enjoy it."

My stomach roiled in protest. He made me so sick. He wasn't getting anywhere near me with his dick. Little did Tristan know if he did attempt to get in between my legs tonight, he'd have a wakeup call. Aiden insisted on getting me a knife to strap to my leg just in case. It wasn't exactly the most comfortable thing in the world to wear, but at least it was concealed in my inner thigh. No one knew except him and me.

"Evening Frazier," I said, ignoring Tristan completely as his father approached us.

"Happy birthday, Avery," he said, giving me a nod. "Your uncle spared no expense this evening."

"Thank you. He wanted everything to be perfect what with the world watching."

He smiled. The sight of it made me ill all over again. It took every last bit of strength I had to stand being near these two men without wanting to tell them how much I hated their guts.

"I take it you didn't tell him about your engagement to my son."

"No, I haven't had time. Things have been hectic at the office."

And I wanted my uncle to be just as shocked as everyone else. I was kind of surprised no one had found out about me getting married to Aiden given how thorough Frazier was. It had only been a week since we'd said yes to each other in front of the registrar. That was the best moment of my life.

"Well, I do hope you two will decide on a date very soon. You know these places get booked up years in advance."

I gave him a bright smile.

"Of course, the sooner, the better."

Inside, I rolled my eyes. There was no fucking way I was ever setting a date to marry Tristan. There wasn't going to be a wedding. I just had to wait until next week when I would be having dinner at Frazier's to celebrate. Then I could get what I needed and this whole thing would be over. At least, I hoped it would be. I hoped I could get enough evidence to expose him for who he truly was.

"Perhaps we'll discuss it next week. Susan is looking forward to seeing you. It has been an age since you've been to the house."

Frazier's wife, Susan, was the only decent person in his family. If you looked past her doting on her son like the sun shone out of his arse. Tristan was the apple of her eye. He put up this fake façade whenever he was with her. This dinner was going to be hell on earth for me.

"It will be nice to see her. I hope she's been well."

I wondered if she knew how sick and sadistic her husband truly was. How he liked to torture women before he fucked them. I tried to keep the smile plastered on my face, but this evening was already getting to me.

I glanced around, trying to spot my husband in the crowd. He was standing by the wall with my uncle. He'd been there the whole time. I was surprised he was still talking to Uncle Charlie at this point. They seemed to be deep in discussion until my uncle turned and stared right at me. I almost shrank back at the look he gave me. Irritation and pure frustration in his eyes. I knew he wasn't going to be happy about me getting engaged to Tristan. Too bad for him.

He said something to Aiden before he made a beeline for me. I wanted to excuse myself, but I didn't get a chance to open my mouth. Uncle Charlie descended on me, took me by the arm and looked at Frazier and Tristan.

"Excuse me for a moment, my niece and I need to have a little talk."

He didn't wait for them to respond, dragging me out of the ballroom without so much as a backwards glance. I didn't protest. This conversation was going to happen whether I liked it or not. He shoved me into an alcove in the hallway outside and glared at me.

"What the fuck is going through that head of yours?" he hissed, his voice low. "Tristan fucking Shaw. I warned you about him."

I straightened, brushing my dress down.

"I have my reasons."

"Are you going to enlighten me?"

"No."

He let out a low growl of frustration.

"You really do fucking try my patience. What the fuck is going on with you?"

"Nothing."

He grabbed my arm and pulled me closer, staring down at me with hazel eyes which matched my own.

"Do not bullshit me. What exactly happened to you when you were taken? What were you shown?"

My stomach dropped. I didn't want to think about what Rick forced me to watch. All the memories came flooding back, causing me to swallow back bile rising in my throat. I couldn't think about what my dad had done to Aiden's mother. I couldn't.

"N…n… nothing."

"Don't give me that. You told John, why not me?"

I shook my head, trying to take a step back. I didn't like him getting up in my face nor did I want to talk about this any further. As strong as I'd become, all the memories of what kind of sick, disgusting people my family and their associates were still haunted me. I still felt self-loathing that I was a part of this.

Except now, I'd been freed from the shackles of having the Daniels name.

"Tell me what happened."

"I can't," I whispered, shaking my head again.

Something in his expression softened. If I wasn't staring at him so intently, I wouldn't have noticed it.

"Was it really that terrible?"

The only person I hadn't seen in those videos was him. It seemed my uncle didn't involve himself in the abuse of the women my family kept. I knew why that was. He only liked girls of a certain age. The thought of it made me feel queasy all over again.

Is this what Aiden had been talking about to him? Did he tell him I'd seen something? Why? Why did he put me in this position? Did he want me to tell Chuck I'd seen videos of women being abused? I had too many questions. My uncle had backed me into a corner I didn't know how to get out of. What I needed was to speak to my husband and ask him what the fuck he was playing at.

"Can we not do this now? We're neglecting our guests."

"Fuck the guests. You already gave them enough to fucking well talk about."

I flinched. He really was angry with me. In some ways, I deserved it. I'd gone and announced my engagement without telling him. Gone behind his back and done something he didn't want me to do. Why I felt any sort of sympathy or regret for this was beyond me. My uncle wasn't a good person. He'd tried to rape me when I was a kid. I was sure he'd touched other little girls too. And yet, the fact still remained, he was my family. Even if I hated that concept now. I hated being related to such monsters.

I made a decision. I no longer cared what Aiden thought about it because he'd put me in a difficult position by revealing that I'd been forced to watch something when I was kidnapped. Taking matters into my own hands was a huge gamble. I just hoped this one would pay off.

"Uncle Charlie, please, I don't want to talk about that tonight. I'm going to tell you one thing though. One thing which has to stay between you and me."

His eyes narrowed, but he dropped my arm.

"What is it?"

"I'm not going to marry Tristan. It's not real. None of it."

His eyes widened a fraction.

"What?"

"They want the money. Our money. Dad put a stupid clause into my trust fund. It makes it legally possible for anyone who marries me before I'm twenty five to take it all away from me. That's the real reason I went back to the penthouse. To get the paperwork. Frazier wouldn't leave me alone, so I did this to stop him pestering me. I'm going to destroy them, Uncle Charlie. Tristan tried to rape me. Do you think I really want to be married to a man like that? Did you think I'd do any of this without a reason? I'm not stupid even if you think I am."

He stared at me, eyes wide as his mouth dropped open. I was relatively sure he hated the Shaws after what he'd said to me about them. It just depended on how much. Would he keep his mouth shut long enough for me to execute my plan?

"He wants the money. Our family money. That fucking cunt."

I nodded. He stepped back, running a hand through his hair. I noticed it had started greying, just like my father's. The stark memory of his face before Aiden had come into the kitchen and taken his life flittered across my vision. Those last moments I'd seen him alive. My uncle reminded me so much of him, except they were almost polar opposites. My dad rarely lost his temper, whilst Uncle Charlie could fly off the handle at any moment.

"Fucking sick cunt. All this time. He acted like him and Mitch were the best of friends but really, all he wanted was money. I knew he was a fucking snake. I fucking knew it. He drew up the paperwork for your trust fund personally. Mitch told me so. Fucking cunt."

He paced away from me, tugging at his suit jacket in clear agitation. I'd known he didn't like Frazier, but this reaction surprised me. The venom in his voice chilled me to my core.

"What exactly are you planning?" he asked as he turned to me again.

"Frazier isn't a saint. I'm sure he's hiding things. All I need is evidence to bury him."

I didn't elaborate on the fact I also needed evidence to bury my uncle too. Bury him and my family's sick operation.

"And how do you propose to get that?"

"I have a plan. That's all you need to know."

He shook his head, running a hand through his hair again.

"I hope you know what you're doing."

I hoped I did too. I was terrified of this dinner next week. Terrified I wouldn't make it out of that house alive and unharmed. It was a risk I had to take.

"We'll see."

He looked towards the ballroom doors.

"This conversation isn't over, Avery. I expect you to tell me everything."

I nodded. He turned and walked back into the ballroom. I slumped against the wall of the alcove. That had not gone to plan at all. What the fuck would Aiden say when I told him Chuck knew my engagement to Tristan was fake and that I planned to destroy the Shaws? That was a bridge I'd have to cross later. I had a party to get through.

I straightened, patting myself down to make sure the knife was still strapped to my thigh.

I was going to be strong even if my mind was running riot.

I stood tall and walked back into that ballroom.

Five Weeks Prior

Frazier stood in front of my desk, his eyes shining with glee.

"I cannot begin to tell you how delighted I am."

I held back from rolling my eyes.

"I've thought about it long and hard. This is the right move for our families. It's what my father wanted and I'd like to give him that even if he's not alive to see it."

Frazier nodded, his expression solemn for a moment. I really, really fucking hated this man with a passion. I couldn't look at him without seeing that awful look on his face when he'd tortured that girl in the video Aiden showed me. Not only that, I had a new memory of him. One of the videos Rick had shown me. It was worse. He'd used a knife to slice into the girl's skin. Her body was completely covered in small cuts. Each one made his eyes light up further and his erection grow bigger. I hated that I even knew what he looked like naked. Hated that I'd watched him fuck her afterwards until they were both covered in blood.

I swallowed, the revulsion I felt about those memories threatening to consume me. I couldn't be sick in front of Frazier. Not now.

"Yes, it is terribly sad he won't be here to see his daughter get married."

I didn't want him here. I was marrying the man who'd murdered him and my mother. Anyone would think I was certifiable. It didn't matter. I knew Aiden and I belonged together. Knew it deep in my soul. We'd fallen hard for each other. Fallen into the pit of insanity we now both resided in and neither of us wanted to crawl out of it. Neither of us wanted to ever let the other go. Aiden consumed me and I consumed him. It's just how we were together.

"I know it's a lot to ask… but would you consider walking me down the aisle when we do get married? You were Dad's best friend. It would only be fitting."

Frazier's eyes lit up further. The slow smile which appeared on his face made my skin crawl.

"What about your uncle?"

"We've never been close. I'd like it to be you."

The lie almost stuck in my throat. I'd rather fucking die but reeling him in with my web of lies was paramount. The further I convinced him I'd been taken in by his bullshit, the easier this would be for me to infiltrate his home. I had to make Frazier and Tristan trust me.

"I'm honoured. I cannot replace your own father, but I do hope you'll think of me as your father one day."

I smiled at him, trying not to show my distaste at such a thing ever happening. He would never be my father. Not if I had anything to do with it.

He took a seat in front of me, drumming his fingers on the arm.

"I'm sure Tristan will be very pleased when I tell him. There are a few matters we should discuss first."

"Such as?"

"I'm aware your uncle is holding an event for you."

I nodded. It was common knowledge now. There was already media speculation as to what would happen at it. Were we going to announce something big? How would the company move forward in light of the tragedy of my parent's death and me taking up my father's mantle?

"I'm wondering how you would feel about making the announcement then."

My smile dropped. I couldn't help it. Announcing publicly was not a part of our plans. Not at all. The look in his eye told me he wouldn't drop this subject. Wouldn't let me get out of it.

"So soon?"

"It is the perfect opportunity."

I supposed in his eyes it was. The world would be watching. What better way to secure my fortune than to announce it and make sure I'd have a hard time backing out of it. My skin crawled. I knew the stakes in this game were high. I'd known that from the moment Aiden told me about what my family really did.

"I will think about it."

"Not too hard now."

"Wasn't there something else?"

He nodded, his dark eyes flickering with emotions I didn't understand, but nevertheless made me feel like I should be on my guard.

"Well, Avery, this arrangement should be mutually beneficial. I know you bear no love for my son. I imagine you'd prefer to be his wife in name only."

It was true. If I was really going to marry him, I didn't want him to touch me physically. The thought of that made my skin prickle. The memory of him pressing me up against the counter in the ladies and his disgusting hands on me was more than enough.

"You're correct."

No point lying about this aspect.

"I would like to draw up an agreement between you. Of course, it wouldn't be legally binding, but it would be beneficial to both parties to make their positions clear."

"That's fair. Is Tristan going to agree to it?"

He gave me a smile.

"Oh, have no fear on that score. I will make sure he does."

His expression told me I had a lot to fear. He was just as psychotic as Tristan. The two of them were shining examples of men who lacked any sort of morals.

"Well, okay. Do you want to maybe start drawing something up and I'll think of what I want out of the arrangement?"

He inclined his head before standing. I stood too, putting my hand out to him. He took it, his cold, papery skin sending a chill down my spine. Giving my hand a firm shake, he smiled.

"I'll be in touch."

I smiled back, trying to keep the nervousness out of my expression.

"I look forward to it."

He released my hand, turned and left without a backwards glance.

And I knew I was in deep shit.

Whatever Frazier had up his sleeve, I wasn't privy to it. I knew he wanted my money, but everything else was a mystery to me. For now, I had what I wanted, but at what cost? What had I really signed myself up for?

I could only hope marriage to Aiden would keep me from whatever it was Frazier had planned for me. Because if it didn't. I wasn't entirely sure if I'd ever recover from it. Knowing Frazier. It wouldn't be anything good.

I needed this to work.

Needed it desperately

My future with Aiden depended on it.

And the thought of it all falling apart around me chilled me to my very core.

FOUR

Aiden

*A*very was sat up in bed drawing when I got in. I'd told her I'd be late due to a bunch of shit Chuck asked me to do. I was growing tired of being at his beck and call. The sooner we finished this shit with her family, the better. All I wanted was to settle down with the girl I loved. Whether that made me a fucking pussy or not, I no longer cared.

I dropped a kiss on the top of her head before going over to the cupboard to strip out of my clothes.

"What you drawing?" I asked, tugging my jumper off.

"Ben texted me a couple of his sketches. Was just working on the one for us."

She'd been back and forth with him for a few days now. At night, she'd taken to drawing or painting. She was working on something for our living room having insisted on taking a bunch of photos of us together for reference. I had told her I wanted more of her paintings for our walls, but I wasn't counting on her wanting to paint us again. She told me it was going to be a proper portrait rather than fantastical like the one above our bed.

"And Frazier?"

"He was obviously happy, but he wants to have some kind of agreement put in place since he knows this isn't a love match."

I could go over the footage of her conversation with him tomorrow. I moved to the bed, having stripped down to my boxers and slipped in next to her, looking over at her sketch. She paused, taking her pencil away so I could see it. A pair of angel wings, but it was only half done.

"It looks good."

"Thank you. I should hope so since it's going on you too."

I grinned. Another set of matching tattoos. Ben was going to tattoo them next week so she'd have them done in time for the wedding. She set the drawing down on the bedside table and turned to me. She looked a little concerned.

"Something weird is going on with Ed."

I reached over, tucking her hair behind her ear.

"What makes you say that?"

"I know Saskia is new and all, but she followed me into the ladies earlier and told me she overheard him having a shouting match with someone on the phone."

I frowned. From what Avery told me, he was a very amenable guy who never raised his voice to anyone. I'd not met him in person, but I knew his father, Troy, a little. At least I'd seen him often enough on footage of him and Mitchell to know he was just as bad as his cousin.

"Did she happen to hear anything he said?"

"Not much. Just that someone had really fucked up and they needed to sort it out before Charlie finds out. I don't know whether it's to do with the company or… if it's perhaps because he's involved in the other shit."

I had my suspicions about her cousin. She knew that. Something about him didn't add up quite right.

"Perhaps we can look at the footage from his office at some point. Maybe we'll hear the whole thing."

She shook her head.

"He wasn't in his office, he was in the photocopier room which you know doesn't have any cameras."

I wondered if that was on purpose. If he didn't want his conversation filmed, then it might well be.

"A little too convenient."

She took my arm, wrapped it around her and put her head on my shoulder.

"That's what I thought."

"I'll look into it, but we have to focus on Frazier."

She nodded. That really was our main priority. So far, Chuck hadn't found out about Sophie and Cora. We were in the clear on that for the time being. Tina said they were both doing a little better since she'd moved them to her place in Cornwall. She was down there with them at the moment, but she'd return before the wedding.

I'd had lectures from her about how soon it was, but she'd still been happy for me. By most standards, it probably was too soon. Avery and I knew what we wanted. Each other. No other girl would match up to her in my eyes. No one would love me the way she did. Accept me flaws and all. Especially after what I'd done.

"I hope I find a dress this weekend. It's going to be difficult at such short notice."

"You will. I don't care how much it costs. I want you to be happy."

Honestly, I'd pretty much do anything to make sure this day went off without a hitch. I'd already arranged a tiny reception along with rooms for everyone in the hotel so she didn't have to worry about it. I never thought I'd be sorting out a fucking wedding, but then again, there was a heck of a lot of shit I never imagined I'd do before I met Avery.

"James is begrudgingly coming with us. He asked me if he really had to when I rang him earlier."

I laughed.

"I'm sure he'd rather be doing anything else than putting up with you two doing girly shit all afternoon."

"He'll have John."

I raised my eyebrow. I was admittedly a little bit fucked off that he'd get to see Avery in whatever she picked out before I did. Half the fucking wedding party would. It was necessary for him to protect her given that we knew Rick would come after her again. He'd promised that. It reminded me I hadn't yet told Avery about the night my mother died. I should, but finding the words was harder than I realised. It really was my worst fucking memory with the exception of Christmas Day when Avery left me. I didn't want to think about that shit right now. Not when she was right here and was about to become my wife.

"I'm sure the two of them can console each other."

"I'm not that bad. It's Gert they should be worrying about. She's constantly texting me pictures of dresses she thinks will suit me. I swear she's more excited than me."

"What? You're not excited about getting all this for life?"

I pointed at myself, biting my lip to keep from smiling. She eyed me, giving me one of those 'are you serious?' looks.

"You're such an idiot," she muttered, brushing her fingers across my chest.

"You wound me, princess."

"Boo hoo."

I kissed her forehead. She pouted so I shifted, kissing her properly.

"Better?" I whispered as I pulled away.

She nodded. Her eyes were drooping a little. No wonder she was tired considering she'd had a long day.

"You want to sleep?"

"Yeah… is that okay?"

"Why wouldn't it be?"

She smiled, sitting up and pulling the covers out from underneath us.

"Well… because… someone usually has an insatiable appetite for me."

I laughed, shaking my head a little as I got under the covers with her and leant over to turn out the light. I tucked her up in my arms, giving her a kiss goodnight.

I wasn't a complete fucking animal who couldn't control himself around her. Some days were bad, but others, like today, I was content to just fall asleep with her close to me. The girl who soothed me and kept the nightmares at bay. She's who I wanted for life.

The shouting hurt my ears. I had my hands over them, my eyes squeezed shut against the onslaught.

"Let go of me."

"You bitch. You've always been a fucking little troublemaker."

"You're not supposed to be here."

I heard a loud slapping sound. Opening my eyes, I peered through the crack in the cupboard door. I couldn't make out the man she was talking to, but I could see Mummy.

I wasn't supposed to be in here. In her room, but I'd been looking for a toy I'd lost. My favourite race car. I remembered I'd been playing with it in here a few days ago with Mummy. I'd run in the cupboard and closed the door when I heard loud voices in the hallway.

"It's time you learnt your fucking place. You think just because you had that bastard kid, you're above everyone else? Let me make something fucking clear to you. You're not."

"No, I don't think that, sir. Please. I haven't done anything."

Mummy was pulled out of sight by a suit-clad arm.

"That's where you're wrong, Lizzie. You've done everything wrong since the moment you came to us. Getting knocked up and now this bullshit. You know how much fucking trouble you've caused me? No, you don't because you're a stupid little bitch who we have no use for any longer."

"No. No, please."

I heard a smack. It made me flinch. She fell back into my eyeline, holding her face.

"Please, sir. I'm sorry. Please."

"Sorry, are you? Sorry for being alive and making trouble for my whole family?"

"I'm sorry. Please, sir, don't."

"It's too fucking late for that."

REVENGE

The hand reached out, spinning her around. I couldn't quite make out who was holding her to their chest, but I knew it was a man by the sound of his voice. It was a familiar voice to me. That's when I noticed something else in his other hand. A blade.

"Any last words?"

"Please, please don't. He'll be all alone."

"You should've fucking thought about that before you fucked up, Lizzie."

"Please," she whispered.

He raised his arm up and dragged the blade across her neck. Blood pooled immediately. She gurgled. The man released her. She put her hands to her neck, the blood pouring out of the wound. Then she collapsed to her knees. I heard the man's footsteps retreating from the room. When the front door slammed, I pushed open the cupboard door. She lay on her back, staring up at the ceiling with her hands by her sides.

"Mummy?"

There was no answer.

"Mummy!"

I jolted awake. My skin felt clammy. What the actual fuck? I'd not dreamt about her in so long. So fucking long. I sat up, trying to reorient myself to the present. That fucking memory. Why had I dreamt about it? Was it because I'd thought about her before I'd gone to sleep? Fuck. Fuck. I couldn't deal with this shit.

I jumped out of bed, pacing the room before I walked out and along to the bathroom. I splashed water on my face and the back of my neck. Staring at myself in the mirror, I had dark

49

circles under my eyes and a haunted look on my face. Fuck. Frustration tore through me. I shouldn't be having these fucking memories attacking me from all fucking sides. I'd had enough. This shit needed to end.

I dried my face and went back into the bedroom. Slipping into bed, I lay there staring at the ceiling. Avery shifted, her hand reached out and connected with my chest. She moved, tucking herself back up under my arm and curling her own around my stomach.

"Where did you go?" she whispered, her voice groggy and full of sleep.

"Bathroom."

"Are you okay?"

I shouldn't be burdening her with this shit in the middle of the night. She needed to sleep, but the memory wouldn't fucking leave me alone. It wouldn't disappear. I could see her face. Her glazed over eyes staring back at me.

"No."

Avery raised her head, staring down at me. I could just about make out the concern on her face from the light streaming in through the gap in the curtains.

"What's wrong?"

"It's nothing. You should go back to sleep."

"Don't do that."

"Do what?"

She sat up properly, resting a hand on my chest.

"Shut me out like that. Talk to me. What's wrong?"

I looked away. How could I tell her? She'd been burdened with enough shit for a lifetime. My mother's death didn't need to be added onto that list.

"Before you came into my life, I used to dream about my worst memories every fucking night. I thought they'd stopped for good, but clearly not."

"Aiden…"

"It's shit, princess, but I'll deal with it."

She shook her head.

"No, you don't get to just say you'll deal with it. You dealing with things by yourself doesn't end well."

Fuck. I was beginning to realise Avery had noticed far more about me than I ever expected her to. And she was fucking right about me not dealing with things well.

"I dreamt about her."

"Your mother?"

"Lizzie… that's her name. I try not to think about her even though I'm doing all of this for her."

I sighed. One day I had to tell her, so why not now? I'd never told anyone about that day. Tina was the only one who knew because she was there after it happened. I never told her I'd watched the man slit my mother's throat.

I had to tell someone and it should be Avery. The girl I loved more than anything.

"The night she died was the worst night of my life."

Avery looked at me with concern but stayed silent as I explained in detail exactly what occurred. My heart broke all over again. Reliving that fucking memory always hurt. She took my hand at one point because my voice faltered on the moment I realised she was dead. When I was done, she crawled over me and settled her head on my chest, holding me tightly. I could feel her tears soaking into my skin. Fuck. She was crying for me.

"I'm so sorry," she whispered.

I wrapped my arms around her. Avery was the only anchor I had left in the world. She kept me from descending into rage, despair and not wanting to feel any longer. My girl kept me grounded.

"When I found out about your father, I thought for a long time it was him, but his voice wasn't exactly the same. I don't know who it was, princess. That's the truth."

I'd wanted it to be Mitchell so I could have the satisfaction of knowing her murderer was dead. Deep down, I knew it wasn't and it fucking killed me.

"I thought you said you did know."

"I wish I did. I just realised it didn't add up with what I remember about that night."

"When Rick took me, he told me to ask you who it was. He said that you had it wrong."

I stiffened. She hadn't told me that part.

"Why didn't you say anything about that before?"

"I don't know. I wish I had. I'm sorry."

I stroked her back.

"No, you didn't do anything wrong. He knows who killed her then."

She raised her head. I reached up, wiping away the tears which were still falling down her cheeks.

"I guess so. He could be bluffing."

I wasn't sure he was. Rick knew far too much. Always had.

"We'll just have to see. I don't want to talk about him."

She sniffed, sitting up and straddling me. Her doe eyes were wide and she looked so fucking beautiful even though she'd just been crying.

"Thank you for telling me."

I rested my hands on her legs, stroking them lightly with my fingers.

"You told me to let you in. I'm trying."

She leant down, pressing her lips to mine for a moment. She cupped my face, resting her forehead on mine and staring down at me intently.

"I know and I appreciate it. I love you so much, Aiden. All I've ever wanted was to help you. Make you happy. I hate seeing you in so much pain."

The crazy thing about this is that Avery knew exactly what it was like to see your parent die in front of your eyes. I should've told her sooner. She didn't have to say anything because she already understood.

I kissed her again, needing to feel that connection between us. Needing to get lost in her. She'd calm me. Soothe away the memories with her gentle touch and delicate skin. She let me grab her t-shirt and pull it off. Soon, there was nothing between us and I could feel every inch of her body pressed against mine.

For once, we didn't fuck each other. We made love. Our feelings exposed and raw for one another to see. And it was everything I needed right then.

Fuck, I loved her so much. I'd do anything for Avery.

I'd fucking bow down at her feet.

I'd worship her.

And I'd die for her.

FIVE

Avery

Present Day

The rest of the night passed by in a blur. Sitting in the back of the car with John driving, I gazed out of the window, but I wasn't really looking at anything. I was exhausted. Talking to so many people, having to deal with congratulations for my engagement, becoming the owner of Daniels Holdings and it being my birthday, the whole night had taken a toll on me. All I wanted was to curl up in bed and go to sleep. Except I wasn't going to get that option. Aiden and I needed to talk.

This felt like a running theme in our relationship. One of us would do something without telling the other and we'd fight over it. I wasn't in the mood for that. We'd both done things this evening. Honestly, now I had time to think about it, this wasn't exactly unexpected. This evening was always going to bring up challenges and surprises.

John dropped me off at the door and watched me go in. I was just thankful to be home. When I got upstairs into the flat, I realised he wasn't home yet. I hadn't seen him at the venue when I left so I assumed he'd gone already. Perhaps my assumption was wrong.

I let my hair down and removed my makeup before slipping into shorts and a t-shirt. I picked up my wedding ring from the bedside table and slipped it back on before crawling into bed and turning the lights out. I felt sort of exposed without it. Having it back on my finger made me feel right again. Whole somehow. It reminded me of how insanely special that day had been. Our wedding day.

I never thought I'd have a simple and quiet wedding, but even if we hadn't done it in secret, I wouldn't have wanted it any other way. Aiden and I had made our own family, free from the awfulness of our blood relations.

That day meant everything to me.

The day I'd become Aiden's wife.

One Week Prior

"Gert, seriously, stop fussing," I said, waving her away.

"But, Ave, it's your fucking wedding day. You have to look perfect."

I shook my head. I was nervous enough as it is without her readjusting my dress for the millionth time. We were standing outside the room together with James. I'd roped him into walking me down the aisle. Who better to give me away than my best friend who'd been with me through thick and thin? It's not like my dad could be here. I shut down that thought immediately. He didn't deserve it anyway. Not after what he'd done.

"He is here, right?" I whispered to James whilst Gert shifted on her feet in front of us, waiting for the music to start.

"Of course he is, why wouldn't he be?" he hissed back.

"I don't know. I haven't spoken to him since last night… It felt weird being away from him."

I'd stayed in my own flat with James and Gert. We'd all curled up together in my bed last night, talking about how insane this all was until we fell asleep. I woke up missing Aiden like crazy. I hated spending the night away from him. We promised we wouldn't contact each other until we saw each other today. James took my phone away from me and hid it. I'd almost begged him to tell me where it was at one point because my heart ached so much. Perhaps it was nerves, but I wanted Aiden so fucking badly.

"Cold feet?"

"What? No. I want to marry him. I just don't want him to bolt."

James rolled his eyes.

"He hasn't. Don't forget, he asked you to marry him."

I tried to keep that in mind. It didn't help my nerves in the slightest. They coiled in my stomach, making my heart feel tight. I wanted this moment to be special.

The music started. Gert looked back, giving me a wink. Fuck. This was it. I was getting married. Shit. Who'd have thought this day would actually happen. That Aiden and I would make such a huge commitment to each other.

I tucked my arm into James' as Gert went through the open doorway. I couldn't see past the first row of empty chairs at the back of the room.

"You got this, Ave. You two love each other, don't be scared."

I nodded at him. It was now or never.

James knew the truth. We'd also had to tell Gert a little about what was going on because otherwise next week she'd be confused as to why I was announcing my engagement to Tristan Shaw. I hadn't revealed the whole truth about my family, only that we were doing it to take down the Shaws. She wasn't unhappy about it considering she hated Tristan just as much as we did. But she was also super excited about us having a wedding.

James squeezed my hand before indicating with his head we should move. I took a deep breath and then we both walked towards the door.

I didn't turn my head to look when we walked through, trying to keep my nerves in check. I had to get through this short walk, then I'd see Aiden and things would be okay. When we turned up the aisle, I first looked at our guests. Skye had Josh in her arms and she was standing with Tina on one side. John was on the other with Gert.

Finally, my attention turned to the man standing waiting for me at the end of the aisle with Ben. My heart pounded in my ears.

Aiden.

And fuck did he look good. My beautiful tattooed angel. He wore a dark grey suit, white shirt and grey tie. In his buttonhole, there was a navy flower which matched the rest of the men and Gert's dress.

My eyes met his grey ones. Love and complete adoration shone within them. I couldn't stop staring at him. I trusted James to get me up the aisle in one piece because my legs felt like jelly.

"You okay?" he whispered.

I nodded, still completely unable to tear my gaze away from the man who was about to become my husband. Our entire relationship flashed before my eyes. Every moment passing by in quick succession. From the night we met under the worst sort of circumstances to yesterday when we'd kissed each other goodbye for the last time before we became husband and wife.

Did I regret a single moment between us?

No.

Would I change anything?

No.

As crazy and as fucked up as it was, it brought us to today.

Before I could process it all, I was standing in front of him and James gave me a kiss on the cheek. He let go of my arm, placing my hand in Aiden's. Then he stepped back and took up his place next to Gert.

"You look beautiful, princess," Aiden said, his deep voice vibrating through me.

"Thank you," I whispered, not quite trusting my own.

The dress. An almost see-through lace bodice cinched in at the waist with an A-line flowing skirt falling to my feet. I hadn't wanted a huge princess style dress even though that's what Aiden called me. Something simple. Sexy but elegant. Gert had sobbed when I came out of the changing room in it. I think even John got misty eyed whilst James told me it was perfect.

Aiden squeezed my hand, smiling at me. The registrar started talking but I barely paid attention to her words. I couldn't look at anyone else. All I saw was Aiden. He enraptured me. And he was about to make me his wife.

I was promptly brought back to reality when the registrar asked Aiden to make the legal declaration.

"I declare that I know of no legal reason why I, Aiden Lockhart, may not be joined in marriage to Avery Charlotte Daniels."

I spoke the returning words when asked, staring up into his beautiful face. I didn't falter even though my hands trembled in his. And when he spoke the contracting words, I thought my heart might burst out of my chest, it was pounding so hard.

I took a deep breath when the registrar asked me to repeat after her.

"I, Avery Charlotte Daniels, take you, Aiden Lockhart, to be my wedded husband."

The registrar asked Ben if he had the rings, which he brought over and gave the first one to Aiden. They were one of the first things we'd purchased so they'd be ready for our wedding day. Mine was a very simple white gold band and his was slightly thicker and palladium.

He pressed it onto my finger and held it above my knuckle.

"I give you this ring as a symbol of our love and marriage. I promise to love you, care for you, protect you and above all, support you in everything you do throughout our lives together."

He pressed the ring fully on my finger. I couldn't breathe. My heart raced out of control. Aiden pledging his love to me was more than I could take. I held onto his hand tighter. I felt a tear slip down my cheek. He smiled, reaching up to brush it away.

"It's okay, princess, I've got you," he whispered, nodding at me.

Ben brought up my ring for Aiden and pressed it into my hand. I shakily put it on his finger and held it.

"I give you this ring as a symbol of our love and marriage. I promise to love you, care for you, listen to you and above all, support you in everything you do throughout our lives together."

I managed to get the words out without choking up as I pressed the ring fully on his finger. I wanted to kiss him so badly and when she finally said, "I now pronounce you husband and wife, you may kiss your bride," I practically threw myself into his arms. Aiden kissed me without any sort of care that all eyes were on us. We drowned in each other for a long minute.

When I pulled away, I stared up into those grey eyes I loved so much and tears filled mine all over again.

"Princess, don't cry," he said, stroking my cheek.

"I'm just so happy."

I didn't want to leave his arms, but we had to sign the register. It took a fair few minutes and when we were done, we finally got to walk back down the aisle together. Those moments we'd just shared were the single most beautiful and amazing ones of my life.

In Aiden's pocket were our official copies of our wedding certificate. Legally bound as husband and wife. I felt so secure and loved, holding his hand.

As soon as we were out of the room, he pressed me up against the wall and devoured my mouth, his hands running down my sides.

"Fuck, I love you, princess. I love you so much," he whispered against my mouth.

My body felt tight almost immediately. A throbbing started in my core. I wanted him. My husband.

"I want to rip that off you and fuck you so hard, you won't be able to walk properly," he told me, pressing kisses to my jaw. "You're so beautiful. So fucking beautiful."

I almost lost all sense of rationality, but I couldn't get carried away in the moment. I pressed my hands on his shoulders, pushing him back slightly. His grey eyes were wild with lust and desire.

"Aiden… now isn't the time."

He shook himself visibly.

"Fuck, I know, but can you fucking blame me when you look like a fucking goddess?"

I felt my face heat up. Hell, he'd never described me that way before. And I really wanted to throw caution to the wind, find an empty cupboard and let him fuck me up against the door. Except I wouldn't do that because our guests were starting to file out of the room along with the photographer we'd hired and paid handsomely to keep quiet.

Aiden stepped away from me, taking my hand. Gert winked at me and James gave me a knowing look. I wanted the ground to swallow me up. I was rarely overly affectionate towards Aiden in front of them, preferring to keep our insatiable lust for each other under wraps.

It wasn't time to feel embarrassed. This was our wedding day. If there was one time I was allowed to show how much I loved Aiden to the world, then this was it.

We all filed out of the registry office and piled into John and James' cars. When we got to the hotel, they greeted us with smiles and took us into a private dining room Aiden had reserved for the reception. There were various canapés and champagne. The photographer insisted on whisking us away for a while for couples' photos before involving the rest of the guests.

I finally got a chance to take a breath and sit down when the wedding breakfast was served. I couldn't stop smiling as we ate and talked. This wasn't like any other wedding I'd been to. So small and intimate. Even so, the rest of our guests insisted we have a first dance together.

As I stood up with Aiden, swaying from side to side, I felt content. I was Aiden's and he was mine.

"You really do look perfect," he told me, his voice low.

"So do you."

"I want to take you upstairs."

I smiled. He'd wanted that since we'd said our vows to each other. I saw it in his expression and the way his hands roamed over me when he thought no one else was looking.

"And neglect our guests?"

He narrowed his eyes.

"Are you trying to make excuses?"

I raised an eyebrow. Did he really think I didn't want him to strip me down and fuck me without mercy? I'd missed him so much last night.

"I want you too."

Once those words were out of my mouth, there was no stopping him. The song ended and we stuck around for a little while longer before he whisked me away up to our room. I barely got in the door when he was on me. He pressed me back against the wall next to the door and kissed me. His hands roamed over my body, tugging up the skirt of my dress.

His fingers were in my underwear before I could take a breath, stroking and coaxing me. The urgency of his movements set my body ablaze.

"I need you, right fucking now," he growled against my skin.

Holy fuck.

I hadn't really thought about how much he might have missed me too. Too wrapped up in my own nervousness about the wedding. I shouldn't have been worried. This was Aiden. I'd known he would be there. Known this was what he wanted.

He tugged my underwear down my legs and I shimmied out of them until they lay at my feet. I hadn't even taken my heels off. He tugged open his fly, freeing his cock. He hitched one of my legs up around his hip before plunging inside me without much warning. My skirt was bunched up at the front in between us, but it didn't stop him thrusting into me.

"Aiden…" I groaned.

"Fuck, Avery. I'm going to fuck you so hard."

"Please, please fuck me. I missed you."

I wrapped my other leg around him as he picked me up and pressed me into the wall. He fucked me ruthlessly, grinding into me with powerful thrusts until I was panting and moaning, my fingers digging into his shoulders. I felt so hot in this dress. Sweat beaded at the back of my neck, but I didn't ask him to stop and take it off. All I wanted was the sweet release he'd give me.

He bit down on my earlobe, causing me to cry out. The sensations rushed through me all at once. I came apart on his cock, completely undone by the magic of the day. He grunted through his own end. My head lolled on his shoulder. Fuck.

Aiden really did give me the most intense orgasms. I couldn't get enough of them or him.

"I love you," I whispered. "I'm yours forever now."

"My wife."

Hearing him say that made me smile. Happiness bloomed inside me.

"My husband."

He pulled me away from the wall and carried me into the room on his hips, still nestled inside me. He laid me down on the huge bed, which was covered in rose petals, and stared down at me.

"You couldn't be more beautiful if you tried," he told me. "You're everything to me. My reason for existing."

He knelt on the floor and slipped off my shoes before tugging me up so he could unzip the back of the dress. He slowly pulled it off me, leaving me naked before him since he'd already discarded my underwear. He folded it over the back of a chair so as not to ruin it before coming back over to me. He let me help him out of his clothes.

"I should really put cream on your tattoos before we go to sleep," he said as he pressed me back down onto the bed and crawled over me. "Remind me."

I nodded. I'd had to get Gert to help me yesterday. She'd done my shoulder whilst I'd made sure to do my arm and wrist. I'd only got inked two weeks ago by Ben. Whilst it was healing up nicely, it still itched like crazy on occasion.

I reached up, cupping his face with one hand and running my thumb over his lip.

"Aiden… You've always been the one. You found a way into my heart and branded yourself on it, making it entirely impossible for me to ever really walk away from you. We've hurt each other, done things we're not proud of, but today… none of that matters. I love you forever. I'm yours. Every part of me. Whatever happens, remember this as the day I gave myself to you freely. Remember I love you unconditionally. Remember that no matter how much pain and heartbreak we go through, we always have each other."

There was a long second of silence as he stared down at me.

"Fuck… princess," he said, his voice breaking on the word.

A single tear slipped down his right cheek. An emotion I'd never thought I'd ever witness from Aiden. My strong, fiercely protective husband cried. I knew they weren't tears of sadness, but something else. Something so much deeper. He hadn't even cried when he told me about his mother's murder. This was the moment I realised the true depth of his feelings for me. We didn't need words any longer.

I pulled him towards me and kissed him. Despite his threat earlier to fuck me roughly, Aiden pressed my legs open and took me with gentle thrusts. I savoured every moment his hands were on me, fingers brushing across my skin as mine wound around his back. The whispered 'I love yous' as we kissed and made love to each other.

As we both lay there, wrapped up in each other's arms after we'd reached a mutual conclusion, I knew that if everything else fell apart after this, I'd have this one day to hold onto. This one memory of a day between us which was perfect and untainted.

Little did I know it came to be the only thing which kept me from falling into a dark pit of despair.

And Aiden… he was the only person who would ever understand the pain my actions caused.

REVENGE

The ones that left a permanent stain on my soul.

SIX

Aiden

Present Day

I wasn't sure why I'd decided to come up to the roof of the building instead of going into the flat. It was a little chilly and windy up here, but I didn't care. I used to come up here when I needed a minute just to breathe. Tonight had been fucking shit. Having to watch my wife pretend to be engaged to another man drove me fucking crazy. Avery was mine. Mine for fuck's sake.

I twirled around the ring on my finger, having slipped it back on when I got in the car to leave the venue earlier. The symbol of our love for each other. We had a few of those now. The rings we wore and the ink tattooed on our skin.

I'd die for that girl. I'd really fucking die for her if it came to it. I didn't trust Frazier nor Tristan. I was fucking worried about this dinner she had to go to next week. The one where she'd finally get the evidence we needed. Our focus had been on them, but John and I had still been looking into who The Collector was. The person who ran the girls for Chuck. The biggest issue was he rarely spoke to the person. They apparently had full control of the whole fucking thing. And things would only get worse now they knew Sophie and Cora had escaped their clutches.

It couldn't be helped. Those girls needed saving. It would've weighed too heavily on me if I'd left them in Robert Bassington's hands. It reminded me I should probably pay that prick another visit considering he'd blabbed to Chuck. I wouldn't though because Avery would fucking kill me. She'd tell me I'd be putting us in even more danger than we were already in. And we were in a fuck ton, especially her. It wasn't just me on my own any longer. I had to think about her too.

We'd only been married a week. It didn't change much between us. If anything, it'd only strengthened the bond we shared. Cemented our partnership. Bound us together for life.

And I really wanted to have her in my arms.

I walked back into the building, shutting the door behind me and took the stairs two by two until I reached our floor. Unlocking the front door to our flat, I stepped in. It was silent and dark. I wasn't sure if she'd be back yet having left before her. I loosened my tie and kicked off my shoes before going into the bedroom.

There she was, huddled up in the covers. My beautiful wife. Fuck. I tugged off my clothes and crawled in next to her. She was fast asleep so I didn't want to wake her up. She had to be exhausted.

I kissed her shoulder and wrapped an arm around her waist, holding her to me. She felt so small and delicate. I'd always seen her as such a tiny, fragile girl even though she possessed an inner strength which knew no bounds. The urge to protect her never went away. The need to keep her safe.

The reality was I couldn't always do that. She kept walking into dangerous situations in order to secure our future. Each and every time, it killed me. Tearing my insides to pieces. I didn't want her to go to this dinner. I hated the thought of her being alone with Tristan and Frazier without anyone to protect her. They were capable of anything. Anything and everything. Tristan had tried to rape her the last time they were alone together.

"Where were you?" she mumbled.

She shifted, turning in my arms and staring up at me with half-lidded eyes.

"The roof."

"Why?"

"Needed a minute is all, princess."

She snuggled closer to me, pressing her face into my chest and wrapping an arm around me, her fingers trailing down my back.

"You told my uncle Rick took me and that he showed me some sick shit."

Her voice was low, but devoid of any accusations. It was merely a statement.

"Robert told him about Sophie and Cora and mentioned I'd threatened to kill Rick. I had to say something."

"He wouldn't leave it alone. So I told him I was taking Frazier and Tristan down to shut him up."

I stiffened.

"You did what?"

"You put me in a difficult situation. If I told him I know about the girls, what do you think he would do? Like you, I had to give him something."

Fuck. We'd really fucked up tonight. Nothing was ever going to run smoothly. You could make all the plans in the world, but when it came to reality, there was always some thinking on your feet when unexpected situations arose.

"What did he say?"

"Just that he hoped I knew what I was doing. Plus he was pretty pissed about Frazier wanting our money. I think that outweighed anything else. He hates the Shaws. I mean full on loathes them."

Chuck didn't like many people and he trusted less than a handful. Paranoid little fuck, but we could use that to our advantage.

"I don't fucking trust him."

She pressed closer, her whole body flush with mine. I felt every soft curve and fuck did it not help matters. My fingers slipped under her t-shirt, brushing across her bare skin.

"Me either. I feel like he keeps trying to get me on side so he can manipulate me."

Her body distracted me. I knew she could feel my cock pressed into her stomach, but she didn't say or do anything about it. Fuck. I'd already had her earlier. Had her in that dress, on her hands and knees in our bed. And right now, I wanted to tie her up even though she was exhausted.

"Most likely," I whispered, pressing my face into her hair and breathing in.

She smelt of coconut, her perfume and sex. It made my cock twitch in anticipation of being buried deep inside her. I pushed up her t-shirt slightly so I could have access to her skin, needing it against mine. It wasn't enough. I wanted her fully naked body pressed against me.

"Take your clothes off, princess."

She shifted, staring up at me.

"I'm tired, Aiden."

"Clothes, please. I want to feel you."

She sighed but tugged her t-shirt over her head before discarding the rest of her clothes. I didn't take my boxers off because I knew if I did, I wouldn't hold back. I pressed her to me, savouring the way her skin felt against mine.

"Thank you," I whispered, pressing a kiss to her forehead.

"This is really all you wanted?"

"Mmmhmm."

She kissed my chest, wrapping her arm around me again.

"You don't usually ask me to sleep naked."

"Feeling you soothes me, princess."

I trailed my fingers down her spine. She trembled at my touch, so I didn't stop. I couldn't. I brushed my fingers over her side and down across her stomach. Her breathing became a little heavier and her palm flattened on my back.

It struck me that we didn't argue or fight over what happened with Chuck this evening. A couple of months ago, we'd be at each other's throats leading to explosive makeup sex. Now, we just talked and it felt good. Although, I couldn't deny I missed the desperate way we fucked each other. The anger and the pain bleeding into it. I just didn't want that with her now. I hated Avery experiencing any sort of pain or hurt.

"Aiden," she breathed, pulling me back to the present where I was still stroking her skin.

"Mmm?"

"Please."

She trembled in my hold. I had a feeling I knew what she was asking, but I wanted her to tell me. Wanted her to say it.

"Please what?"

"Touch me, please."

"I am."

She bucked, moaning quietly.

"No, touch me properly."

"You're going to have to elaborate."

"Aiden, please."

I shouldn't tease her but hearing her beg was always so fucking sweet.

"Tell me what you want, princess."

"Please, please touch my clit, make me come. I'm so wet for you."

I trailed my fingers down her stomach and lower until they brushed against her entrance. She wasn't lying, but then again, she told me sometimes I only had to look at her to get her wet.

Fuck. I coated my fingers in her arousal and did as she asked. Her responding moan was like music to my ears. This girl did things to me. She made me ache with want and need. I loved her with an intensity which threatened to break me in half. I needed her. I fucking well needed her like I needed air.

I pulled her head back by her hair and kissed her, devouring her mouth like I was fucking drowning. She arched into me, pressing harder against my fingers. Fuck. The heat radiating from her drove me fucking crazy.

She moved, pressing her hands on my chest and forcing me flat on my back. Tugging my boxers down enough, she freed my cock, swung a leg over me and sunk down on it. I grunted, feeling her tight heat encasing me fully. Fuck. She rocked back and forth, her hands on my chest. Her doe eyes were wild with desire and affection.

"Fuck, you feel so good," she told me.

"I thought you were tired."

"Shut up and kiss me."

I didn't have a chance to respond. Her lips were on mine, taking exactly what she wanted. I gave in. Letting her have control. Letting her set the pace. Allowing her this moment to fuck me. I'd worked her up and this was my fucking reward for it.

Perhaps I should've let her fall asleep in my arms. My beautiful dark haired wife who was currently grinding her hips into mine. She grabbed my hand and pressed my fingers between her legs. Avery knew exactly what she wanted and I gave it to her. It didn't take long before she was shuddering above me, her tits bouncing on her chest as she came. Fuck she looked so beautiful, crying out my name as the waves of pleasure rushed over her.

When her trembling subsided, I flipped her over on her back and thrust inside her. I fucked my wife without a fucking care for how erratic and rough my movements were. She held onto me, cursing at the intensity, but never once telling me to stop. I slammed into her over and over until she came again, crying out as her nails dug into my shoulders. And I let go too, giving into the unadulterated bliss she always brought on.

We were both a panting, sweaty mess, lying there together with her head on my chest.

"Tomorrow, Mrs Lockhart," I whispered. "I'm going to tie you up and make sure you don't leave this bed all day."

She squirmed against me.

"I can't wait," she whispered back.

Two Weeks Prior

"So what you're saying is The Collector is someone in her family?" I said, staring at John intently.

He nodded.

"It has to be. I think it's a title handed down. I can't ask Chuck any further questions about it. He's getting really suspicious."

John had been snooping, but we were still running into dead ends. We had to find out who it was so we could find the girls. I had information on them up until six years ago when the trail dried up. Whoever it was had started hiding their tracks better.

"So, it was Mitchell for a time, but it changed when he took over Daniels Holdings after Nick got sick. We know it didn't fall into Chuck's hands. So it could've gone to Troy or Arthur."

The youngest of Mitchell's cousins, Arthur, was a reclusive little fuck who kept to himself. He didn't work for Daniels Holdings. Instead, he'd started his own investment company who mostly owned restaurants across the country along with a few other ventures. I knew he had a hand in the sex trafficking, but he didn't seem to be as deeply involved as Mitchell, Chuck and Troy were. We couldn't, however, completely rule him out.

"Most likely. I'll do some more digging into them. Not easy when I have to look after Avery, but I'm doing my best under the circumstances."

"I know… we need to nail them. They're the key to everything. We get them, the empire falls."

John nodded, looking over at where Avery was sat in the armchair by the window sketching. I knew she was only semi paying attention to our conversation. She'd been a little quiet for the past few days. Nerves about next week and the wedding were kicking in. For both of us.

"How's she holding up?" he asked, dropping his voice low.

"Okay, I guess. Hates Frazier constantly being at the office, but not much else we can do about it."

"And is everything else okay, the planning and all that?"

"Things are as ready as they can be. So far, no one else knows. I think we're in the clear but we can never be too careful."

Anyone finding out about our wedding would fuck all our plans up. When everything was legal, it wouldn't matter as much. They couldn't change it then. We couldn't do anything about the trust fund until all of this was resolved, but at least her money would be safe. I didn't want it. I'd keep it away from Frazier Shaw though. For as long as my lungs still breathed air and my heart beat in my chest. Protecting Avery was the single most important thing to me.

"I'm honoured you two want me there."

"Avery insisted. Said it wouldn't be the same if you weren't. You saw her grow up and have done so much for the two of us."

He smiled, rubbing the back of his neck.

"You're going to make a grown man get all emotional in a minute."

"Soppy git."

SARAH BAILEY

"You're a fine one to talk. Don't forget I've seen how you care for that girl on a daily basis."

I rolled my eyes. Sure, I'd become sort of soft when it came to Avery, but I cared about her. I wanted to make her happy. She had enough of my brutality in the bedroom. Outside of it, she needed someone who'd be her partner, not a man who ranted and ordered her around all the time. I'd tried to leave that version of me behind. So I could deserve her even though I probably never would.

"She's worth it. Watching her smile is like looking at the fucking sun. So radiant."

"I heard that," came her voice across the room.

John laughed, slapping me on the back. It wasn't like it was a secret how I felt about her.

"You were supposed to."

She looked up from her drawing, giving me a grin and a wink. Fuck that girl could really brighten my mood instantly.

"I best be off," John said.

"Yeah, see you in the morning."

"Don't worry, I'll nail this fucker to the wall, Aiden. Whether it be Troy, Arthur or someone else, we'll find him and we'll take him down. Enough is enough."

I nodded. I knew he would find something out somehow.

"See you tomorrow, Avery," he called as he walked out.

"Bye, John."

I went over to her, kneeling at her feet and wrapping a hand around her calf as I heard the front door slam.

"Would my radiant princess like dinner?"

She set her drawing aside, put her feet down on the floor and leant over, catching my face in her hands.

"Yes, please, my beautiful husband to be."

I bit my lip, trying not to smile. Fuck. Anyone else calling me beautiful, I would've told them to fuck off, but Avery said it was her immediate thought when she saw me the first time. Her beautiful avenging angel.

I was trying to live up to that image she had of me.

Even though in reality, I was still battered, broken and bruised and she was no longer innocent, fragile and sheltered.

My girl would see us through even if I never found redemption for all the things I'd done.

Avery was my salvation.

And I would find a way to be the man she deserved.

SEVEN

Avery

Present Day

I poked my head around Ed's office door. He was sitting at his desk, fiddling with a tablet with a frown on his face.

"You look like you could use a break."

He looked up, his expression startled.

"Shit, Avery, you scared me."

I slid into the room, folding my hands behind my back. He'd been acting weird for weeks. Ever since Saskia had overheard him, his behaviour became more erratic. Something was bothering him and I wasn't sure what.

"Sorry, fancy some lunch?"

He looked down at his watch.

"Sure, ordering in or should we take a working lunch?"

"Already sorted… Saskia has it laid out in the conference room."

I wanted to put him at ease so his guard would be down and he might let something slip. Later, I'd have to deal with

Frazier and Tristan, but for now, I could try work out what the hell was going on with my cousin.

"Did you want to discuss something then?"

I shook my head.

"It's all work around here and after all the excitement of my birthday last week I just thought we could talk about how you think everything is going."

He nodded, standing up and coming around his desk. He followed me out of the room and along to the conference room. There were various posh sandwiches, snacks and drinks. Way more than Ed and I could eat by ourselves. When we were seated and tucking in, he turned to me.

"So… getting married to Tristan. I was a little surprised when you announced it."

"I'm not in love with him if that's what you're wondering."

He inclined his head a little, smiling.

"What is your reasoning then?"

"It's what Dad wanted. Joining our families together seems right under the circumstances."

I was lying through my teeth, but who cared at this point? Even though Ed hadn't given me many reasons to suspect him, I still didn't trust him. Just like Aiden said, I couldn't trust anyone in my family. I had to suspect everyone and everything. I didn't want to turn into one of those girls who was paranoid about everything, but my family had done more than enough to warrant suspicion.

"You're doing it out of a sense of obligation?"

"I guess so."

He frowned, fiddling with his glass.

"Not that I have any right to offer you advice on your love life, but don't you think you should marry someone because you want to be with them?"

"You think I don't want to be with Tristan?"

He raised an eyebrow.

"Do you?"

I felt like I was falling into a trap here. Did I answer that question honestly or not? I looked away. Ed's gaze was far too intense, stripping me open and leaving me exposed.

"Does it matter?"

I took a bite of my sandwich whilst I waited for his answer.

"Yes. I think our family has placed far too many obligations on us and this shouldn't be one of yours."

My eyes snapped to his. His expression was neutral but his eyes told me he was serious. What kind of obligations did he have? Was this to do with the dark family dealings? I couldn't ask him outright, but I wanted to know. I needed to. What did Ed know? How deeply involved was he?

"We don't always get what we want in life."

"We also no longer live in a time where you have to marry a man you don't want to."

My uncle didn't want me to marry Tristan. My cousin didn't. What did they have against the Shaws? What exactly was Frazier hiding? Everyone always seemed to get along so well. This made me realise that perhaps more was going on than I'd first thought. I got the distinct impression that my father's death had been the catalyst to all of this. Had he kept them all in line and made sure these divides didn't affect their business relationships? If so, then Aiden had completely disrupted everything.

Was this his plan all along?

Did he know how this would play out?

Remove the key player and all the rest would fall one by one. It certainly looked and felt that way to me. Frazier's insistence on me marrying Tristan. Ed acting strangely. My uncle going from telling me off one minute to apologising to me the next. Rick Morgan involving himself in our family affairs. All of this seemed far too convenient to be a coincidence.

I had to ask Aiden him later.

"You're right… that doesn't mean I'm not going ahead with it. Do you have something against the Shaws?"

He sighed, plucking a bunch of grapes off one of the plates and popping a few in his mouth.

"Not exactly. You just shouldn't trust anyone outside the family. You never know what type of skeletons are living in people's cupboards."

I knew what ones were living in our family's. Horrific ones involving slavery, human trafficking, rape and abuse. Not to mention murder. Aiden's mother can't have been the only girl they'd killed. Whoever it really was considering he was now convinced it hadn't been my father. That left us at a dead end.

Aiden said the voice was familiar to him. The level of detail he'd used to describe the event broke my heart. It wasn't just because I loved Aiden. No seven year old boy should have to watch someone slit their mother's throat and leave her to bleed out on the floor. After witnessing all that shit as a child, it was no wonder he had so many problems. The whole thing was traumatic.

"You saying Frazier has a bunch in his?"

"Maybe he does. Just look at his clients. You can't think they're all innocent with nothing to hide."

Frazier had some very high profile clients. He rubbed shoulders with some of the richest men in England. He had connections. Ones he no doubt used to help my father and all his other associates. It was those connections I needed to find along with his secrets. Frazier had to have covered a lot of shit up.

"I'm not that naïve. There's darkness in everyone." *Even in me*, I added to myself silently.

He gave me a sad smile. It did something strange to my insides. Was Ed struggling with his own darkness? What did he really know? Too many questions.

"Some more than others."

I nodded slowly. I hadn't come in here to talk to him about my engagement to Tristan, but it'd given me a lot to think about.

"How are things with you anyway? Are you happy here?"

He steepled his fingers. A gesture which reminded me of my father. He used to do that when he was contemplating something. The thought of it seared into my chest, causing me to clench my fist under the table against the onslaught of pain I felt when I thought about him. I hated my father so much, but there was still a tiny part of me that would always love him. He'd raised me, loved me and cared for me. How could a man who doted so much on his daughter be such a monster behind closed doors?

I reminded myself he'd been less than a stellar father in the past few years since we'd argued so much over my future. He'd shown the true man he was underneath the mask. The one who got angry when he didn't get his way. Did he take out that frustration on those girls? Did he enjoy dominating them because it gave him a sense of power? Control?

I felt a little ill thinking about it in that way. Mostly because there was such a fine line between the way my dad treated those women and the way Aiden treated me. There was one huge difference. I wanted to submit to Aiden in the bedroom, but those girls my dad abused? They hadn't wanted it at all.

I had an unorthodox relationship with Aiden, sure. Before I left him, he had all the power and he used it to his advantage. I knew how wrong that was. I recognised it and in his own way, so did he. We'd changed. Our relationship evolved into something else. I was his wife now and he was my husband. I'd chosen to go back to him. I'd picked Aiden. I'd taken my side in this war and I was never going back on it.

"I am. Working with family has been rewarding. Seeing the company go from strength to strength in such a short time, despite all the hardships our family has faced. I only hope it will continue."

I didn't know whether to take his words on face value or not. Was there a deeper meaning? Fuck. I really was beginning to sound so paranoid. I wanted to trust Ed. I wanted him to be on my side. Except I couldn't. That niggling voice of doubt in my head assured me trusting my cousin would be my downfall. My biggest mistake.

I steeled my heart even though it killed me to do so. I had to. The alarm bells going off in my head were too strong to ignore. Not listening to my gut instincts would surely land me in trouble.

"I'm happy you feel that way. I'm so glad we're working together. Having an ally in this place is a godsend you know. Uncle Charlie is difficult to deal with at times, but with you, it's easy."

The way he smiled told me everything I needed to know. The excitement in his eyes at my words. He thought I trusted him. The sinking feeling in my stomach almost made me want to hurl up my lunch, but I didn't. Remaining calm and composed was my only course of action.

Ed knew.

He fucking knew.

And I hated that fact.

Hated the realisation I had.

I would have to take him down along with my uncle and the Shaws. I'd have to destroy my family completely. It was the only way. No one was coming out of this unscathed.

So right then and there, I drew a line in the sand.

From this day forth, my cousin was my enemy.

And I would not let my love for him cloud my judgement.

Or so I hoped.

Trudging back into the flat, I realised I didn't have much time before I had to leave for dinner with the Shaws. A pit of dread coiled in my stomach. I didn't want to sit through this evening with them, but I had to. It was the only way. Frazier didn't keep his secrets at his office. They would be in his home, ensconced in his office where no one else would have access to them. I knew though. And I'd get it for Aiden and me.

My husband was in the bedroom, waiting for me when I walked in. His grey eyes were stormy. It concerned me.

"Hey," I said, taking off my blazer and hanging it up in the cupboard.

He came up behind me, wrapping his hands around my waist and leaning down to kiss my cheek.

"Princess," he breathed, inhaling me.

"I've got to get ready."

His hands around me tightened.

"I hate this."

I nodded. I did too. I started to unbutton my blouse, but he spun me around and replaced my hands with his own. He threw the blouse in the wash basket when he slipped it off my shoulders and unzipped my skirt, discarding that too. I stood there in just my underwear. His eyes darkened significantly.

"Stay there," he told me.

He moved away to the bedside table and pulled something off it, coming back over to me. He dropped to his knees, running his hand up my thigh. He secured the strap to my thigh before slipping the knife into its sheath.

"If he tries anything with you, do not hesitate, Avery. Do you understand?"

"Yes."

I didn't relish the prospect of hurting anyone physically, but if it was me or one of the Shaws, I knew who I'd choose. Myself.

Aiden rose to his feet, dropping a kiss on my forehead. Before he could disappear, I grabbed him by the face and tugged him down for a proper kiss. I needed a moment with him. His body against mine. I pressed myself to him, wrapping my arms around his neck. Aiden responded in kind, holding me close, his hands banded around my back.

"Princess," he whispered against my lips. "I love you."

I just about melted on the spot. I wanted him to lay me down on the bed, put me in that harness of his and let him use my body for his pleasure. Somewhere along the line, I'd embraced my own need to be completely at Aiden's mercy. I wanted the restraints just as much as he did. Just thinking about them made my insides clench.

Now was not the time. Not when I had a job to do. It might be the most important evening of my life. Having one up on Frazier Shaw would make this all worthwhile.

I pulled away, staring up into his beautiful features. My avenging angel. I wanted him so fucking much, I could barely think straight.

"This might not be the right time to ask this, but when tonight is done and we've got what we need… Can we celebrate with…?"

"With what?"

I trailed a finger down his chest, staring at it intently.

"I liked what you did the first night we stayed at mine."

He put a finger under my chin, turning my gaze back up to his. The darkness in them simmered with heat.

"You did?"

"Yes… I realise you were punishing me over the James thing, but the way you took complete control, how you spoke to me… it did things to me. I want you to do it again. I want to be at your mercy like that. Fuck, Aiden, it was so hot. Maybe it's really fucked up, but I don't care. We're fucked up together."

I'd never actually voiced out loud how I felt about that night. It had been a couple of months ago, but hell, right now, all I really wanted was for Aiden to help me forget about everything else. I wanted to drown in my husband. I needed it. Desired it. Craved it. It pulsed in my veins. My nerves tingled.

He leant down towards me, brushing his lips over mine as he cupped my backside with one hand, pressing me into his hard cock.

"You want to be tied up so you can't move and fucked within an inch of your life in all three of your tight holes?"

His deep, rich voice vibrated right through me. I squirmed, nodding. I wanted it more than anything.

"Shit, princess. You have no idea what the fuck you do to me."

"I think I do."

I ground into him, my stomach rubbing against his cock. He groaned in response.

"It'd be my fucking pleasure to put you back in the harness and use you like you want me to. Fuck, Avery, why did you have to bring this up now?"

The thought of what I had to do this evening terrified me. Losing myself to Aiden was the only way I could cope with that fear.

"I'm sorry."

"Don't apologise. I wish you'd told me before, but things have been so crazy. I know now… and trust me, when I do tie you up, you'll know exactly how it feels to be mine and at my mercy."

I shivered. I was already Aiden's and had been at his mercy from the day we'd met. I wanted him in control. Putting me through my paces. Pushing me to my limits. Making me come so hard I no longer knew what was up or down. I craved everything about this man. The man who'd become my sole focus in life. My husband.

I kissed him again before I pulled away. He released me although I could see his reluctance to in his eyes. They roamed down my body, falling on my heaving chest. I was so fucking turned on. The pull between us pulsed. Aiden set me on fire and I'd just well and truly stoked the flames.

"Fuck, princess."

He pushed me against the cupboard door, my hair wrapped in his fist as he dragged his teeth down my neck.

"We can't."

Who was I fucking kidding? I had maybe an hour before John picked me up but making myself look like the perfect wife to be would take time and I needed a shower if Aiden was going to fuck me.

He released himself from the confines of his clothes. When his bare cock rubbed against my stomach, it felt like fire against my skin. He was so hot. He dragged me away from the door and pressed me down on the rug on the floor. Both of us were too consumed by each other to move to the bed. He tugged aside my underwear and thrust inside me. I cried out, my nails digging into his t-shirt.

"Fuck, Aiden."

"So wet for me. Wanting your husband to fuck you without holding back, hmm?"

I almost melted on the damn spot hearing him call himself my husband.

"Please."

"When I tie you up, I'm going to leave the gag out this time. Then I can hear you begging and pleading with me. And I can fuck your throat. You won't be able to stop me. You want that, don't you?"

He gave it to me hard and I met him thrust for thrust.

"Yes, I want it all."

I wanted him everywhere. In every part of me. Despite being terrified of anal when he'd first indicated he wanted it, now, it was another part of our relationship I loved. It felt so good to have him take me there with wild abandon. And fuck, did he know it. He made it feel like heaven. Made me beg him to fuck me harder until I came over and over for him.

He claimed my mouth, devouring me from the inside out. He didn't let up until I trembled and shook beneath him, unable to form coherent thoughts any longer. It was exactly what I needed.

He kissed my face and got off me when we both came down from our highs, sitting up with his hands resting on his knees. My limbs felt like jelly, but I needed to get in the shower and wash away the scent of sex on my skin.

When I came out of the bathroom after getting thoroughly clean without wetting my hair, Aiden was sitting on the bed staring down at his ringing phone.

"Who is it?"

"I don't know…"

"Then maybe you should find out."

I went over to my cupboards and pulled out a fresh set of underwear along with the dress I was going to wear.

"Hello?"

I looked back at him, watching the colour drain from his face.

"I'm giving you one fucking minute to tell me why you're calling me before I hang up."

The venom in his voice made me freeze.

His grey eyes met mine. The anger in them made my heart pound.

'Who is it?' I mouthed at him.

He put his hand over the speaker.

And the name he blurted out sent a chill down my spine.

"Rick."

EIGHT

Aiden

ick's voice grated on my ears. I knew as soon as I heard it who he was. We'd never actually spoken before, but I'd heard him enough times from when he visited my mother. What I didn't know is why the fuck he was calling me.

"I suggest you don't hang up on me. What I have to say is important."

Avery's face was full of concern when I told her who it was. She needed to continue getting ready because John would be here soon. I waved her away, pointing at her naked body. She frowned but started getting dressed.

"What do you want?"

"Did you think no one would find out about your marriage?"

I stiffened. It wasn't like I hadn't considered that possibility, but I didn't care any longer. It was done. Legal. Avery was my wife.

"What's it to you?"

"You're walking on very thin ice."

"No shit. Tell me something I don't know."

I hated this man. He might be the reason for my existence, but he was scum. He was worse than fucking scum. Rick Morgan was a cunt of the highest order.

I stood up and paced the room. I hated that I was even giving him the time of day, but I was fucking concerned about him being aware of my marriage to Avery and what he would do with that knowledge.

Why hadn't it occurred to me before that he, of all people, would be the first one to find out? I knew he was watching us and knew things about us no one else did. Intimate details of my relationship with her. I hated him knowing anything. I still hadn't worked out how he found out. I scoured the flat high and low for cameras, but there was nothing. What I hadn't done is check Avery's. I needed to.

"She's a real doll that Avery. Feisty."

I clenched my fist, wanting to punch the fucking wall.

"Don't you fucking say shit about her."

He laughed, making my skin crawl. He had no fucking right to talk about her. He didn't know her. They'd spoken once and if I had my fucking way, they'd never speak to each other again. He didn't deserve to know Avery.

"That little darlin' has you wrapped around her finger. It'd be such a shame if something happened to her because of your recklessness."

"What the fuck are you talking about? Are you threatening her?"

I'd already threatened to kill him and now he was just making it that much easier.

If it came to it, I would destroy him.

And I'd start with exposing his biggest secret.

Me.

His son.

"Me? Hurt your little darlin'? Why no, what kind of father do you take me for?"

"You're not my fucking father."

I felt a hand on my arm. I stopped in my tracks, staring down at my wife. She was dressed now. Even in my agitated state, she looked fucking good enough to eat. It was a demure little black number which fell to her knees. It concealed the knife strapped to her thigh. It was the only form of protection she'd have against Tristan and Frazier considering it was nigh on impossible to get her to agree to take a gun with her. I didn't have time to show her how to shoot one and I didn't have one here anyway. It was too much of a risk to have an illegal, untraceable handgun in the flat. I'd taken enough of those procuring one to take her parents out.

I put a hand around her waist and pulled her into me, holding her to my chest. Feeling her against me helped me focus. I had to stay calm even if Rick was winding me the fuck up.

"I mightn't have raised you, but you're my son by blood, Aiden."

"Yeah? Try telling that to your wife."

Fuck him. He could go to fucking hell.

"This ain't getting us nowhere."

"No. Why the fuck did you call me? To tell me you know about my marriage to Avery? Big fucking deal. Unless you're planning on telling Chuck, then I don't give a shit."

"It's not me knowing you have to worry about."

"Then who?"

Fuck. He was really driving me crazy. Avery wrapped her arms around my back, running her fingers down my spine. She always knew how to soothe me. My girl. My beautiful raven haired princess.

"Anyone can access marriage records."

That didn't mean anyone had the fucking inclination to do so unless they had a reason to.

"If you're not going to give me a valid fucking reason why the fuck I'm still talking to you then I'm hanging up."

I heard him sigh deeply. I wasn't going to let him just talk my fucking ear off. He'd taken my fucking girl once and I didn't trust him. Not one bit.

"Be cautious."

"Thanks for the fucking warning I didn't need."

"Not the only reason I called."

Of course it fucking wasn't. Rick wouldn't fucking break twenty eight years of fucking radio silence to tell me to be careful.

"Did your little darlin' do what I asked her to?"

He didn't deserve a fucking answer to that. He didn't deserve anything from me, but I wanted to know who murdered my mother. I needed to know.

"Yes."

"Good. You can tell her I'll see both of you soon. It will be nice to meet my daughter in law in person."

I almost fucking lost it. I didn't want him anywhere near Avery ever again. She didn't need his shit in her life. Neither of us did.

"Didn't you get my fucking message?"

He laughed. Fucking laughed. Cunt.

"Oh, I heard. Bob was furious with you. I told him antagonising you was a bad idea. He has a habit of not listening to sound advice."

"Then you know I won't fucking tolerate you coming anywhere near her."

Avery stiffened in my arm, raising her head off my chest, her doe eyes wide with fear.

"Your threats are meaningless, Aiden. If you kill me, you'll never know who really murdered Lizzie."

I dropped my arm from around Avery, clenching my fist and grinding my jaw. He was fucking pushing my buttons and he knew it. I wanted him dead. So fucking much. But he was fucking right. I also needed to know who killed my mother. Who took her life. Who slit her throat in front of me. It was the only thing I didn't know and it fucking killed me.

"And what, you're not going to fucking tell me unless she's there?"

"Your little darlin' is an important piece of the puzzle."

What the actual fuck did that mean? He was talking in fucking riddles the worthless piece of shit.

"She has nothing to do with any of this."

"I think you'll find she has everything to do with it."

"You know what, go fuck yourself, Rick. Stay away from me and stay the fuck away from my wife. I meant it. I will fucking kill you."

"Tut, tut, Aiden. Your temper will be your downfall one day if you don't keep it in check. Keep her safe. The vultures are circling. They're out for blood and she's in the crossfire."

He hung up before I had a chance to say anything else. I almost threw my phone against the wall.

"Aiden?" Avery said.

I looked down at her still wrapped around me. What had Rick said? She's in the crossfire? Did he fucking know what we had planned this evening? Was he warning me not to let her go to Frazier's? I wasn't sure whether to listen to his fucking warnings or not. It nagged at me. Avery wasn't safe. She would be in serious shit if she went tonight.

Keep her safe.

"You're not going tonight."

"What?"

"I said you're not fucking going to Frazier's tonight."

She dropped her arms and stepped away from me, eyes full of confusion.

"Why not? What did Rick say?"

"It's what he didn't say. You're not safe."

She folded her arms across her chest.

"We already knew that."

I hadn't wanted her to go through with this before, but after Rick's words, I was even more paranoid about what might happen. Frazier was fucking unpredictable and dangerous. He didn't have my wife's best interests at heart. And his son was a fucking worthless piece of shit who would rape her any chance he got.

"We're calling it off. You're going to phone Frazier and tell him you're not feeling well. Make some shit up, but you're not going to the Shaws."

She stared at me for several seconds before she frowned.

"We've worked towards this, Aiden. This is our chance to set things right."

Didn't she understand? She was more important to me than taking down Frazier. If I lost Avery, I'd have nothing. If they did something unspeakable to her, it would break me. I couldn't live with myself if she went through any more shit. I'd done enough to her as it was. I'd messed with her head. I'd fucking broken her. Fuck. I couldn't have her going into the lion's den without me. I couldn't.

"It's too dangerous."

She sighed, turning away and walking out of the room. I followed her into the bathroom. This conversation wasn't over. She started applying her makeup in front of the bathroom mirror.

"I know it's dangerous. Do you think I'm not terrified about walking into his house unprotected? I have no idea what they have planned, but I can't just let this opportunity slip by."

"Avery—"

"I don't want to hear it. We've known from day one this could go wrong. Why are you acting like this now? I know you're worried about me, but I'll be okay. I have to do this. I need to destroy them. Don't you understand?"

"Do you think I don't want that? I want them all fucking dead, but not at the expense of you. Never at the expense of you."

I ran a hand through my hair, my fear and agitation growing. Couldn't she see? This could be a fucking trap for all we knew. My gut was telling me if she went there, something really fucking shit would happen. Something neither of us could come back from.

"For fuck's sake, I can't do this. I can't let you go there. They'll hurt you."

She shook her head before turning to me.

"I know the risks."

"You don't fucking understand. Frazier is a psychotic cunt and Tristan tried to rape you. Do you think he won't try again?

He fucking told you he was going to fuck you at your birthday party."

She flinched. She'd told me that the day after. I was fucking mad about it. His dick was not allowed anywhere near her. He was not having access to my wife. My fucking wife. I wasn't even being a possessive or jealous piece of crap. I was worried about her fucking safety. It wasn't fucked up to not want my wife to get raped by someone who'd threatened it on more than one occasion. I took his fucking threats seriously. I didn't trust him near Avery.

"I know what he said."

"Then why are you arguing with me about this?"

She turned away, continuing with her makeup. I couldn't fucking stand this. She was acting like my concerns meant nothing. Maybe I was going off the deep end because of my conversation with Rick, but that didn't negate how helpless I felt. I couldn't protect her. Fuck. This reminded me of how I'd felt the day Rick took her.

I strode towards her, grabbed her arm and forced her to look at me.

"Stop. Just stop. I don't want you going to their house."

"Aiden, you agreed to this. You said it was our best chance. You don't get to change your mind now. I have to do this. I need them out of my life. This is the only way I can expose them all. Don't you get it? I'm married to you, but I can't openly admit it. I can't tell the fucking world I'm not a Daniels any longer and that I love you. You. My husband. Do you know how that makes me feel? Like shit. I can't carry on like this. It has to end and it has to end now."

She wrenched her arm out of my grasp. I knew this was tough on her, not being able to be honest about us being together. But this is how it'd always been from day one. Things didn't just change overnight. We had to work towards it. Did she think I wanted to hide it any more than her? Fuck. I wanted everyone to know she was mine. I was fucking proud to be her husband. I was proud to have her on my arm. She was the fucking world to me. The most beautiful girl I'd ever seen. So fucking smart. So fucking radiant. And she picked me. Me of all people to be her man.

"I get that you're angry about Rick phoning you and taunting you with whatever bullshit he decided to sprout, but you don't get to take that out on me."

"Take it out on you? I'm not fucking taking it out on you. I'm fucking well scared for your fucking life and wellbeing."

She didn't soften. Her doe eyes hardened.

"You are. You're shouting at me and getting pissed off because you think I'm not listening. I am. I understand what this is doing to you. Do you think I want to go over to their house and make small talk with two people I hate? I don't. I really don't want to do this, but I have to. I can't go on like this. I want to have a normal fucking life without all of this bullshit. I want a life with you. What we have now is not a fucking life. We're living in the shadows. I'm living in hell because of my family and Frazier fucking Shaw."

Tears welled in her eyes. The sight of it fucking killed me. Her words destroyed me.

"I love you, Aiden. I love you so fucking much, but you're not going to stop me doing this."

She turned back to the mirror, finishing up her makeup whilst I stared at her silently. What the fuck could I say to any of that? I wanted a life with her too. A life that didn't include her shitty family and the Shaws. And one where Rick fucking Morgan left us alone.

I followed her out of the bathroom. She slipped on a low pair of heels and her coat.

"Avery, please don't do this."

She didn't look at me as she opened the front door. I couldn't let her fucking go. I walked out of the flat with her, grabbing my keys on the way. She fiddled with her phone, doing her best to ignore me as we rode down in the lift to the ground floor. My heart was in a fucking vice. I needed her to come back upstairs with me. How was I going to convince her? I understood what she was saying, but the threat the Shaws posed to her was more important.

Why the fuck had I even agreed to this stupid idiotic plan in the first place? Why had I ever thought this was a good idea? It was the worst idea. Absolute worst idea ever. She fucking knew that. This is what broke us apart in the first place.

I stopped her from opening the door when we reached John's car, turning her to face me. I had to try. I had to convince her.

"Avery, please. Just stop and think about this. Think about what you're walking into."

She took a deep breath, her doe eyes softening.

"I know what I'm doing. Please, stop making this harder for me."

She reached up, placing her hand on my cheek.

"I love you. I'll be back with what we need."

She stepped back out of my grasp, opened the car door and slid in. I watched the car pull away, unable to stop the sinking feeling in my stomach. The one that told me this was going to end badly. Avery was walking into a trap of Frazier's making and I couldn't stop her.

"Fuck."

I turned away to walk back into the building when I felt a sharp pain radiate from the back of my skull. I staggered, reaching up and touching where someone had clearly slammed something into my head. My vision blurred a little, but I kept upright. I swung my fist, connecting with something soft. The person grunted.

"Fuck," someone said.

"Just get him already, we don't have time for this," said a second voice.

I put my fists up. Whoever the fuck these guys were, they were not taking me down easily.

"Do I look like I want to get beaten the shit out of? Just fucking knock him out already."

I swung at the first man who came into view. The knock to my head really fucking hurt. What the fuck did they hit me with? I should've concentrated on the others, but the first one came at me, distracting me. I swung again, managing to hit him straight in the jaw. He grunted but didn't go down. I wasn't sure how hard I'd hit him considering I could barely fucking see straight.

The next thing I knew, a needle was jabbed into my neck and I was drowning. I felt my feet fall out from underneath me. Someone caught me. I tried to look up at them, but I couldn't make out their features properly.

"There we go. That wasn't so hard, was it?"

"Hurry the fuck up and get him in the van before someone sees us."

I felt the sensation of being lifted up and carried by two people before I was unceremoniously dumped on a cold metal floor. Before I had a chance to try and regain my senses, I was plunged into darkness.

Whatever they'd given me was working. My limbs wouldn't function. My head felt fuzzy. What the fuck had they given me? What the fuck was happening? Why the hell would anyone fucking knock me out? Who'd sent them?

The questions in my mind blurred into one. I was sinking further and further. I didn't know what was up or down any longer.

I closed my eyes and the last thing I thought before I lost consciousness was that I was truly fucked and my wife was in serious danger.

NINE

Avery

*M*y heart was torn to shreds. Completely. Aiden's fear seeped into me. Everything he said made sense. Absolutely everything. I was tired of this shit. So tired that I couldn't stop now. We'd set this plan in motion and I was ready for it to all be over.

"Are you okay?" John asked, looking back at me through the rear view mirror.

"Not really."

"Aiden didn't look happy."

I sighed, fiddling with my coat.

"He's not. We had a fight. He doesn't want me to do this tonight. Rick called him then he went mental at me."

"Rick called him?"

I nodded, but then realised he was paying attention to the road so couldn't see me.

"Yes. Not sure what he said other than he knows Aiden and I got married and I got the impression he still wants to meet me in person."

John drummed his fingers on the steering wheel for a moment.

"Rick's never got in touch with him before from what he's told me."

Aiden hadn't exactly been unreasonable with me and it made this worse. I knew him talking to Rick would piss him off. I just wanted to know what the man said to cause my husband to go completely off the deep end over me going to the Shaws tonight. Except instead I'd got angry at him too. And now I felt like the world's worst wife. I should've pressed him about what Rick said. I should've made him tell me.

"No… It'll be okay, I'm just worried about him and what he might do. I mean last time he beat the crap out of Robert Bassington."

John gave me another look through the rear view mirror. He seemed concerned too.

"Are you sure you still want to do this?"

"Not really, but do I even have a choice at this point? If I don't do this now, then it'll just be later down the line and I think we've all had enough."

He nodded slowly. He'd dealt with my family for a long time. He knew a lot of their darkest secrets. John wanted a quiet life now, just like Aiden and me. One without threats and dark family deeds hanging over us. I'd meant what I said to Aiden. I wanted a life with him where we could be free to love each other in the open.

Was it so wrong that I wanted to be able to walk down the street and hold my husband's hand without being scared we'd be exposed by the press or some random person snapping a picture of us? I wanted to be able to wear my fucking wedding ring. I just wanted to be normal. Not that our relationship could ever be described as normal. Not with how it started and the ways in which we desired each other.

"As long as you're sure. I can take you back if you're not."

"I'm sure."

The rest of the journey to Frazier's was silent. I was too busy dwelling on my argument with Aiden. I wished we hadn't got into a fight. It made this so much worse. My nerves coiled in my stomach, destroying my appetite and giving me a slight headache. I needed Aiden's support and I didn't have that. I pulled out my phone, settling for sending him a message.

ME: I'M SORRY.
ME: I LOVE YOU XXX

I didn't get a response. He was probably still cooling off. Something in my gut told me I should be worried about him not responding. He hadn't even seen the texts. Aiden didn't usually ignore his phone going off. I was about to try calling him when we pulled up in Frazier's driveway. I stuffed my phone back in the pocket of my dress. I'd picked it deliberately because a dress with pockets, who didn't want one of those?

John helped me out the car and gave me a sharp nod.

"I'm only a text message or phone call away."

I put a hand on his arm.

"I know. Thank you… Hey John, can you try calling Aiden and see if he's calmed down yet? I don't know why, but I feel like something's wrong."

He gave me a tight smile.

"I will. I'm sure he'll be fine if you give him time."

I wasn't sure of that, but I smiled back at him before turning and walking up the steps to Frazier's front door. I rang the bell and waited. Two minutes later, Tristan opened the door.

"Hello, Avery."

"Hi, Tristan," I ground out.

Fuck did I hate him. He was wearing a collarless blue shirt with the sleeves rolled up. He stepped back, allowing me to walk in. When the door closed behind me, I felt a sense of dread prickle against my skin. I was fucking terrified of what tonight would bring.

I shuffled out of my coat and he took it from me, hanging it up in the cupboard. They had a grand hallway which had a sweeping staircase. I'd been here so many times throughout my childhood.

He placed a hand in the small of my back and directed me towards the formal dining room. My skin crawled. I didn't want his hands on me, but objecting was useless. I had to play my part tonight or things could go very wrong.

The room was well lit with a huge chandelier hanging over the middle of the table, which was a large dark wooden antique. Frazier had informed me about its origins when I was younger, but I'd hardly been listening. The man had a taste for expensive furniture. Nothing but the best for the Shaws.

Frazier was sat at the head of the table and there were only two place settings either side of him. I looked up at Tristan.

"Is Susan not joining us?"

"Mum's sister has been taken ill."

I wasn't sure if he was lying or not, but this didn't bode well at all. I would've felt safer with his mother here.

"Oh, I'm sorry. I was looking forward to seeing her."

"It's unfortunate, yes."

I sat to Frazier's left whilst Tristan walked around and placed himself across from me. His mud brown eyes were intent on my face. I fidgeted under his gaze.

"Thank you for coming, Avery," Frazier said, giving me a nod.

"Of course."

I didn't want to be here. I wanted to run back to Aiden. Tell him I was sorry. Bury my face in his solid chest and never let go. But that was the coward's way out. He might be my husband but I couldn't hide behind him. I had to face up to reality. The only way we were ever going to get out of this mess was by taking matters into our own hands.

There was a pensive silence for a long moment before we were served by Frazier's staff. The two men made polite small talk with me throughout the starter. It felt strange being so civil to them. When the staff had served us the main meal and withdrew, Frazier turned to me.

"The Radisson Blu in Marylebone have had a cancellation in August. I have made a provisional booking."

I froze, my fork halfway to my mouth.

He fucking did what?

I couldn't believe he'd gone behind my back and looked at reception venues for this bloody summer. Was he crazy? I hadn't even agreed to a date with Tristan yet. I took a breath, setting my fork back down. I couldn't get mad about this. I had to remain calm. This was still a fake engagement and I wouldn't be marrying Tristan. So what if Frazier had booked a venue? It could always be cancelled again.

"Isn't that a bit soon?"

"Why, no. I will hire you the best wedding planners, you won't have to lift a finger."

I knew why he was so invested in this. He wanted my money. No matter how sick it made me feel, I had to keep a straight face.

"Well, okay, perhaps Tristan and I can go see the venue together?"

I'd rather die than spend time with him, but it didn't hurt to show a little willingness. Tristan rolled his eyes.

"That can certainly be arranged."

I smiled and went back to my food, hoping this conversation was over. I had come here to talk about our engagement and subsequent wedding plans but that didn't mean I had to like it. And I had another job to do. When the dishes for the main course were cleared away, I excused myself to the bathroom.

Hurrying along the corridor when I got out of the dining room, I headed towards Frazier's office, keeping my eyes peeled for any of the staff. Thankfully they were too busy preparing dessert so the coast was clear. I slipped in and shut the door behind me. I didn't bother turning the light on as I crept towards his computer. It was on, but password protected. Pulling out the little memory stick Aiden had given me a couple of days ago, I plugged it in. He'd taught me how to hack into it. When I got through the password and it brought up the main screen, I ran another program he'd put on there. It would search all the files for me and download any relevant ones.

I breathed a short sigh of relief when I saw it was working, but too many minutes had gone by. I left it running as I slipped out and walked towards the bathroom. Once inside, I took several deep breaths. I couldn't stay here long, but I checked my phone. Aiden still hadn't responded to me. I sent him another message.

ME: GOING OKAY, GOT TO THE PC BUT WAITING FOR IT TO DOWNLOAD.

No response. He hadn't looked at his phone at all. I was beginning to worry. Why hadn't he checked his messages? Was he that pissed off with me? Surely, he'd want to know I was okay. Fuck. What was going on with him?

Aiden might not have responded, but John had sent me a message. When I opened it, my heart tightened uncomfortably in my chest.

JOHN: CAN'T GET HOLD OF AIDEN. GOING OVER TO CHECK ON HIM.

ME: OKAY. LET ME KNOW IF YOU FIND HIM PLEASE.

I splashed my face with water, flushed the toilet and walked out, almost barrelling straight into Tristan.

"I was just coming to look for you, dessert is about to be served."

His eyes were narrowed as I stared up into his hateful face.

"Right, uh… let's go then."

I didn't look towards Frazier's office. I didn't have time to go back in there. Not now Tristan was here. I had to hope the program would finish downloading all the files and I could get to it later.

He planted his hand on my lower back again. I glared at him.

"I'd rather you didn't touch me."

"Get used to it, Avery."

His hand moved lower, brushing over the top of my behind. I tensed, shifting out of his grasp. The revulsion I felt at having him touch me over my clothes would be nothing compared to him actually touching my skin.

"You can threaten me all you want. You and I both know this marriage is a sham. I'm not letting you feel me up."

He grabbed me by the wrist, stopping me in my tracks before he shoved me against the wall. Caging me in with one hand up by my head, his eyes roamed down my body.

"I'll feel you up all I fucking want. You're going to be mine. So if I want to touch you, I will."

His other hand ran down my bare arm. I shoved him away from me.

"Get fucked, Tristan."

I walked away back into the dining room. I heard his footsteps behind me, but I ignored him.

"There you two are," Frazier said.

I took my seat, finding dessert of a chocolate fondant with raspberry sorbet had already been served. Tristan threw himself back down in his own seat, scowling at me over the table. Frazier eyed us both. I started on my dessert, not wanting to talk about what happened in the corridor.

One of Frazier's staff came into the room and leant down to say something to him which I couldn't quite hear. He nodded at them with a gleam in his eye. Something about it set me on edge. Tristan seemed nonplussed by the exchange, too busy scowling at his plate. I'd pissed him off. Who knew what type of shit he was plotting? Honestly, I was surprised nothing untoward had really happened to me yet. What the fuck did they have planned?

"So, Avery, we have much to discuss. Have you finished?" Frazier said.

I'd cleared my plate without noticing.

"Um, yes."

"Shall we retire to the drawing room?"

Pretentious prick. Who still calls it a drawing room?

I shrugged. He rose and put a hand out to me which I took as I stood up. He tucked my hand into the crook of his elbow. Tristan followed us from the room.

"This has been a long time coming. Our families finally being one."

I wasn't sure how to respond to that, so I settled for staying silent. What I did notice was I wasn't being taken to the drawing room. No, we were walking further down the corridor to rooms I hadn't been in before. I looked up at Frazier, but his expression remained neutral.

He stopped outside a door, let go of my hand and opened it. Before I had a chance to say anything, Tristan grabbed me by my arms from behind and shoved me into the room. He held me in place in the pitch black until an overhead light came on.

I blinked rapidly, my eyes falling on someone cable tied to a chair. Someone I knew intimately.

"Now, Avery, tell me… do you know who this is?" Frazier said, turning to me.

I shook my head. His expression hardened.

"Come now, don't lie to me."

"I don't know what you're talking about."

"You do," Tristan hissed in my ear. "Have you conveniently forgotten what happened when I came to your office?"

Tears pricked at my eyes. It didn't look like they'd hurt him, but he was clearly unconscious.

"Why are you doing this?"

Frazier's eyes darkened, his expression suddenly turning vicious.

"Because you've been lying to me since day fucking one. Did you think I wouldn't find out?"

I froze. What exactly did he know? He wasn't telling me much so I knew I had to be careful of what I revealed. Tristan's hands around my arms tightened painfully. I was fucking terrified, but I had to stay strong.

"I haven't lied to you."

I knew it was the wrong thing to say because Frazier advanced on me and smacked me across the jaw. My head snapped to the side from the impact. A sharp pain radiated up my face and I couldn't help the slight groan emitting from my lips.

"If you keep lying, I will only hurt you further. Now, do you know who this is?"

I looked up at him, trying to keep my emotions locked inside.

"Yes."

There was no point me denying it further. My heart was shattering in my chest. I wanted so badly to go to him, but Tristan's grip was too tight.

"Good. We're getting somewhere. Keep this up and maybe we'll go easier on you."

My hands started to tremble. This was the worst possible situation. I was defenceless, but I still had to tread very carefully. A wrong move and all of this could come crashing down in front of my face.

"What do you want?"

"I want to know what he's told you."

"What do you mean told me? Why would he have told me anything?"

Frazier's eyes narrowed.

"You've been with him for months. Don't tell me you two don't talk about anything or does he just keep you around so he can fuck your pretty little cunt? Is that what you are to him? His little whore?"

I flinched. He leant closer.

"Wouldn't surprise me. You are Mitchell's daughter and he hates your family after what they did to his mother. What better way to get revenge than to ravage daddy's little princess? Pity your father isn't around to see how far you've fallen."

I felt sick to my stomach. Not only had he knocked out and tied up my husband, but he was also now taunting me and calling me a whore.

"What do you know?"

"I don't know anything," I said.

"More lies. Why don't you admit it, Avery? Admit you're his whore."

I shook my head.

"No. That's not what it is."

Frazier leant back, his dark eyes betraying a slight hint of confusion. He walked away a few paces, looking between me and Aiden. My heart hammered in my chest. All I wanted was to know he was okay. Fuck. We'd argued with each other. And then this. They'd taken him. But how did Frazier know? How? This made absolutely no sense.

"Then what? Are you telling me it's more than that? Hmm? Is this a little love affair between the two of you?"

A single tear slipped down my cheek. The words stuck in my throat. Tristan's breath was hot on my ear.

"Oh, I think it is, Father. Look at her, she's trembling."

Frazier turned to the both of us, his eyes roaming across me.

"Well, well, well… that just made this far more interesting."

"How did you know about us?" I blurted out.

His smile was deadly.

"So you admit it. I've kept an eye on you for quite a while. Especially after you came to me and told me you'd marry my son. Except you had no intention of doing that at all, did you? You came here for something else. What is it, Avery? What do you know?"

Did Frazier know how long Aiden and I had been together? Did he know about Aiden keeping me captive? Did he know we'd got married? He would've said something if he did. He wouldn't have accused me of being Aiden's whore. That meant we were still in the clear somewhat, but it didn't bring me any sort of relief. I was still in serious shit and so was Aiden.

"I don't know anything."

Frazier was silent. He watched me for a minute then he walked over to a small desk and pulled out a drawer. He tugged something out of it and snapped the drawer shut. Walking towards Aiden, he lifted his hand and pointed a gun at my husband's head.

"No! Don't, don't hurt him, please. Please, don't kill him."

Tears fell unbidden. I couldn't help it. He was pointing a gun at my unconscious husband's head. Frazier was a fucking bastard. I hated him. And yet he knew exactly how to manipulate me. Fuck. I'd fallen headlong into this trap. Aiden was right. I never should've come here tonight. We never should've left the flat.

"Then tell me the truth."

"Please," I sobbed. "Please don't hurt him."

"What do you know?"

I was fucking done. I'd do anything to save Aiden. Anything. Even revealing what I'd tried to keep hidden this whole time.

"I'll tell you if you put the gun down. Promise me you won't kill him, please."

He stared at me. I must've looked like a fucking state right then. A sobbing mess of streaked makeup. He lowered the gun slowly.

"I won't kill him. Now, tell me what you know and don't leave anything out."

I took a breath, a wracking sob escaping my lips.

"Everything," I whispered. "I know everything, Frazier."

TEN

Aiden

I heard screaming. It rang in my ears. Why was it so loud? What the fuck happened to me? I tried to raise my head, but it ached like a bitch.

"No, stop it, let go of me. Please, you promised. You said you wouldn't hurt him."

I knew that voice.

"Take her out of here. Do whatever the fuck you want with her. It's no fucking less than she deserves."

That sounded distinctly like Frazier Shaw, but I couldn't be certain. I opened my eyes. There was a woman struggling in someone's grip whilst another man stood next to me.

"Please, stop. No," she screamed. "Let me go."

"Stop struggling, Avery. It'll only be worse for you," said the voice of the person holding her.

Holding my fucking wife. I raised my head, staring at the scene. Tristan had Avery by the arms. She was kicking and screaming, trying to get away from him. Frazier stood next to me with a gun in his hand.

What the actual fuck?

"Let her go," I said, my voice sounding hoarse and groggy.

Frazier's head snapped to me.

"Oh, look who's decided to join the land of the living."

"Let her go," I said more clearly this time.

He gave me a fake sympathetic look. I wanted to punch his fucking stupid face in. What the hell was going on? I struggled to move as the effects of whatever the fuck drug they'd given me began to wear off. I looked down at myself. I was fucking cable tied to a chair.

"Aiden," Avery sobbed. "Aiden, I'm so sorry."

"Come on, Avery, it's time you and I got well acquainted, don't you think?" Tristan said.

The grin on his face made me want to smash his head against the fucking floor. He was going to fucking rape her. She knew it. I knew it.

"Let her go," I growled. "Don't you fucking lay a hand on her."

Frazier clocked me around the jaw with the butt of the gun he was holding.

"Shut up, you don't get a fucking say in what happens to her, you hear me?"

I ignored him. He would get what was coming to him later.

"Avery, I'm going to come for you. I promise you, princess, I promise. I'll always find you. Remember what you said to me, remember that day."

Her eyes met mine. Her face was tear streaked and her eyes bloodshot. Fuck. I wanted to go to her so badly. I wanted to wipe away those tears and kiss away her pain. What did they do to her?

She gave me a slight nod to say she understood what I was trying to tell her. Remember our wedding day when everything was perfect between us and none of this shit had happened yet. I just hoped it would keep her from falling apart completely.

I didn't know how, but I'd get out of this fucking situation and I'd get her. And I'd fucking kill both these cunts for this shit. They wouldn't make it through the rest of the night. I vowed that silently to myself and her.

Tristan locked his arms around her, beginning to walk backwards. She kicked out, trying to stop him. My princess, so fucking strong. She wouldn't go down without a fight. I knew she'd never give in willingly.

"Aiden," she screamed as Tristan dragged her from the room. "Stop, let go. Aiden!"

I heard her screams all the way down the hall. It shattered my heart. My fucking wife was about to be tormented and I couldn't fucking stand it.

My jaw ached. The back of my head hurt. I still felt groggy as fuck. I tried to shake it off and concentrate. I had to work out how to remedy this situation.

Frazier turned to me, his eyes narrowed and expression tense.

"You and I need to have a little talk."

He waved the gun in my face. Didn't surprise me that he had it and probably knew how to use it. Posh twats like him usually did some shit like clay pigeon shooting at the weekends. He did rub shoulders with some of the richest men in London. I questioned whether he acquired it legally or not, but it didn't matter. He was the one with the weapon and I was currently incapacitated. When my head stopped spinning, I'd work out how the fuck I was going to turn this around.

"Why did you send her here, hmm? To dig up dirt on me?"

"Seems you've already got all the answers."

His eyes flashed with irritation, but he paced away from me. Good. If he kept his distance, he'd be less likely to see me trying to get out of these fucking cable ties. Each ankle was attached to the chair legs and my hands were in front of me. He should've fucking had them put behind me. Idiot. Then again, Frazier had likely hired a bunch of thugs to knock me out and bring me here, so they weren't to know I was ex-army. That would be his first mistake.

I shifted a little, testing how much resistance they had. Eying them, I noticed they weren't heavy duty. I could probably snap them if I put my weight behind it. It just meant waiting for the right moment. Bide my time and when I did get the fuck out of them, I'd fuck Frazier up. He wasn't coming out of this encounter with me alive. The cunt had given my wife to Tristan. That was fucking unacceptable. Not to mention all the other shit he'd done to women over the course of his lifetime. I dreaded to think how many and the extent of the damage he'd inflicted on them all.

"What did you send her here for?"

"As if I'm going to tell you shit."

He took a deep breath and turned on me. Dark eyes blazed with unconcealed fury.

"You'll fucking talk or I'll put a bullet in your head. Then you won't see your precious Avery again. And don't try bullshit me into thinking there's nothing between you, because she admitted it. She's in love with you."

"What's it to you anyway?"

His eyebrow raised.

"She didn't like being called your whore. In fact, she cried when I threatened to kill you. Tell me, Aiden, was telling Tristan to let her go an act? Is she your whore? Have you enjoyed abusing that little cunt of hers to get back at her father? I bet Mitch is turning in his fucking grave. You've had her for months now. I saw you two together before New Year. Black Night didn't seem like your type of haunt, but you were there with her and that Benson boy."

I clenched my fists but kept my expression neutral. He'd called my wife a whore to her face. The fucking prick. Avery had never been that to me. She was the sun. The only light I had in all the fucking darkness.

There was no point me denying I knew Avery and that we'd been together. Not when he'd seen us when I'd taken her out on that date so she'd come back to me, but I could keep my emotions out of it. I could lie to Frazier's face about my feelings for her. Then he couldn't use those against me. I'd be fucking damned if I was going to show that mother fucker how much his words cut into me like a knife.

"What do you want me to say, Frazier? You've worked it out yourself."

"I want to hear it out of your own goddamn mouth. Is she your whore?"

"Yes."

It killed me to say that, but fuck, there was no other way. A grin spread across his face. It made me sick.

"I made her fall in love with me so she'd do what I wanted, but I don't give a shit about her. Why would I? She's Mitchell's daughter."

His grin got wider. He was such a sadistic fuck. Clearly got off on knowing I tricked her into thinking I cared about her.

That was so far from the fucking truth it was laughable. I was so fucking glad she wasn't here to hear any of this. She wouldn't believe it, but it'd break her heart and I couldn't abide by the thought of that.

"How did you do it? How did you convince her?"

I shrugged.

"I told her the truth. Figured she'd come around eventually if she knew how fucked up you all are. Wasn't hard when you have access to your employer's security footage."

He nodded slowly, putting his hands behind his back and pacing in front of me.

"Quite the talented hacker. I've wanted you on my team for a while, but you always refuse the request from Chuck. I don't forgive consistent denials easily." He paused, cocking his head to one side as he paced. "That little bitch doesn't spread her legs for just anyone. You must've laid on the charm. Anyone can see why a woman would fall at your feet."

I almost laughed. Heck, I'd tried to stop it all happening. I hadn't wanted to want her. I certainly didn't pursue a physical relationship with her, but the pull had been impossible to resist. The need to have her submission. And when she'd given it… fuck it was the best thing to ever happen to me. Her body was my solace. Her love was my balm. Her kind and perfect soul, my salvation.

"She can't get what I give her anywhere else. I showed her what she truly needed."

"And what would that be?"

His eyes glinted, his face eager to know more. I didn't want to fucking tell him anything about our sex life, but Avery's life was fucking on the line and so was mine. If I could keep him talking and get him to drop his fucking guard, then I'd have the upper hand. I worked my wrists in the cable tie, testing their strength a little as I leant forward to disguise my action.

"She likes being dominated, told what to do and when to do it. She likes it rough and dirty. She screams when I tie her up and fuck her ruthlessly. She loves every part of it. And you know what the best bit is, Frazier? I'm the first one she let into that tight little virgin arse of hers. Took some persuasion, but it was worth it. She begs for it now. Gets down on her hands and knees and begs me. She's so desperate for my cock and the things I do to her, she can't help it. She's addicted to me."

I felt so fucking sick saying these things about my wife. Whilst some of it was true, the way I'd said it made it sound like I was some sick bastard who didn't care anything about her. I loved her so fucking much and the fact that she even let me do any of that to her, that she enjoyed it, it made me insanely fucking lucky.

I watched his expression grow gleeful as if what I was telling him made him happy.

"I knew she'd be a dirty little slut. I have to thank you, Aiden. Trained her to be the perfect whore. When Tristan's broken her in, she'll be a toy for us to share."

Bile rose up in the back of my throat. Neither of those fucks were going to get their dicks wet in my wife. Fuck. I couldn't stand this. His words fucking killed me. The thought of him going anywhere near Avery made me want to tear his head from his neck.

"Good luck with that. She's tougher than she looks. You think she hasn't seen what you're capable of? She has. She's seen it all. She won't go down without a fight. I admire her spirit even if she's Mitchell's daughter."

Frazier stopped pacing, putting a hand on his chin.

"I'm sure Tristan is capable of handling her. I taught him well."

I shrugged.

"All I'm saying is, don't underestimate her." *And don't underestimate me either.*

He turned his back on me. Big fucking mistake. He should've kept both eyes on me at all times. It was time to fucking end this sick shit's life and get my wife. I'd stalled long enough. Avery didn't have time for me to keep Frazier chatting all night. I needed to get to her and rip Tristan a new one.

I pulled my wrists apart. The cable tie dug into my skin, but I ignored the pain. It strained for several moments, trying not to buckle under the onslaught, but I worked out every single fucking day. I wasn't going to let a stupid piece of plastic stop me from getting to my wife.

When it snapped, it made a slight noise. Frazier began to turn around, but I was faster. I stood, tugged the chair up, slipping the cable ties around my ankles off the legs and stepped forward. I swung the chair around and it connected with his chest. He let out a grunt, stumbling backwards. I was on him immediately, tackling him to the ground. He tried to raise the gun. I knocked it out of his hand, sending it skittering across the floor.

His dark eyes were full of shock and rage. He shoved against me, but I was bigger and stronger than him.

"Get the fuck off me," he grunted.

He bucked wildly and clocked me on the side of the head. I reared back, the pain radiating across my ear. The momentary distraction allowed him to struggle out from under me. He tried to crawl towards the gun, but I grabbed hold of his ankle and dragged him back towards me.

"You're a fucking dead man, Frazier."

I wrestled him into sitting position and locked my arm around his neck, squeezing. He flailed against me, trying to dislodge me but I had him held too tight.

"I've got some news for you. Avery isn't my whore. She's my wife. You and your son just wanted her for her money. Don't think we don't know about the trust fund clause. You were stupid enough to think she'd marry your son and give you what you wanted. Newsflash, that's never fucking happening because right here, right now, I'm going to kill you. Just like I killed Mitchell and Kathleen."

He struggled harder and I tightened my grip, cutting off his airway. His hands clawed at my arm.

"That's right, Frazier. It was me. I murdered them in cold fucking blood and I took their daughter captive. I only meant to use her to take you and the rest of the fucking Daniels down. Turns out, Avery is everything I never knew I needed. She's the bravest fucking girl I've ever met. She'll put up a fight with Tristan. She won't let him use her. Trust me on that. It's too fucking bad for you that you'll never get to watch her destroy everything you and your sick fucking friends built."

His movements were becoming weaker. This wasn't how I usually took people out, but he'd made me so fucking angry. He was the sickest mother fucker I'd ever met. What he did to women was disgusting. Even my sick fuck of a father didn't torture the women he raped. Frazier loved to cut them, drill into their bones, slice pieces of their flesh from their bodies before he fucked them. He got off on having their blood all over him. Sick fuck.

"We're going to rid the world of all the scum like you. You don't deserve to breathe the same air as Avery. You're a disgusting excuse for a human being."

I watched his eyes bulge in their sockets as I took away his last breath. He lost consciousness, but I kept my arm across his throat. I kept strangling him until I knew he was dead. Only then did I drop the sick fuck to the floor. He lay there, his eyes wide and unblinking. It wasn't enough. I needed to make sure he wouldn't fucking be able to get back up ever again.

I walked over to where the gun lay on the ground. If I picked that up, my fingerprints would be all over it. I'd have to dispose of it, but I was fucking done. I squatted down and collected it off the ground. Straightening, I turned. Frazier was still flat out on the floor. Not breathing.

I raised my hand, aimed and fired. The sickening sound of the bullet piercing his skull rang in my ears.

He was dead.

Frazier Shaw was fucking dead.

And I was fucking glad of it.

Now, it was time to take out his mother fucking son. If he'd managed to fucking rape my wife, I'd lose my fucking mind. I didn't have time to think like that. I had to get to her. I had to keep Avery safe.

I stormed out of the room. I'd fucking clean this shit up later. I ran through the house, searching for where he might have taken her. Then I heard screaming upstairs followed by silence.

I ran as fast as my legs could fucking carry me, taking the stairs two by two. I had to get to her. I had to fucking stop this.

And when I threw open the door to the bedroom, the scene I was met with shook me to my fucking core.

"Avery?"

ELEVEN

Avery

I kicked out at Tristan, trying to dislodge him as he dragged me down the corridor away from Aiden and Frazier. Aiden's expression killed me. I knew he would still be groggy from whatever they'd used to knock him out with, but the agony in his eyes knowing what Tristan had planned sliced into my skin, ripping my heart to shreds. There had been determination too. He told me he'd come for me. Promised me. Aiden didn't break those. I had to stay strong for him.

"Let me go, you fucking arsehole," I screeched, trying to elbow Tristan.

"The more you struggle, the worse it will be for you," he told me.

Up the stairs we went, him dragging me with some considerable effort.

"For fuck's sake, Avery. Calm down," he grunted as I managed to kick him in the shin.

"No! Fuck you. I'll fucking kill you."

"I'd like to see you try."

Tristan didn't know I had a knife hidden under my dress. I had to reach it before he found it. I had to defend myself against him. I couldn't wait for Aiden to get away from Frazier because Tristan would no doubt take me if I wasn't careful.

He grabbed me by my hair and dragged me down the corridor when we reached the top of the stairs, throwing open his bedroom door. My scalp burnt. I tried to hit him, but he threw me in the room and slammed the door shut behind him. I didn't get a chance to recover. He dragged me up off the floor by my hair and shoved me against the wall, pinning me there with his body.

"I like it when women fight back, but you're causing me too much fucking trouble," he hissed.

I spat in his face, struggling against him. He smiled, wiping my spit away with his sleeve.

"You'll pay for that."

He pulled away and backhanded me across the cheek. I cried out, putting my hand up to my face. I glared at him. My cheek really hurt, especially after Frazier had smacked me around the jaw earlier. I was sure I'd be black and blue before this was over. Better than being raped. Anything was better than that. I didn't want those memories. I only wanted to remember the way Aiden touched me. I only wanted him between my legs.

Tristan stared at me, his mud brown eyes narrowed. I didn't move for a long moment and neither did he. Perhaps he thought if he hit me, I'd stop fighting him. He was fucking stupid.

I launched myself at him, knocking him off balance. We both crashed to the floor. I scrambled away from him before he had a chance to recover. I ran for the door, pulling it open and making a dash for it down the corridor.

I only got a few feet before Tristan tackled me to the floor. I screamed, pain lancing across my chest, arms and legs at the impact with the floor and Tristan's added weight.

"You really are fucking determined to piss me off."

"Fuck you," I wheezed.

"I've told you so many times, Avery. The only one who's getting fucked around here is you. I'm going to rip your cunt in half then I'm going to fuck your little rosebud. If you're good, I might ease up on you a little, otherwise, I'm going to stick my dick in you without lubrication. You better fucking wise up before I destroy all your holes completely."

I froze underneath him. Tears pricked at my eyes. I didn't want to imagine it. How much he'd make it hurt. He'd ruin me forever if he did any of those things. How could I ever come back from that?

My heart hammered in my chest at a million miles an hour. I felt sick to my stomach. What if Aiden didn't get to me in time? I couldn't stand the thought of it.

"Don't," I whispered. "Please don't."

"There now, have you decided to give in?"

I would never give in to him, but perhaps if I could convince him to let his guard down just a little, I could get myself out of this mess. I still had the knife. I could feel it pressed against my skin in its sheath. I had to be strong enough and brave enough to use it. To protect myself against the man who was going to rape me.

"Don't hurt me."

He stroked my hair back from my face, leaning in and rubbing his cheek across mine.

"Shh," he cooed. "I won't hurt you if you stop fighting me."

I didn't believe that for a second.

"You promise?"

"I'm going to punish you for trying to escape, but after that, I'll make it feel good. I'll fuck you better than Aiden ever could."

I was pretty sure no one would ever compare to Aiden and how he made me feel, but I wasn't about to voice that to Tristan.

"Punish me how?"

"You'll see. Now, if I let you up, are you going to be a good girl?"

I nodded, my face brushing against his. I felt the stubble on his cheek grazing my skin. Little did he know I was bluffing.

Either he was stupid or he wanted me so much, he didn't care if I fought him again because he moved off me. I flipped myself over onto my back, staring up at him as he stood. He put a hand out to me. It was now or never. I had to get out of here.

I put my hand in his, letting him pull me up. As soon as I was on my feet, I wrenched my hand out of his grasp and pushed him away from me, dashing back down the corridor. I could hear his footsteps after me, but I kept moving.

I'd just about reached the stairs when he slammed me into the bannister, winding me.

"I should've known you'd never give in," he growled.

He wrestled my arms behind my back and dragged me back to the bedroom, throwing me down on the bed. I held my stomach, trying to get my breath back. He went to the door and slammed it shut.

When his back was turned, I pulled the knife from its sheath, knowing it might well be my only chance to access it. I flattened it against my palm, hiding it from view. I had no choice. It was me or him now.

He turned on me, his mud brown eyes blazing with fury and lust. It made my skin crawl. Advancing on me, he shoved me down onto the bed and started pulling up the skirt of my dress. I struggled, trying to stop him, but he held both my arms down and sat on my legs.

"Don't even think about it you little cunt. You've just pissed me off. So now I'm going to make it hurt. You and I could've been good together, Avery. I could've given you exactly what you needed."

"Never. You're sick."

He smiled, his teeth glinting in the low light.

"You're just a little whore to him. He could never truly want you."

"You don't know anything."

"Don't I? Enlighten me then? Why would a man like him want anything to do with a little bitch like you? He just fucked you because he wanted to get back at your father. You're the idiot who thought it was more than that."

I shook my head. The knife dug into my skin where he was pressing my arms down on the bed. It reminded me I still had a way out. I could still hurt him and stop him coming after me.

"The joke is on you, Tristan. You're just too fucking stupid to see it."

His eyes narrowed.

"What are you talking about?"

"I know what your father wants. My money. Well, he's not fucking getting it and neither are you. You know why?"

He looked at me, eyes widening as he took my words in.

"Because I'm not Avery fucking Daniels any longer, you stupid fucking prick. You know who does have control of my trust fund?"

He reared back a little, letting go of my arms.

"Oh, that's right. You thought he was just using me as a good lay."

"You're lying."

"Am I? Are you sure about that? Too fucking bad for you, isn't it? That I'm Avery Lockhart now."

We stared at each other for several seconds. Tristan's face morphed into something monstrous. His mud brown eyes darkened and he snarled.

"You fucking bitch."

He backhanded me across the face. My head snapped back. He tugged my dress up, fumbling with his own trousers as he tried to rip my underwear off my body at the same time. I was frozen for all of ten seconds.

I palmed the knife and lashed out, screaming at him. I brought the knife up and it plunged into his neck. I felt the blade pierce his flesh. I pulled my hand back and the blood poured out of the wound, dripping down onto my face.

He stared down at me, shock flittering across his features before he put his hand to his throat, trying to stem the bleeding. It was too much, it flowed faster, covering me in it. I couldn't believe I'd just done that.

I stared at him as the blood got in my hair and face and on my dress. He couldn't stop it. I was pretty sure I'd just nicked his carotid artery. He was going to bleed out all over me.

I pushed him off me. He fell back against the covers, the blood still flowing and seeping into the bedding. I scrambled back, falling off the bed and crawling backwards with the knife still clutched in my hand.

I got to my feet, staring at the bed in shock. Tristan gurgled and shook before he went still. Very, very still. And I knew in that moment, he was dead.

I'd killed him.

It had been self-defence, but I'd killed him.

I couldn't believe it. None of it made any sense. I'd actually killed another human being. Guilt flooded me, coursing through my veins.

"Oh god," I whispered.

I could feel his blood all over me. My stomach roiled. I heard footsteps outside the door and then it opened. On the threshold stood my husband, his eyes going wide as he looked over the scene.

I dropped the knife, tears falling down my cheeks as I fell to my knees and wailed.

"Avery?"

"I killed him," I sobbed. "I didn't mean to, but he's dead."

He strode towards me but I put a hand up, stopping him in his tracks.

"Don't, I'm covered in blood, his blood. You'll make it worse. Oh my god, there's blood everywhere."

He looked over at the bed where Tristan lay unmoving.

"Princess… it's okay. I'm here. Did he hurt you?"

"Yes and no. He didn't… I didn't let him… Oh god, Aiden. I killed him."

His silver eyes burnt with compassion and it broke me further. Aiden knew what it was like to take someone else's life but I didn't. I had no idea how much it would destroy me inside. I trembled, feeling everything crashing down on me at once.

"I need you to stand up for me, princess. Can you do that?"

His voice was so calm. I didn't know how he could be so calm about this situation. I'd killed another person. I'd stabbed Tristan in the neck and he'd bled all over me.

I nodded slowly. I could get up off the floor. Staying here in this room would only make it worse for me. I rose, picking the knife up with me. He put his hand out. I walked towards him and dropped it into his outstretched palm.

"I know you're in shock right now, Avery, but I'm going to need you to take a shower. You need to wash away all the blood, okay? I'm going to sort this out."

I stared up at my husband. I trusted him. Aiden would make this right. He was the only one who could. His expression softened. He reached up, cupping my face and stroking my cheek.

"It's okay, princess. I promise."

I let him lead me away into the en-suite and help me out of my blood-soaked clothes. He turned the shower on and made me get in. I watched him wash his hands in the sink as well as the knife, which he left on the counter. He gave me one sharp nod, pointing at the toiletries before slipping out of the room.

I looked at the shampoo, conditioner and shower gel. These were all Tristan's. It made me sick to think I had to use a dead man's products. A man I'd killed. I dissolved into tears again, putting my face in my hands as the water rushed over me. I could see it turn red as it flowed down me through my fingers. The sight of it was awful. Knowing what I'd done cut me to the core.

I had to pull myself together. Aiden told me to wash away all the blood so I would. I released my face, reaching for the shampoo and begun the laborious process of washing my hair and my body.

When the water finally ran clear, I knew it was gone. All the blood. Somehow this made me feel a little better. I turned the shower off and stepped out, grabbing a clean towel from the rack and wrapping myself in it. I picked up a smaller towel and dried my dripping locks as much as I could.

I stepped back out into the bedroom, finding Aiden had stripped the bedsheets and unceremoniously dumped Tristan back on the bed, carefully angling him so that it was clear he'd been attempting to have sex with whoever had killed him. That girl happened to be me, but I didn't want to think about it any longer. I wanted to curl up in a ball and cry my eyes out. That wasn't an option.

He looked up from where he was cleaning the floor and nodded at a pile of clothes he'd left by the door. I picked them up and dressed on automatic. I knew they were Tristan's clothes, but I didn't care at that moment. A pair of boxers, followed by shorts, a t-shirt and a jumper which I had to roll the sleeves up on. I slipped on the pair of flip flops, which looked ridiculously big on my feet.

When he was done, he stripped off the gloves he was wearing. He went into the bathroom and came out with my clothes and the knife. He stuffed my clothes and the towels into a black bag before, taking me out of the room.

"Take these downstairs and leave them by the door, please. I know this is hard, princess, but I need you to stay strong for me."

I stared up at him, tears welling in my eyes.

"Okay," I whispered.

His expression softened. He dropped the bags he was holding on the floor and cupped my face.

"Listen to me, Avery. I love you. We got out of this alive. I'm not going to let you go down for this either. No one is going to know we were here."

I'd known that's why he was cleaning up the scene, but somehow it made me feel worse. I should be punished for killing Tristan. I took his life. I had no right to do that.

But look at what he tried to do to you? He was going to rape you. You had no choice. You know that.

"Where's Frazier?"

"He's dead."

I didn't know whether that made me feel any better or not.

"What happened?"

"We'll talk about it later. I need you to go to Frazier's computer and make sure all the data transferred to the memory stick. Then you need to get rid of everything related to the company."

He'd read my text messages then.

"What about the staff?"

"I think Frazier made them leave before he brought you to see me."

I shivered. All the planning we'd done to make this evening a success had gone up in flames. Frazier already knew about us and had made his own plans. And now the Shaws were dead. This wasn't clean at all. It had been messy. So very messy.

"Okay. The data. You need me to check the data."

"Yes. Stay in his office until I get you, okay?"

I nodded. He leant down and placed a chaste kiss on my lips before he walked back into Tristan's bedroom. I knew there were still things he needed to clean up before we could walk away from this.

Picking up the two bin bags, I carried them downstairs, careful not to trip over with the oversized flip flops. I left the bags at the front door and walked along the corridor to Frazier's office. I flipped the light on and sat at his desk. The data had finished transferring.

I clicked on the folder and started looking at the files. There was so much here. So many incriminating documents. He'd covered up fraud, drunk driving and even a hit and run. There was more, but I wasn't sure I could look at all of it.

And there was stuff on Daniels Holdings. Things that made me ill. Some of it was the same evidence Aiden had shown me about the bribes, but there were other things. Like how they'd circumnavigated a case against the company regarding shoddy building work. There was blood on their hands. A kid had died because of their negligence.

I felt sick. So fucking sick. How could they do this shit?

I sat back in his chair, drumming my fingers on the armrest. I wanted him to pay for this. Frazier was dead, but I wanted to burn his legacy to the ground. I opened one of his drawers, finding several blank memory sticks inside.

I set about selecting several of the cases that didn't involve Daniels Holdings and put them on one of the blank memory sticks. Next, I typed up a message on the computer and printed it out. I folded the message up and put it in an envelope along with the memory stick.

The last thing I did was erase all the evidence Frazier had on my company. The police might check his computer and anything incriminating Daniels Holdings would ruin our plans to destroy my family.

Aiden walked into the office. He looked a little haunted.

"Is it all there?" he asked.

I nodded, holding the envelope out to him.

"What's this?"

"I want you to put it on Frazier's body."

He frowned, taking it from me.

"Why?"

"So that when the police find him, they'll know what a dirty solicitor he was. I want him exposed. After what he's done, he deserves it."

He stared at me for a long moment before he peered inside the envelope at the memory stick.

"What did you put on this?"

"Nothing that ties back to the company. Just enough to incriminate him. I know we can't expose my uncle and my family yet."

He nodded.

"Okay. I trust you."

"Can we go yet?"

"Give me five more minutes, okay? I need to make sure there's nothing on Frazier which can tie back to me. I've done my best with Tristan."

I walked out of the office with him, turning out the light on my way. The memory stick with everything we needed was in my pocket. I walked back towards the hallway, leaving Aiden to deal with what he needed to.

I grabbed my coat out of the cupboard in the hallway, knowing I couldn't very well leave it there. I waited patiently by the front door until Aiden came back. He picked up all the bags there and we walked out. John was waiting outside for us.

"I need to get rid of this shit," Aiden said to him.

"You sure you got everything in there?"

"I did the best I fucking could under the circumstances."

John looked down at me.

"Are you okay?"

I shook my head. I was never going to be okay after what I just did. Never. I wasn't sure what Aiden had told John, but it didn't matter. What happened in that house would stay between the three of us. I knew that. Aiden had covered up what we'd done.

Aiden put the bags in the boot and helped me into the back of the car. John drove us for a while, but I didn't look at where we were going. We pulled up at an abandoned warehouse. They went inside with the bags and came out twenty minutes later.

I wasn't sure what they'd done and I found I didn't want to know. This night had been hell from start to finish. All I wanted to do was forget about it.

Aiden pulled me into his lap and held me whilst John drove us back to Aiden's flat. He stroked my hair, soothing my aching soul.

"It's okay, princess," he murmured. "I know this is a lot to handle. I know you feel awful about what you did, but what matters is you're safe."

"He didn't rape me," I whispered. "I didn't let him. I put up a fight."

He clutched me tighter.

"I know, you've been so brave. So fucking brave. You're going to be okay. We'll be okay. They're gone now. They can't hurt you any more. They've paid for what they've done."

I trembled, trying not to remember the look in Tristan's eyes when he realised I'd stabbed him in the neck with a knife.

"Shh, it's okay," he whispered, kissing my forehead. "I've got you."

Tears leaked out of my eyes. The despair I felt sunk into my bones. How could I have ever been capable of taking another person's life away? How?

"Aiden," I sobbed. "I'm so sorry. I'm so sorry I didn't listen to you. I should've. I never would've done that if I'd just stayed. I'm sorry."

"Princess, please don't apologise. It's not your fault."

"It is. It is. I killed him. I can't do this. I can't. I'm sorry. I didn't mean to do it. I wanted him to stop."

"Shh, shh, I know, princess, I know. Shh. It's okay. You had no choice. Just let it out, okay? I'm here. I'll help you get through this. I will, I promise. I'll make it okay."

I shook my head, sobbing into his chest. Nothing about this was okay. Nothing at all. My soul fractured in half. I wasn't sure how to live with myself.

"How?"

"By loving you every single day and reminding you of how strong you are. How brave you've been. How much good is in you. You survived and you'll keep on surviving. It'll be okay because we're going to make sure the rest of them pay. We're going to rescue all those girls and we'll make sure no one hurts them again. That's how."

I wrapped my arms around Aiden's neck and buried my face in his shoulder.

I just hoped he was right because if he wasn't, then I'd die inside a little more every day.

I didn't want to be a broken girl.

And a small part of me realised that perhaps after this, I'd never be able to put myself back together ever again.

TWELVE

Aiden

"urther details have been released regarding the ongoing investigation into the deaths of Frazier Shaw of Shaw Associates and his son, Tristan. The two were found by their housekeeper in what appeared to be a violent altercation. Frazier Shaw was found strangled to death with a gunshot wound to the head. Tristan Shaw died from massive blood loss due to a severed carotid artery. Police are appealing for witnesses…"

I looked over at Avery who was sat in the armchair staring at the window. She'd been this way for two weeks and I had no fucking clue what to do to get through to her.

"Police have raided the offices of Shaw Associates. They have declined to comment on what they were looking for, stating the investigation is ongoing…"

Avery told me exactly what she put on the memory stick she made me leave on Frazier's body when we lay in bed together that night. I'd made sure to wipe it down so her fingerprints didn't remain. I'd stayed up with her all night.

Listened to her sob and tell me every single detail of what happened between her and Tristan. A part of me fucking died inside knowing what she went through whilst I dealt with Frazier.

"Princess, do you want some tea?" I asked.

She nodded but didn't look back at me. I hauled myself off the sofa, turned the TV off and went into the kitchen, flipping on the kettle.

Avery hadn't gone to work. She told them she had flu, which gave her a few days breathing space. When the news of the Shaws' deaths broke, she'd had Chuck on the phone demanding answers. She told him she was taking a few weeks leave and she'd talk to him about it upon her return. He wasn't happy about it. The whole thing had caused a ripple effect across their community. We had no choice, but until I got her to come back to me, dealing with the consequences of our actions could wait.

Avery refused to talk to me. She nodded and shook her head at me when I asked her if she wanted things, but that was it. It was like the light inside her died.

To the outside world, Avery was a girl in mourning over her fiancé dying, but here, in this flat, she was slowly deteriorating because she'd killed him. I'd tried everything to get her to come back to me. I held her when she cried. I fed her, bathed her and tried to get her to talk. No matter what I did, she just sat there staring out the window, barely acknowledging I was there. It fucking killed me to see her like this.

My phone rang. Digging it out my pocket, I answered it. "Tina."

"Aiden, how are things? Is she still the same?"

"If by the same you mean she won't talk to me or move from the chair, then yes."

I hadn't told Tina what happened but she put two and two together when she saw the news.

"I'm sorry. This is hard on both of you."

Having Frazier's death on my conscience didn't bother me much, but it did bother me that my wife was suffering over that little shit's death. It should've been me. I should've saved her from having to take his life. There was nothing either of us could do about it now.

"I don't know how to get through to her. It's breaking my fucking heart seeing her like this."

"Are you sure you've tried everything?"

I frowned. What else could I possibly do?

"I think you know deep down what she needs, Aiden."

"I don't follow."

"You and her have never had an orthodox relationship, have you?"

I wondered for a moment how the fuck Tina knew that, but then again, she knew me. Knew my issues surrounding control. Did she suspect it had bled into my personal life? She must know. Fuck. The last thing I needed was her prying into the intimate details of my relationship with Avery, but who else did I have to talk to about this? The only people who knew anything about what really happened that night were her and John. And I certainly wasn't about to discuss this shit with him.

"No, we don't."

"I don't think kind and caring is working for either of you."

"So what, I should just be a dick to her all over again?"

"I didn't say that. I'm going to make a huge assumption here, but from watching you two, it's clear who is in control and I'm relatively sure she's on board with that."

Fucking hell. Was Tina actually suggesting I made my wife submit to me when she was clearly in emotional pain? I wanted to put my head in my hands. Her assumption was correct, but it didn't make it right. Not when she was like this.

"Have you been listening to the therapist bullshit from Sophie and Cora?"

She sighed.

"No, Aiden, I'm trying to help. Sometimes you need to try a different approach to get someone to snap out of it. She can't just sit there mute and numb for the rest of her life and she can't talk to a therapist considering what happened. You're the only one who can help her."

She wasn't even talking to her friends. Not that either of them knew what had gone down that night. James called me daily to check on her. I could hear the agony in his voice every time I told him there was no change.

"I can't do that to her."

"You mean you won't."

"Do you even know what you're asking me to do?"

"I don't need to know. Do what you need to do to snap her out of it. Give her what she needs."

I just couldn't. No matter how much I missed her, forcing her to submit wasn't right. She had to want that from me. How would I know if she was really consenting to it if she wasn't fucking talking to me?

"I have to go."

"Aiden…"

"Just drop it, Tina."

150

I hung up. I didn't need a lecture from her. What I needed was to take care of my wife. That meant making sure she was well fed and had enough to drink. I wasn't going to allow her to starve herself.

I made her tea and brought it to her. Kneeling at her feet, I put the mug in her hands. She held it to her chest.

"Princess, will you talk to me?"

Nothing.

"Avery, please."

Silence.

I put my hand on her knee, giving it a squeeze.

"I know you're hurting but you can't keep shutting me out. You have to let me help you. I made you a promise that we would get through this together."

She kept staring at the window, holding the mug and completely ignoring me.

"Avery, this has to stop. I can't keep begging you to speak to me."

I dropped my hand from her knee. Even after her parents died and she got taken by Rick, she was never like this. Never just numb to everything and everyone around her. She'd cried and raged at the world. She didn't retreat and completely cut herself off. She was a fighter. This wasn't her. This wasn't the girl I knew. The girl I loved.

"Princess, please. I love you. I need you to come back to me."

I stood up when she didn't move and walked away unable to face seeing her like that for one more moment. I had no idea what the fuck it would take to get her to just say something. My heart shattered every time I had to watch her blank expression. I missed her so much. The way she smiled when I teased her. Her infectious laugh. Those doe eyes which held so much love and affection. Fuck.

All I wanted was my Avery back.

And I had no fucking clue how to achieve that.

Two days later, there was no change and I was desperate enough to contemplate doing what Tina had alluded to. I'd lain in bed last night alone wondering if she'd look at me with those doe eyes of hers full of love and affection ever again. I'd reached breaking point. I couldn't take it any longer. She stayed on that fucking armchair all night. I was done watching her deteriorate further.

Striding into the living room, I stopped a few feet away from her. I took a deep breath. This was about fixing her and I was fucking determined to do that no matter what it took.

"Look at me."

She stared out the window.

"Avery, I'm only going to say this one more time. Look at me."

Nothing. I wasn't sure what I expected.

"Don't make me repeat myself. You know what happens when you disobey me."

She stiffened at my words. The first sign she'd actually been listening.

"Look. At. Me."

Very, very slowly, she turned her head towards me, doe eyes wide as she met mine.

"Good girl."

She didn't speak, but I could see a tiny spark of recognition in her eyes. Was this working? Was Tina right? Fuck. Who knew. I had to keep going now she'd actually responded. I had to try.

"Get off that chair and kneel at my feet."

It took her several seconds to comply. She slid off the armchair, the blanket falling to the floor and knelt in front of me. I almost fucking died. My girl. My wife. She was finally fucking there. Finally present.

"What do I want?"

My words reminded me of that day in the forest. The first day I had my cock in her mouth. The day which changed everything between us.

"My submission," she whispered.

My heart cracked wide open and bled. She sounded so fucking broken. It was the first thing she'd said to me in over a week.

"Good girl."

The spark in her eye remained. I had to keep this up even though all I wanted was to hold her in my arms and kiss her. Tell her it was going to be okay.

"You're going to do everything I tell you without hesitation. Can you tell me why that is?"

"I'm yours."

"That's right. Mine."

She closed her eyes for a moment, her expression betraying just how much she savoured my voice. Like it was her lifeline. Fuck. I didn't want Tina to be right, but maybe she was. Maybe I'd just been too fucking stubborn to see it.

"Stand up and come with me."

153

She did as I asked, opening her eyes and raising herself to her feet. I wasn't going to do things for her any longer. She had to remember how to do them for herself.

I walked out of the room, down the hallway and into the bathroom. She hadn't had a wash in days. I pointed at the shower.

"Strip, get in and wash yourself thoroughly. I want you clean for me."

She took off her clothes, watching me the whole time. Seeking my approval that she was doing this right. That she was obeying me.

I tried not to stare at her naked body. It made mine ache with longing. I missed her skin on mine. Her curves pressing against me as we slept. How she'd lay there, wide open and begging me to take her. I wanted that Avery back. I wanted my wife.

"You're taking too long. Get in the shower."

She flipped it on and walked in, shivering under the stream of water. Reaching for the shampoo, she lathered up her beautiful dark locks. I sat on the edge of the bath and watched her, making sure she did as I told her to. She kept glancing my way as if checking I was still there. I wasn't about to leave her alone now she was beginning to come back to me.

When she was done, she turned the shower off and stepped out. Water droplets scattered across her pale skin. Fuck. Avery was such a goddess to me. So beautiful.

"Pick up that towel and wrap it around you, then you're coming into the bedroom and drying your hair. Do you understand?"

"Yes."

She picked up one of the towels from the rack, dried herself so she was no longer dripping and wrapped it around her slim frame. I'd been making sure she ate so she hadn't lost any weight. I doubt she would've taken care of herself without me.

She followed me into the bedroom and sat in front of the mirror with her hairdryer and brush. She methodically dried her hair. I sat on the bed, waiting patiently until she was finished. She set her brush down and turned to look at me.

"Come here."

She stood up, placed the towel over the mirror and walked over before dropping to her knees in front of me.

"You've been a good girl for me so far, princess."

Her eyes tracked my hand as I reached out and tucked her hair behind her ear. She leant into my touch.

"Do you want me to touch you?" I asked her.

Her doe eyes met mine.

"Yes, please," she whispered.

I retracted my hand. I watched her expression. Her eyes burnt with longing.

"You have to earn that. Show me how much you want it."

She hesitated, looking up at me with wide eyes. Fuck. I really didn't want to push her, but she needed to snap out of this shit. This was the only thing which had worked so far. I'd got her to do things for herself and talk to me. It was progress even if this felt painfully slow.

I leant my arms back on the bed, waiting to see what she'd do. Whether she'd cave in on herself or fight her way back to who she really was deep inside.

"You're testing my patience, Avery. Earn my touch. Do you want to go back to the chair in the living room and forget we're husband and wife? Forget you belong to me and that you should obey me. Because you can. If that's what you really want, you can go back there and hide away again. But if you want this, if you truly want me, you'll stay here and prove it to me. You'll come back to me so I can help you through this. So we can move past this."

My words seemed to cut through whatever it was holding her back. She reached out, her hands running up my thighs as she crawled between my legs. Her hands moved higher before her fingers found their way to the bottom of my t-shirt. I let her pull it off me. Her fingers trailed down my chest, causing me to stifle a groan. Fuck me. Having her touch me was wonderfully torturous after two and a half weeks of her indifference.

She unbuckled my belt, unzipping my fly and tugged at my jeans. I moved to allow her to take them off. She tentatively reached out and ran her hand across my cock. I couldn't hold back a groan then. Perhaps it spurred her on because she insisted on removing my boxers without preamble and wrapped her hand around my cock.

"I'm sorry," she whispered, looking up at me with those fucking beautiful hazel doe eyes of hers. "You've put up with so much from me."

Without letting me respond, she circled the head of my cock with her tongue. Fuck. Avery was the sweetest damn fucking girl in the world. Her mouth was heaven as she wrapped it around me.

"That's it, princess," I grunted. "Fuck."

I shifted off my hands, curling one into her hair and holding the back of her neck. I needed to touch her. I gently massaged my fingers into her scalp. She needed to set the pace. I wasn't going to force anything on her.

Her fingers dug into my thigh as she bobbed up and down, setting a slow, drawn out pace. Neither of us were in a hurry. I certainly didn't want to blow my load too fast down her throat. No, I wanted to savour every moment because I was fucking terrified she'd retreat into herself again.

Pulling away, she stared up at me.

"Aiden, please touch me."

She looked so fucking lost. I couldn't deny her it any longer. I put my hand out to her.

"Come here then."

I shifted back slightly and she crawled into my lap. I held her to my chest and stroked her back. She rested her head on my shoulder, letting out a soft sigh as she curled her hands around my sides.

"Do you want to talk about it?" I asked.

"I don't know how you deal with it."

How I dealt with having killed people? There wasn't a simple answer to that. I never started out wanting to end anyone's life. In many ways, it was revenge and a skewed sense of justice which drove me. Not to say it didn't weigh on me. I didn't enjoy killing. It wasn't some kind of sport to me. The only real satisfaction it gave me was knowing they couldn't hurt anyone any more.

"I don't have an easy answer for you. I never wanted it to be on your conscience. Your reaction is perfectly normal. You should feel remorse, normal people do. I'm not normal nor do I pretend to be. You don't want to be like this, trust me."

"I thought if I could stop feeling it would make it easier, but it's worse. I keep remembering his face and all the blood."

She raised her head from my shoulder and looked at me.

"No more bloodshed. I can't face it. No more death. I want them destroyed but not like this."

I cupped her cheek. She looked so lost and alone.

"Okay. We'll find another way."

After everything she'd been through, I couldn't say no. I was tired of it all too. We had to end it so we could live a normal life together. So I could care for her for the rest of our days. Avery might never get over killing Tristan, but I'd be there for her all the same.

"Are you sure? I understand why you want them gone. I really do, but more death isn't the answer. No matter what we do, it won't bring anyone back. Haven't we had enough pain, Aiden? Haven't we suffered enough? Haven't you?"

Her words dropkicked me right in the chest. She was right. I had. And now, so had she.

I stroked her cheek.

"I'm sure, but I'm not going to make you any promises because we can't predict what will happen. That night is proof we can't account for everything."

She reached up, placing a hand on mine.

"I know. Thank you for understanding."

I stared into her eyes, hoping this meant she was back, but nervous she wasn't all the same.

"You're not going to disappear on me again, princess?" I whispered.

She shook her head.

"I don't want to live like that. I'm trying… for you… for us. It hurts. It's like there's a black mark on my soul and I can't rub it off. I don't know if this guilt will ever go away. I'm so sorry I dropped out on you. I didn't know how to handle what happened. I didn't know what to think, say or do. It's like a part of me died that night. I feel so broken, Aiden. I don't know how to fix it. I don't know how to make it better. My soul is crying out for something and I don't know what."

She clutched my hand on her face.

"Please help me. I don't want to feel like this. I shouldn't have shut you out. You're the only one who understands. You know me better than I know myself. You know what I need."

I leant forward, capturing her mouth in mine. I understood her. She needed me. That's what her soul was calling out for. Me. I could feel it. I took her pain away. I always had. Even if I didn't want her to be reliant on me in the way she had been when we first met, I had to give her what she needed. I'd build her back up to the girl she'd been before this all happened. The one who possessed an inner strength unlike any other girl I'd met.

She sighed into my mouth, pressing closer. I dropped my hand from her face to her throat, holding her in place with a loose grip. Pulling away, I pressed kisses to her jaw until I met her ear.

"I'm going to give you exactly what you need," I told her in a low voice. "What you've always needed. You want my control, don't you, princess? You want me to take away all your choices. You want to submit. Give me everything. Every part of you. Even the darkest parts of your soul are mine."

I bit down on her earlobe, eliciting a mewl from her lips.

"Yes, please. I'm yours. I'm all yours."

I almost groaned in anticipation of being inside her. Her submission was everything to me. To us. The desire to have her at my mercy never really went away. It pulsed in my veins. She might be my wife now, but I still needed this side of our relationship. I always would.

"I want you on your knees on the bed. You won't be able to run. So tell me now if you want to stop."

"Please, Aiden. Please, I want you. I need you."

"On the bed then."

I released her throat. She crawled off me and knelt on the bed with her back to me, her hands resting by her sides. I got up, going to the cupboard and selecting a set of restraints I'd never used on her before. I walked back over to the bed and made her stand up as I slipped both sections up her legs until they rested on her upper thighs. Settling her back on the bed, I wrapped the next part around her waist and attached her wrists to the cuffs, securing them to the sides of her hips.

I put a hand on her lower back, forcing her to take her weight on her shoulders with her face half pressed into the covers, which she turned to the side so she could breathe. This left her open for me. Open but restrained. Fuck she looked so beautiful bent over like that for me.

"Is this what you wanted, princess?" I asked, running my hand over her behind. "You want to be tied up and fucked?"

"Please, please fuck me. I want you so much. All of you. Everywhere."

"Everywhere, hmm?"

She wriggled.

"Fuck me, Aiden. Fuck me in both my holes. Please."

Fuck. I stroked my cock. She was so fucking beautiful with a dirty mouth. I'd taught her to let go of her inhibitions. So she wouldn't be ashamed or scared of telling me what she wanted.

"Don't worry, you're going to get all of me. I promise."

I'd selected another thing from the cupboard. I picked it up off the bed and ran it across her wet pussy.

"I'm going to make sure you're satisfied completely. You want both? You're going to get both."

I flicked the cap off the lube and coated the plug before pressing it to her. I was careful, slowly inserting it so as not to hurt her. She moaned as it stretched her.

"Please, oh fuck, please."

When it was fully inside her, I moved closer and ran my cock along her pussy. She wriggled against me. I could tell she was desperate for more. She needed this. So I gave it to her. I sunk my cock in her pussy. It was that much tighter because of the plug nestled in her arse.

"This is what you wanted. No mercy, princess. None at all."

I gripped the harness at her thighs and thrust inside her to the hilt before pulling back and slamming into her again. Fuck she felt incredible. She clenched around me, moaning as her hands flexed at her sides.

"Please, please, Aiden, fuck me harder. Harder."

I gave her what she begged for. The pace was brutal and completely unforgiving. Her moans got louder. Sweat beaded on her back, coating her delicate skin in a light sheen. Not having her in over two weeks made it almost impossible to hold back, but I did it for her. I ignored the tightening in my stomach. I thought about how much she needed this from me.

"Fuck, you're going to come for me. I want to feel you all over me," I grunted.

She was the most intoxicating girl I'd ever fucking met. And she was mine. Fuck. I was going to lose complete control.

"Now, Avery. Fucking come for me now."

I thrust harder and deeper, feeling her pulse and clench around me as she cried out, screaming my name. Fuck. I let go, emptying everything I had to give inside her delicious heat.

161

I panted hard, stroking a hand down her back as I stilled. She stared up at me, her doe eyes wide with lust and complete adoration. Fuck. Even though I'd just come, it wasn't fucking going down. I was still half hard for her. I needed more and I was pretty sure she did too.

I pulled out the plug, discarding it beside us. Picking up the lube, I pressed more inside her. She watched me, not saying a word when I shifted out of her and slicked my dick up further, stroking it in her eyeline so she could see what she did to me. Her tongue darted out, running across her bottom lip.

"More, princess?"

"Please," she whispered. "Please take my pain away."

A few minutes later, my cock was rock hard again and I pressed it against her other entrance. It slid in easily given I'd already opened her up with the plug. I grunted at the heat and tightness. Fuck. She always felt so good here.

I wasn't rough, taking my time as I fucked her slow and deep. She groaned, pressing back against me as much as she could in the restraints.

"That's it, princess. Show me you want me."

"I do. I want you so much. Always. Please, I want to come again."

"Oh, don't worry, my love. I'll make you come all over my cock."

She looked up at me. I'd never called her that before, but at that moment, it just felt right. I leant over her, pressing a kiss to her cheek.

"I love you," she whispered.

"I love you too, princess."

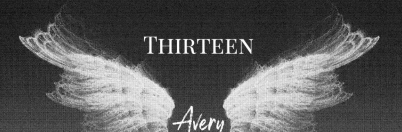

THIRTEEN

Avery

rapped up in Aiden's arms, I felt a sense of belonging which I hadn't felt in two and a half weeks. I hadn't really noticed the time passing, so lost in my own self misery. When I told him I had a black mark on my soul, I meant it. I'd killed to protect myself. To protect us. If Tristan had managed to force me into having sex with him, raped me, I don't think I'd have ever come back from it. That would've destroyed Aiden and me.

But could I ever live with myself after I'd killed him?

Tristan wasn't a nice person. He was fucked up in the head.

Did that mean he deserved to die?

Probably not.

I didn't have the right to decide who lived or died. But it had happened and I couldn't take it back. Self-preservation kicked in, forcing me to do the unthinkable.

The images of his shocked expression branded themselves on my retinas, causing my heart to ache. Tears sprung to my eyes. Would this guilt ever go away? When I'd been lost in my own misery, I hadn't really felt much, but now, it all came crashing down on me once again. Tearing my insides to shreds. No matter how much I tried to justify it to myself, I'd still taken a life. And that was unforgivable.

Aiden kissed the top of my head, stroking my back as my tears leaked out of my eyes. I couldn't hold back the pitiful sob which followed.

"It hurts," I cried.

"I know, princess," he said, his voice soft and soothing. "I'm here. I've got you. It's okay. Just let it out, okay?"

I nodded against his chest. I clutched him tighter, sobbing onto his bare skin. If he minded, he didn't say anything. Aiden had become my sole source of comfort since the day we'd met. The day he'd held me and let me cry on his chest after he'd killed my parents. We'd been on a collision course from the time our eyes met until we'd finally given in. I should've known back then just how much trouble I was in. How much of a mess my life would become. How every step, every action had led us to this.

"I didn't mean to kill him. It all happened so fast," I sobbed. "I just wanted to stop him."

"I know it hurts, but you're so strong, Avery. You were so brave that night. So fucking brave. You could've given in, but you didn't."

He released me only to take my face in both his hands, staring at me intently.

"I'm not supposed to say this, but I'm so fucking proud of you."

"You are?" I sniffed.

"You fought so hard. You've already been through so much shit and yet, you refused to give up."

I reached over, placing my hand on his heart.

"Because I have something to fight for."

And that was the honest truth. I wasn't just fighting for myself, I was fighting for him. I wanted to help him destroy it all. Aiden deserved so much better than what he'd been lumped with in life. I knew he'd done a lot of bad shit, but loving someone was about accepting them, flaws and all. That was the thing. I had always loved him without conditions.

He told me what he'd done to Frazier. I knew exactly what he'd said. That night, rather than bottling it all up, we'd shared our mutual experiences. I'd sobbed on his chest just like I'd been doing now. My heart was still in tatters on the floor. I didn't get mad about him telling Frazier I was his whore because it wasn't true. I only had to look in Aiden's eyes to see that. I only had to remember our wedding day and how he'd cried in my arms at my private declaration of love.

"I didn't just do it for me, I did it for you. For us," I whispered. "I killed for you, Aiden."

His silver eyes darkened. He leant down and kissed me. The gentlest of kisses which seemed to go on forever before he leant his forehead against mine.

"I know you did," he whispered across my lips. "I don't want you to do it again. I don't want you to suffer any more pain. You're my light. Don't forget that. Don't ever turn yourself out again. You hear me?"

I nodded. I could never forget that. He told me not to turn myself out and I had. I'd fallen into some sort of catatonic state where everything around me just faded away. Even him. I'd known he was there and trying to talk to me. I'd heard him beg me to say something. The Avery he loved was locked inside, screaming to get out. Crying out for him. Desperately needing the man who gave her everything.

Tears fell down my face all over again. I reached out, cupping his face with one hand.

"You have no idea how sorry I am for the past couple of weeks."

"It's okay, you're back now. I have you right here."

"No. It's not okay. You needed me too. Where was I? Wallowing in my own self misery. You did so much for me. You made sure it couldn't be traced back to us without me asking. You knew what I needed that night and since then, you've been taking care of me even though I've been a shit wife to you. I'm so sorry and at the same time, I'm so grateful. Do you have any idea how much I appreciate you? You think you're not a good person, but you are. At least you are to me. I don't care what anyone else says or thinks. I love you so much, Aiden. I can't live without you. I have no idea what I would do if you weren't here. I'd have lost myself completely."

He kissed me again, wiping away my tears with his thumb.

"It's very simple, princess. I'd do anything for you because I love you. I promised to protect you and I meant it."

I buried my face in his chest, sobbing my heart out all over again. He just held me and stroked my hair. When I was all cried out, he told me he was taking me out and I wasn't allowed to object. I hadn't left the flat since we got home that night. I wasn't sure it was a good idea to be seen together, but I kept quiet as I got dressed.

If Aiden thought it would do me good, then I was going to go along with it. I had to remember I needed to stay in the present. And I'd do that for him after everything he'd done for me.

REVENGE

Walking into the office, I felt a sense of trepidation. I'd been away for three weeks. I knew Uncle Charlie would ambush me the moment I got in, but what I was not expecting was to find him and Ed waiting in my office.

I walked in, shrugging off my coat and hanging it up on the hook before having a word with John and asking him to wait outside. I sat down at my desk and levelled my gaze on both of them.

"How are you feeling?" my uncle asked.

"I'm okay, thank you."

He and Ed gave each other a look before turning back to me. I eyed them warily. What did they want?

"Was what happened to the Shaws part of your grand plan?"

I took a deep breath. This was always going to come up, but I wasn't sure when my uncle had decided to confide my secret to Ed. It aroused my suspicions further.

"What makes you think I had anything to do with that?"

"Well, you tell me, Avery. You said you were getting engaged to Tristan to find dirt on Frazier and then low and behold less than a week later, both of them are dead."

I tried not to flinch. The memory of that night came flooding back. Images of Tristan lying dead on the bed flashed before my eyes. I blinked them away.

"I don't know what happened. It's like I told you, I came down with the flu that night. I could barely get out of bed. What else do you want me to say?"

"Then why the fuck are the police raiding his office?"

I sighed. That had been my fault admittedly, but I wasn't going to tell him about it.

"Why? Concerned about what they might find?"

Ed's eyes darted between me and my uncle. He'd not seen us interact much recently. Didn't know how strained our relationship was.

"Why would I be concerned?"

I sat back, drumming my nails on the desk.

"Well, if you were, there's no need. Shaw Associates no longer represents Daniels Holdings."

They both stared at me, eyes wide.

"What?" Ed asked.

"As of six weeks ago, we moved everything in house to our own legal department. The board signed off on it."

My uncle slammed his hand down on my desk.

"Why the fuck did you not think to inform me of this?"

I shrugged.

"I didn't think I had to."

It'd taken me a week to convince Frazier it would be a conflict of interest having his firm represent us if he was going to be family. I wanted a clean slate. To be honest, I think he agreed because he thought it was the only way he'd get his hands on my money. Idiot.

"Fuck. You could've fucking well told me. I wouldn't have spent the past week trying to find out what the fuck the police had found."

"Well, sorry. I didn't think it was that important. I mean, you don't get involved with the legal department."

The thing is, even though everything had reverted back to our own legal department, I'd known Frazier would've kept his own personal records on Daniels Holdings in his home. That's why when I found all that shit on his computer, I'd erased it so when the police searched it, they'd find no trace of anything related to my company. The rest I didn't care about. They could dig up all the dirt they wanted on everyone else. Daniels Holdings was in the clear until I decided to reveal the truth.

"It's fucking important, Avery."

I didn't think he'd get this pissed off about it. Honestly, I thought he'd be happy Frazier didn't have his hands on our legal paperwork any longer. My uncle looked at Ed again, his eyes narrowing.

"So you really don't have any idea what happened to Tristan and Frazier?" Ed asked.

"Other than what's in the news? No. The police haven't spoken to me yet. Don't know what Susan told them."

"Yes, well, Susan made one statement to the press and that's it. No one else has heard a peep out of her," my uncle said.

"Can you blame her? Her husband and son were killed… kind of violently if you ask me."

Tristan's shocked expression flittered across my vision again. I wrapped my hand around the arm of my chair, trying not to let my expression betray my inner turmoil. I had to forget about this. I had to keep it off my mind. It was so fucking hard.

My heart felt tight. I was not going to freak out in front of them. Shit. I wished Aiden was here. I just needed him to hold me and tell me it was going to be okay. He'd get me through this. I needed him so fucking much.

"Quite… I've been wondering if it was the same person who murdered your parents."

I shuddered, unable to stop myself. Little did he know how on the nose that was. Now, I really did need Aiden. I had all sorts of awful images in my head and I felt like my whole entire world was about to come crashing down around me. Gripping the chair arm tighter, I took a steadying breath.

"Does it matter who killed them? I thought you hated the Shaws."

"I do… I did."

"Is this all you wanted to talk to me about? I've got a lot to catch up on."

What I actually needed was to go into the ladies and call Aiden before I completely lost my mind. The sooner I could get Uncle Charlie and Ed out of here, the better.

"No. Ed and I have something important to discuss with you."

I looked between them. What the hell was this? I wasn't sure I could deal with it all at that moment. I felt sick to my stomach. All I could think about was all the death I'd seen. The room started to spin. I couldn't think straight. See straight.

Dead.

Dead.

I abruptly stood up. Both of them looked up at me, frowning.

"Um… excuse me, I'll be back in a minute."

Before either of them could say anything, I walked out of the room, past a confused looking John and dashed into the ladies. I put my hands on the counter, trying to breathe whilst panic set in all around me. I could see their faces. My dad. My mum. Frazier. Tristan. All staring at me. I was going crazy again. Completely fucking batshit crazy.

I slid down onto the floor, turning so my back was to the sinks and fumbled with my phone in my pocket. I managed to unlock it and dial Aiden's number, hoping he'd pick up. I couldn't breathe. I held my chest as I put the phone to my ear, trying desperately to suck in air.

"Princess?"

"I…I… help me."

I took a shuddering breath, feeling my heart pounding out of control in my chest. I could hear my blood rushing in my ears. What the fuck was happening to me?

"What's wrong? Did someone do something to you?"

"N…No… I… I… can't breathe."

"Where are you?"

I could hardly get my words out. The four faces were staring at me, unblinking. Why the hell were they there? What was going on? My chest felt so tight. I didn't know what to do or say.

"Avery, are you still there?"

"Y…yes."

"I'm going to need you to put your head between your legs and just breathe, okay?"

I shifted, putting my knees up as I bent over them. I tried to take a deep breath, but it wasn't working. My lungs burnt.

"Breathe, princess. Just breathe."

I took a shuddering breath, trying to focus on Aiden's voice.

"That's it, and another."

I did as he said, breathing in and out.

"Good girl. Keep breathing."

I took five more breaths, feeling the panic begin to subside. My heart rate started to slow. I could no longer see their faces.

"Aiden," I whimpered.

Coming to work had been a stupid idea. I couldn't do this. I wasn't ready. How could I face the world when all I could think about was how I'd killed another person? When all I could see was death.

"What happened?"

"I don't know," I whispered. "I was talking to Uncle Charlie and Ed and I just felt so sick and weird. And I saw them again… but this time Frazier and Tristan were there too."

"You saw your parents again?"

"Yes."

There was a long pause. I hadn't hallucinated them in months. This didn't bode well. I was deteriorating all over again. I could feel it.

"Okay, I'm going to come get you."

"What? No, you can't."

"Avery, you're having hallucinations again. Do you really think I'm just going to leave you there alone?"

"But you can't come to the office, you know that."

He sighed.

"Do you think I give a shit if anyone finds out you're my wife? I don't. Not any longer. I'm fucking done with this now. No more lies. No more secrets. I'm coming to get you and that's the end of the fucking discussion."

"But, Aiden…"

"No. Do not argue with me. I'll be there in twenty minutes. Do not fucking get John to drive you home. Wait in your office. Do as I say or I won't be fucking responsible for my actions. Do you hear me?"

I swallowed.

"Yes," I whispered.

"Good."

He hung up on me. I raised my head, my hand dropping to my side. What the hell? I had no idea what had gotten into Aiden.

There was a knock at the bathroom door, followed by a muffled, "Avery, are you still in there?"

I got to my feet, slipping my phone in my pocket. I looked at my face in the mirror. I looked like a fucking ghost. Shit. I had twenty minutes to work out what I was going to say when Aiden got here. How I was going to explain this?

I pinched my cheeks, trying to bring back colour into them, but it was useless. Trudging towards the door, I opened it. John was waiting there, a concerned look on his face.

"Are you okay?"

I shook my head, coming out of the room and standing with him in the hallway.

"What's wrong?"

I rubbed my head, looking down at the floor.

"I think I had a panic attack and now Aiden is on his way here and I don't know what to do."

"Well shit."

I couldn't bring myself to laugh at that. This had turned into an absolute mess.

"He said he doesn't care if they find out we're married."

He put a hand on my arm, giving it a squeeze.

"I can't leave, he'll get really mad," I continued. "I have to deal with Ed and Uncle Charlie. I don't know what to say to them. They want to talk to me about something, but I don't know what it is. What do I do? If Aiden turns up here, he'll completely ruin everything we've worked so hard for."

He released my arm and gave me a sympathetic look.

"You can't stop him, you know."

I nodded. When Aiden decided on a course of action, he just did it. The consequences be damned. He wasn't thinking straight because I was involved. The ramifications of them discovering we were together were potentially huge

Was he doing this because I'd retreated into myself for over two weeks? Did he think I was going to go back into that state? Or was he worried I'd completely fall apart like I did last time I hallucinated my parents?

Either way, I'd worried him enough for him to say fuck it to everything else. I felt like kicking myself, but there was no point. I'd needed Aiden. No one else would've got me to calm down. I knew that.

"I suppose I better go face the music."

"Are you sure you're ready?"

"No, but I don't have a choice. When Aiden gets here, everything's going to hell anyway."

He shrugged.

"Maybe it won't be so bad."

"You know Uncle Charlie isn't that stupid. He's going to put two and two together and then where will we be? He'll know what…"

I stopped. John didn't know about my parents. Didn't know Aiden had taken me captive. I couldn't reveal that no matter what. Even if John knew about what we did to Frazier and Tristan, it didn't matter. No one could know how Aiden and I met. No one.

John cocked his head to the side as if urging me to go on.

"It's just not going to end well."

I sighed. Time was ticking down and I couldn't continue wasting it with John. I gave him a smile before turning away and walking back to my office. He didn't call after me.

Ed and my uncle were still seated in front of my desk. They both looked at me with concerned expressions. I put my hands up as I sat back at my desk.

"Before you ask, I'm okay. I haven't been feeling right since I got the flu, but I'll go see a doctor or something if it carries on."

My uncle nodded.

"Are you sure?"

"Yeah… Now, what did you want to talk to me about?"

The two of them looked at each other for a moment. I felt a sense of trepidation at their eager glances. I looked at the clock on the wall. Too much time had passed. Far too much. Any second my whole life would come crashing down.

Uncle Charlie turned to me, about to open his mouth when my office door was flung open. Ed and my uncle twisted around at the noise. I gripped the arms of my chair. Aiden stood there, his grey eyes dark and stormy. My heart thumped erratically in my chest at the sight of him.

He walked into the room with so much self-assurance, I let out a small squeak of surprise. Hell. My husband looked so deadly in that moment.

"Aiden…?" Uncle Charlie said, standing up and looking between the two of us.

Aiden completely ignored them, striding around my desk, taking my hand and tugging me to my feet. I stared up at him as he dropped my hand only to cup my face with both of his. His eyes searched mine for several moments. My breath caught in my throat. His fear and concern bled into me.

"What is going on?" I heard my uncle ask.

I couldn't tear my eyes away from my husband. He commanded my full attention. My beautiful tattooed god. Every inch the man who stood up for me and protected me through thick and thin. As if I could ever look away.

Neither of us spoke, just staring at each other as if we were silently communicating.

Are you okay? Tell me you're okay, princess, Aiden asked me with his eyes.

Yes. I'm okay now you're here, I responded without words.

His grey eyes softened. I wanted to melt into him. To have him hold me and soothe away all my pain. He was all I ever needed.

He dropped his hands from my face, slipping one of his into his pocket. He grasped my hand and slipped my wedding ring back on my finger. I stared down at it and his own hand which held mine. Both our rings glinted in the harsh light of the overhead lamps.

He'd just made a declaration to my family.

I was his.

Legally Aiden's girl.

His wife.

Mrs Avery Charlotte Lockhart.

FOURTEEN

Aiden

I knew I had to face the consequences of coming down here and showing her fucking family she was mine. I was just so fucking tired of everything. Tired of living a lifetime of lies and secrets. Tired of hiding in the shadows. After what went down with Tristan and Frazier, especially Avery's reaction, I was fucking done. All of this had only brought us more misery. I couldn't fucking stand her pain. So now, I was fucking well doing something about it.

I turned to Chuck and her cousin, Ed. Chuck looked like he'd seen a fucking ghost and Ed had a frown on his face.

"I wasn't lying when I told you Avery is married to me," was the first thing out of my mouth.

Chuck spluttered, put his hand on his mouth and sat down abruptly. Silence descended over the room. Avery's hand in mine tightened. I could feel her trembling next to me.

I watched her cousin carefully. I had my fucking suspicions about him. There was curiosity in his expression as well as surprise.

"When?" Chuck asked, dropping his hand from his face.

"What, when did I start seeing your niece? Months ago. When did we get married? A week before her birthday."

"And you kept this a fucking secret from me this entire time? What the fuck is going on in that head of yours?"

I shrugged. There were a lot of reasons why we hadn't told Chuck. Mostly because I didn't want him to suspect it was me who'd killed his brother.

He stood up, pacing away with his hand in his hair.

"Christ, Aiden. After every-fucking-thing I've done to try help you after all the shit with Mitch, this is what you do? You go behind my back and get married to my fucking niece. To his fucking daughter. Have you completely lost your fucking mind?"

He turned back to me, his eyes blazing with fury.

"Tell me right fucking now, when did this fucking happen and how? I will not tolerate any more shit from either of you. You're going to tell me the fucking truth."

Avery flinched at my side, her fingers digging into mine. I looked down at her. Her doe eyes were wide, almost as if she'd never seen her uncle so incensed before.

"The truth?" I asked.

"Yes, the fucking truth."

Avery looked up at me, shaking her head. Her eyes pleading with me not to tell him anything. Not to reveal the one thing which could bring everything crashing down around us.

"It started the night Mitchell died."

Avery almost caved in on herself. I turned to Chuck, who was about to open his mouth, but I put a hand up. The real truth of that night was going to remain between Avery and me.

"I had nothing to do with that shit. I was walking past the building when she ran out in tears. I was there because of that shit you asked me to do with those dealers. Anyway, she ran into me and I recognised her. I felt kind of shit about leaving her there in tears so I told her who I was and asked if she wanted to talk about it."

I looked over at Avery. She regarded me with an almost neutral expression, but her doe eyes told me she hadn't expected me to come up with some bullshit story about how we met. I'd become rather adept at thinking on my feet. I had to when dealing with the Daniels and their bullshit.

"I tried to take her home, but she didn't want to go, so I did the only other thing I could. I brought her back to mine and let her tell me about her argument with Mitchell. So when you called me the next day, she was asleep on my sofa. That's why the police couldn't find her because when I told her about Mitchell and Kathleen, she was a fucking mess. She begged me not to tell anyone where she was. So yes, we lied to everyone including the police."

"You're telling me she was with you the entire time?"

I turned back to Chuck.

"Yes. And trust me, I didn't mean for any of it to happen. It just did. I didn't take advantage of your niece, so you can stop looking at me like I'm some fucking scumbag who started screwing a girl who was in clear emotional distress. I'm not that fucked up."

Chuck's expression cleared a little. He ran a hand through his hair.

"Why didn't you tell me when she came back? Hmm?"

"She didn't want to tell anyone because of how it would look."

Chuck paced away, clearly agitated. I wasn't sure he'd bought what I'd told him.

"Is this true, Avery?" he asked, not looking at either of us.

"Yes," she said, her voice a little unsteady.

He was silent, his back to us. Ed was still seated, watching all of us with trepidation. Time felt like it wasn't passing. We were all just stuck there, waiting for someone to say something.

And then the last person any of us were expecting strolled into the room with his hands in his pockets. He eyed the scene for all of ten seconds.

"Well, this is quite the party."

My fist clenched. Avery let out a quiet moan of pain so I loosened my grip on her hand a little. What the actual fuck was he doing here?

"Rick?" Chuck said.

"Charles, long time no see, old friend."

Holy mother of all fucks. This fucking man knew no fucking bounds. Walking in here like he owned the fucking place.

"What are you doing here?"

Avery wrapped her other hand around my arm, giving it a squeeze. I was not fucking prepared for this shit today. Not one bit.

"Are you okay?" she whispered.

"No, I'm fucking not."

I was practically shaking with rage. How fucking dare he turn up here. How fucking dare he come to my fucking wife's office. I told him to stay away from us. I warned him.

"I'm here to meet my daughter in law," Rick said, his voice as smooth as fucking butter.

"You knew about this?" Chuck asked.

"Now, now, Charles, did you think I wouldn't keep an eye on my own son's activities?"

"Does everyone fucking know about this shit except me?"

"I didn't know," Ed piped up.

Chuck turned and gave him a death stare. Ed shrank back in his seat.

"Did I interrupt something?" Rick asked.

His expression told me he knew full well he'd walked into a shit storm. Chuck put a hand up.

"No, no, Ed and I were just leaving."

He turned, walked over to me and gave me a warning look.

"You and I are not done. I'm not buying this shit from you and her," he told me in a low voice.

Then he turned, aimed a finger at Ed and pointed at the door before he walked out. Ed got up and hurried away after him, leaving Avery and me alone with my scumbag sperm donor.

He quietly closed the door behind them. Turning to us, he didn't bother plastering a smile on his face.

"I warned you, but y'all hell bent on throwing caution to the wind now."

"I didn't fucking well ask for your opinion. What the fuck are you doing here?"

Avery let go of my hand and curled into my side instead. I wrapped an arm around her, but my gaze stayed on Rick.

"You not going to properly introduce us?"

"I told you in no uncertain terms to stay the fuck away from me and Avery."

Avery clutched me tighter. I could feel her vibrating with fear. Last time she'd been near Rick, he'd had her tied up and forced her to watch disgusting videos of his sick twisted friends. Not even I wanted to show her any more of those.

"Your little darlin' is shaking like a leaf. It's okay, doll, I don't bite."

"Aiden," she whispered. "Please make him leave."

The terror in her voice made my heart fracture in two. Fuck. I wrapped my other arm around her, pulling her against my chest.

"It's okay, princess, I've got you," I told her, my voice low.

This was too much for her. She'd started hallucinating again, then dealing with her uncle going off the deep end, and now Rick. He needed to get out of my sight before I did something I couldn't take back.

"I will call security if you don't leave right now."

Rick raised an eyebrow. I looked at him closely. I hated the sight of him. Especially since I could now see myself in him. His light brown hair, jawline and the way he carried himself. The difference between us? He was a weedy little shit compared to me. Standing there in his expensive suit, tie clip and brogues, he looked like a Class A fucking twat. Trying to pass himself off as the British elite when he was just a jumped up fuck.

"No need. I'll say what I need then I'll be on my way. I expect you and your little darlin' to have dinner with me tonight at the Ritz. Be there at eight."

He gave me a self-satisfied smirk before he turned, pulled open the door and strolled out.

Was he out of his fucking mind? Dinner with him? No fucking way. I was not about to subject Avery to that shit nor did I want to spend the evening with that sick as fuck cunt.

"Is he gone?" she asked.

"Yes, princess."

She pulled away from my chest slightly, staring up at me. Her bottom lip trembled.

"Everything's gone to shit."

She wasn't wrong about that. Everything had blown up. We could fix it though. Chuck just needed to calm down. And Rick could get fucked.

"Are you okay?"

"No, I'm not. I can't deal with any of this. You told my uncle and he doesn't believe us. Rick wants us to have dinner with him and I know you don't want to go but we both know we have to."

She looked away, her arms tightening around me.

"I'm kind of mad at you for coming here," she whispered. "I know you're worried about me, but it wasn't necessary and now we're in even more trouble."

I took a breath, trying to tamp down on the rage I felt at that moment. It wasn't directed at her, but she couldn't possibly understand what it was like when I got that phone call from her. I almost lost my shit hearing how distressed she was. It'd taken a lot of fucking self-control to stay calm enough to help her.

I wasn't going to apologise for it either. It was fucking time. All these secrets had only led us to more problems. Yes, we might have got rid of the Shaws, but it'd created more issues than it'd solved. It'd been to the detriment of Avery's mental health. Every day I could see how wracked with guilt she was over Tristan's death. How much it destroyed the good inside her. How she couldn't think of herself in the same way any longer.

I backed her towards the desk, picked her up and put her down on it before sitting in her desk chair and pulling it up between her legs. I rested my hands on her thighs. She stared down at me, those doe eyes intense and appraising me with no small amount of trepidation.

"You come first, no matter what. Everything else is insignificant if you're suffering. I'll deal with Chuck. This has to end, Avery. You know it does."

I was careful about what I said given where we were.

"We can keep hiding away in the shadows or we can take the bull by its fucking horns and do something about it. All I want is for you to be happy, for us to have a normal life. We can't do that when all these secrets threaten to tear everything apart. All I'm doing is being here for you because I know how much you're suffering, princess. That's why I came. You need me. Don't you know I'd do anything for you? I'd risk everything just to make sure you're okay."

She put one of her hands on top of mine, giving it a squeeze.

"How can I ever stay angry with you when you say stuff like that?"

I could see her trying to hold back a smile.

"We just need to take a minute. We'll work out what to do, okay?"

She nodded. Staring down at me, she raised an eyebrow.

"You're sitting in the boss's chair. I mean… you know technically I'm your boss's boss."

I smiled as she raised one of her legs and set it on the chair in between mine. A slight change of subject, but honestly, I didn't want to talk about that shit any longer. I wanted to make sure she was okay after her panic attack. We hadn't had a chance to discuss it.

I leant back, staring at her. Fuck. She looked so hot right then. I tried not to think about how much I wanted to bend her over her desk.

"What's the company policy on inter-office relationships? Am I going to get in trouble for screwing my boss's boss?"

Her smile took on a seductive note to it. Fuck. We should not be playing this game with each other right now.

"There's no rules against fraternising with colleagues, but we wouldn't want anyone to think I was showing favouritism."

Shit. Fuck. Hell, her fucking eyes were inviting me to take advantage of the situation. Was she doing this to avoid thinking about the world of shit we were in? Why did I even care when she was practically offering herself up to me on a platter?

I shook my head, smiling at her. I was not going to fuck her across her desk. I repeated that to myself over and over again as I watched her slip off the desk, turn around and place her palms on it. She looked back at me as she bent over slightly.

"Avery…"

"Isn't this one of your fantasies?" she said, her voice low.

I'd completely forgotten I'd told her about that months ago. Fuck.

"You do realise I'll have to go erase all of the footage unless you want security to get a surprise view of the boss getting a seeing to?"

She smirked.

"It's lucky my husband is so handy with technology then, isn't it?"

"You know I want to, but this isn't the time or place."

Not after all the shit today. We could fuck at home where I didn't have to hide my darker desires. I'd make her feel better then. Take her pain away when we had privacy and weren't in danger of being interrupted.

"What triggered your panic attack?"

She sighed, straightening and turning to me. I put my hand out to her. She sat in my lap and wrapped her hand around my neck, staring at me.

"Talking about what happened with my uncle and Ed. It just reminded me of everything. I guess it's going to take a while for me to feel normal again. I don't know if I ever will to be quite honest. I'm ready for this all to be over. I want to heal in peace and quiet rather than having to deal with all this shit."

"You're a lot calmer about this than I expected."

She shrugged, giving me a half smile.

"I'm fed up of crying over what happened. I don't want to be an emotional wreck. All that does is bring me more pain. Besides, we have more important things to worry about than the past even though I feel like it's going to come back and haunt us."

"The past has a funny way of catching up with you."

"I keep worrying everything is going to blow up in our faces."

"There's always a possibility of that. Whatever happens, princess, remember we have each other. Even if everything goes to shit."

The intercom buzzer went. Avery shifted in my lap, reaching over and pressing down on it.

"Miss Daniels, there is a detective and a police officer here to see you," Saskia said.

I'd met her assistant on the way in here. She hadn't wanted to let me in the office, but when I told her, Avery was my wife, she soon changed her tune.

"Oh… Um… send them in," Avery replied.

She lifted her hand off the button and turned to look at me. This couldn't be anything good.

"What the hell are the police doing here?"

"Fuck knows."

There was a knock at the door. Avery walked over and opened it. Standing there was the detective and a police officer. Detective Reynolds. I recognised her from when she questioned me.

Shit. Shit. Fuck. Fuck.

"Good morning, Miss Daniels," the detective said. "My name is Detective Reynolds. I have a few things we need to speak to you about."

"Oh, right," Avery said.

Reynolds gave her a sympathetic look.

"It's okay, Miss Daniels, it's nothing for you to worry about."

Avery looked back at me, eyes wide with concern. I took a step towards her. I had a sick feeling this was about Tristan and Frazier. She turned back to the detective.

"I'm not Miss Daniels."

Reynolds frowned.

"Excuse me?"

"It's Mrs Lockhart now. I just want you to have your facts straight. This is my husband."

Reynolds looked past her and her eyes landed on me. They narrowed.

"Mr Lockhart," she said.

I walked towards them, coming to a halt next to Avery.

"Hello, Detective Reynolds, it's nice to see you again."

It wasn't, but she didn't need to know that.

"I think you have some explaining to do considering last time we spoke, you claimed to have never met Miss Daniels."

I gave her a smile. This wasn't going to end well. I'd just have to spin her another story. I could manage that.

"What did you want to talk to me about?" Avery asked, pulling Reynold's attention back to her.

"It's regarding your parents' case."

We both stepped back to allow them in. Avery led them over to the sofas in the corner of her office. She sat down in one of them and tugged my hand. I took a seat next to her whilst Reynolds sat on the sofa to our right. The officer remained standing.

"Mis… Mrs Lockhart, this is a conversation we should be having in private."

She eyed me warily.

"Aiden is my husband and he's not leaving."

Reynolds looked put out momentarily before her expression cleared.

"As you wish. You're aware it's been over six months since the death of your parents," Reynolds said as she eyed me with no small amount of suspicion.

"Yes," Avery replied.

"As their immediate next of kin, it is my duty to inform you we believe your parents' murders are connected to the recent deaths of Frazier and Tristan Shaw."

FIFTEEN

Avery

I stared at the detective for the longest moment. How the fuck had they worked that out? I mean, I knew they were connected, but no one else should. Except perhaps all of his sick associates. They must know someone was gunning for them now. That someone being Aiden. I clutched his hand tighter, wanting desperately to be anywhere else but there right now.

But the detective had said it was nothing for me to worry about. Did that mean they had no idea who it was? I hoped so. I couldn't stand the thought of Aiden going to prison. Nor me for that matter considering what I'd done. I still felt so much guilt and remorse over the whole thing, but I had to get on with my life. I had to move forward. No matter how much Tristan's death weighed on my conscience.

"You do? Wait… why haven't you asked my uncle to come in? He's also next of kin."

Detective Reynolds looked at the officer for a moment before levelling her gaze back on me.

"I cannot give you the full details as our investigation is still on-going. However, Charles Daniels is a person of interest in the case and we will discuss it separately with him."

I looked at Aiden. How was Uncle Charlie a person of interest? What the hell had the police found?

"Information has come to light regarding Mr Shaw's involvement in illegal activities, some of which are connected to your father. I would ask that you do not share this information with the public."

"Illegal activities? Do they relate to Daniels Holdings?"

Reynolds shook her head.

"No, they are regarding your father's personal affairs. We suspect the murders were committed by more than one party and that the motive may have been revenge, but nothing is certain. Again, this is speculation and this information is confidential."

I nodded.

"I understand. What's said here won't leave these walls."

Reynolds gave me a grateful smile before her face cleared and she was back to business.

"I understand you recently announced an engagement between yourself and Mr Shaw. Yet, now you've informed me, you're already married to Mr Lockhart. Would you care to explain the circumstances here?"

Aiden squeezed my hand. I hope he trusted me to spin the police a story laced with the truth. Whatever I did, I couldn't allow them to suspect it was me who'd killed Tristan and had been there that night.

"Our relationship was a secret from our family until today," I said. "And I had reason to believe Frazier Shaw wanted me to marry Tristan because he wanted my inheritance. You see, we found out there's a clause in my trust fund which grants my husband full rights to it."

Reynold's raised an eyebrow.

"And this made you pronounce an engagement with Mr Shaw?"

"Well, Aiden and I wanted to find out if we were right. I know we probably shouldn't have hatched our own plan to catch him out, but Frazier had been pestering me for weeks. I just said yes to get him to stop. I never had any intention of going through with it."

The detective gave me a sceptical look, but I shrugged.

"I see. Might I ask when you and Mr Lockhart got married?"

"Five weeks ago."

Reynolds looked directly at Aiden.

"And when did the two of you meet?"

Aiden leant back slightly, eying her with a smile.

"The beginning of the year, when Avery returned to work."

He looked over at me, affection in his eyes.

"Sometimes there's just that instant connection. I must admit, it has been rather fast, but when you know you've found the one, you know."

I tried not to laugh. That was the single most ridiculously sappy thing I'd ever heard come out of Aiden's mouth. Not to mention it was complete bullshit. We'd known each other for more than five months before we got married and even then, we'd been through so much, it felt like a hell of a lot longer.

Reynolds looked between the two of us as though she wasn't sure whether to believe us or not. It's not like she could come out and accuse us of lying. She had no reason to suspect we weren't telling the truth.

"I see. Well… I came here today specifically to ask you if you would allow us further access to your parent's penthouse. I have a warrant, but we would much rather work with you to find the truth."

I'd gone through my dad's office with a fine toothcomb so I knew what was in there. I just wasn't sure what the hell they were looking for.

"I don't have a problem with that. May I see the warrant?"

The officer stepped forward, pulling some paperwork out of his vest and handing it to me. I gave it to Aiden since he probably understood it more than I would. He glanced over it. When he looked up, he gave me a nod.

"Shall I get you the keys?" I asked the detective.

"I would be most grateful."

I stood up and went over to my desk, pulling out the top drawer. I'd been keeping them here because I didn't want the reminder. There was no way I was going back there. Not after I'd dealt with the memories of what happened last time. It'd only bring me more misery. I no longer wanted to think about that night or what Aiden had done to my parents.

I brought the keys back over to the detective before sitting down next to Aiden again. He took my hand, lacing our fingers together. If he hadn't been here when they showed up, I wasn't sure what I would've done. It made me grateful he'd decided to say fuck you to our family and reveal the truth about our relationship. I was sick of the secrets too. All I wanted was normality. And I wanted Daniels Holdings gone. I was ready to wash my hands of it. I was done.

Reynolds stood up.

"Thank you for your time, Mr and Mrs Lockhart. I will keep you updated. In the meantime, if you think of anything that could help us in our investigations, this is my card. You can contact me at any time."

She handed me a business card before giving us both a nod and striding out of the room with the police officer in tow.

I let out a long sigh of relief, staring down at the business card in my hands. Aiden took it from me and placed it on the coffee table before he turned my face towards him.

"I'm not sure she bought our story."

"Neither am I. She was the one who questioned you that time."

"Yeah… Don't think she likes me."

I raised an eyebrow.

"What gave you that idea?"

I knew very well. It was clear Detective Reynolds thought Aiden wasn't an upstanding citizen. She'd be right on some level, but we weren't about to tell her that.

"You know, she was just giving off that type of vibe."

I smiled. Whilst I was glad that was over, it also brought up all sorts of further complications.

"The closer they get to the truth, the more concerned I get," I admitted.

"Hey, they won't find out, princess."

"Do you think we should hand over what we know to them?"

He shook his head.

"No. We need to find out who has the girls first. We can't make any moves against them until we know where they are. If they get tipped off, they'll probably kill them and destroy the evidence. That's the type of people they are. You know that."

I looked at our joined hands, feeling a little sick at the thought. My family were capable of that. They didn't care about the lives of those girls. Aiden was right. We needed to find them and make sure they were safe first. I couldn't live with their deaths on my hands. I had to make sure we rescued them.

"Speaking of girls, how are Sophie and Cora?"

"Tina says they're doing well. She doesn't think she can leave them there alone for too long though. They seem very attached to her. I think this is good for her, you know. Looking after people is what she's done her whole life."

"She doesn't have to take care of you anymore now you have me."

He snorted.

"As if I ever allowed her to really take care of me in the first place."

I stroked the back of his hand with my thumb.

"You let me take care of you."

His grin turned devious.

"You take care of me in ways no one else can."

I gave him a wink, which made him laugh. Hell, I loved it when Aiden laughed. The deep, rich timbre of his voice always did things to me.

As much as I wanted to keep the conversation light and playful, today had brought about way too many problems for us to deal with.

"What are we going to do about my uncle?"

"Right now? Nothing. He needs to calm down. Besides, you heard what that detective said, Chuck is a person of interest. That means he's got bigger problems than finding out we're married."

"I feel like we're skating on very thin ice right now. Uncle Charlie, Rick and now the police, I mean… things were always going to come out sooner or later, but I don't want us to get caught in the crossfire."

He let go of my hand and cupped my face, running his thumb across my cheek.

"We're going to be okay, princess. We're in this together. You and me. We'll make sure the right people are punished."

I nodded. I hoped Aiden was right.

Because if he wasn't...

I don't think I could survive being separated from him again.

Walking into the Ritz on Aiden's arm, I felt a sense of dread. Seeing Rick earlier today had terrified me. It brought back the memories of my kidnapping and him forcing me to watch those videos. Those reminders were very unwelcome, but they also made me even more determined to see this through.

Aiden looked over at me, his grey eyes hard as steel. He wasn't happy about this dinner with Rick. Neither was I, but if we didn't go, he'd just make our lives hell. I knew he was capable of it.

The maître d' showed us to a table. Rick was already seated, his dark eyes glinting as he saw us. He stood, coming around and pulling out my chair for me.

"Hello, little darlin'," he said.

My skin crawled. Aiden stiffened but said nothing. I sat, letting him push my chair in for me. Aiden sat next to me, taking my hand under the table. Rick sat across from us.

"Thank you for coming."

Both of us stared at him. I wasn't sure what the hell to say. He'd basically given us no option but to meet him here. I didn't trust him. Not one bit.

I dropped Aiden's hand and picked up the menu, not wanting to look at the man who'd given life to my husband. I noticed Aiden did the same. If Rick was put out by us basically blanking him, he didn't show it. Minutes ticked by without us saying anything. The waiter came over and took our orders. Then we had no choice but to either talk or stay silent.

"Why did you ask us here?" Aiden said.

Rick steepled his hands, reminding me of my father. I stiffened, trying not to allow panic to set in. I'd already seen his face in my mind today. Another reminder would just send me over the edge.

"Is a man not allowed to want to meet his daughter in law?"

"Let me make something very clear, you're not my father and she is not your daughter in law. We are not family. Tell me why you insisted on this."

"I wish to help you."

Aiden's eyebrow curled upwards, incredulity in his expression. I couldn't believe my ears myself. Why the fuck would Rick want to help us and with what?

"Help me?"

Rick nodded, his expression turning serious.

"If you do as I ask, I will tell you everything you want to know about your little darlin's family… and Lizzie."

Aiden's expression darkened. I put my hand on his arm, reminding him I was there. That we couldn't make a scene in a public place. No matter how much I wanted to tell Rick to get fucked.

"What do you want from us?" Aiden asked through gritted teeth.

I could feel the tension radiating off him. I desperately wanted to soothe him. Needed to take his discomfort and pain away. I knew the mention of his mother's name, especially from Rick, would remind him of it all.

"I wish to know both of you. Spend time with me whilst I'm in England and the day I depart, I will tell you everything."

It seemed like an innocuous request, but I knew better than to think that anything Rick said was innocent. He couldn't just want that.

Aiden looked at me. I could see the disgust and hatred in his face, but I could also see the battle going on inside his head. He wanted to know who'd killed Lizzie. He wanted that desperately. I knew he'd never be at peace otherwise.

I leant towards him, brushing my lips against his ear as I squeezed his arm.

"I think we should consider it," I whispered.

Before I could pull away, he cupped my face, turning it so he could whisper in my ear.

"We can't trust him."

I nodded. I wasn't saying we could. Aiden needed closure and Rick was the only one who could give that to him. No matter how much he hated the man.

He turned back to Rick.

"How long are you here for?"

"Three weeks."

Aiden tensed. Three weeks would be bearable. Just about.

"And how often do you expect to see us?"

"Have dinner with me twice a week."

"Fine."

Rick smiled. It was then that the waiters arrived with our starters. Wanting to save Aiden from having to talk to Rick further, I engaged him in conversation. He asked me about how the company was doing. The small talk continued into the main course. Aiden vibrated with tension next to me. I could see he was becoming more and more agitated by the minute being in Rick's company. I wished I could soothe him, but there wasn't much I could do in a crowded restaurant.

When the mains were cleared, I excused myself to the bathroom. I didn't want to leave Aiden alone with Rick, but I also needed a minute. Thankfully it was empty. I looked at myself in the mirror, sighing heavily. Having to talk to a man my husband hated wasn't an easy task. I wasn't sure how we would survive the next three weeks having to spend more time with him.

I was so lost in my own thoughts, I didn't entirely register the door opening. It was only when a hand wrapped around my arm and I was tugged into a cubicle that I realised I wasn't alone. I looked up as Aiden locked the door behind us.

"What are you doing?" I hissed.

He spun me around and kicked the toilet seat closed. Shoving me against the wall, he tugged my hips back as he pulled my blue dress up.

"Aiden, what the fuck?"

"Shut up," he said harshly in my ear.

Practically ripping my underwear down, he stroked me before plunging two fingers inside my pussy. I bucked, letting out a small sound of alarm. He slapped a hand over my mouth.

"You're going to be quiet and let me fuck you," he told me.

My traitorous body melted at his words, but my mind screamed at me that we were in a public place. What the hell had gotten into him? I knew he was rattled from being around Rick, but that didn't give him the right to shove me into a toilet cubicle and demand I have sex with him.

Even if I tried to tell him no, my body was saying yes. His fingers guaranteed I was dripping for him. I heard him undo his belt and unzip his trousers. The next thing I knew, he'd pulled his fingers out of me and replaced them with his cock. He grunted as he thrust inside me.

"Fuck, princess," he hissed.

I groaned against his hand. Shit, he felt so good. He pounded into me against the wall, his fingers on my clit. I wriggled against him, needing more. Fuck. All my arguments against this evaporated under the intense sensations he was eliciting from my body. I was still worried someone would come in and hear us, but not enough to stop. Hell, I needed to come so badly.

"Harder," I moaned into his hand.

He must've heard my muffled noise because he tugged me closer and fucked me harder. His harsh breath against my ear drove me fucking crazy.

"That's it," he hissed. "You're such a good girl. All mine. Fuck."

I tried to hold back, but my climax erupted inside me. I bucked, moaning into his hand as my pussy clenched around his cock. Fuck. It felt deliciously wonderful. All the pent up tension inside me evaporated. Utter bliss radiated across my skin, making me want to feel like this every moment we were together. I was so fucking addicted to Aiden. And he was all mine. This fucked up tattooed god. My avenging angel. I didn't think 'No' was in my vocabulary when it came to him.

I slumped against the wall when I came down from my high whilst he continued to pound me into submission. His grunts got louder until I felt him pulsate inside me, filling me with his cum.

"Fucking hell, princess," he whispered.

Releasing my mouth, he held me to him with both hands wrapped around my stomach as he kissed my shoulder.

"Not that I didn't enjoy it, but what was that about?"

"You take my pain away," he told me. "Just like I take yours from you."

My heart fractured at his words. I knew he was angry about being around Rick, but I didn't realise how much it'd made him suffer.

"I needed in you, princess. To feel you. To love you. I can't stand being around him."

I nodded. I understood. And I couldn't deny the release he'd just given me was amazing. I felt better equipped to get through the rest of the evening with Rick now.

Aiden pulled away, re-adjusting his clothing. I turned and looked at him. The tension which had lined his face all night was gone.

"Just warn me next time you want to fuck me in a toilet," I said.

He grinned, leaning down to kiss me. I smiled back when he released me. I couldn't be mad at him. Tonight was taxing for both of us. He checked to see if the coast was clear before leaving the room and letting me clean up.

I took a deep breath before I left the toilets when I was done.

This was only the beginning.

We had three more weeks of dinners with Rick.

And I wasn't looking forward to any of them.

SIXTEEN

Aiden

*A*very was still asleep when I woke up. She looked so fucking precious with her hair splayed out across the pillow. She'd been my fucking rock last night. Having to spend an evening with Rick, the man I despised with every inch of my fucking soul, was pure fucking hell. Avery had taken it in her stride. She'd answered his questions about the company and how she was faring since her parents died. I'd barely had to say anything to him at all.

I kissed her forehead, careful not to wake her as I slipped out of bed, picking my phone up on the way. It was before six. Her alarm wouldn't go off for a while so I decided to get a run in. I pulled on shorts and a t-shirt, heading out for half an hour.

Covered in a sheen of sweat by the time I got back in the flat, I had a shower. When I went back into the bedroom, she was still sleeping. My raven haired princess. She'd clutched the covers in her sleep, looking so fucking adorable. I wanted to crawl over her and wake her up with sex. Worship every inch of her body. My wife. The most beautiful girl I'd ever known.

Looking down at my phone after I tugged my boxers on, my heart fucking stopped in my chest. An alert had come up. I'd set it up to go off when Avery's name appeared on various tabloids and news sites. Just so we knew what was being said about her. I clicked on the article, clenching my fist as I read it.

Last night heiress and owner of Daniels Holdings, Avery Daniels, was photographed with an unknown male outside of the Ritz in London. The couple looked very close sparking a hot debate about the nature of their relationship. Only four weeks ago, Avery revealed she was engaged to Tristan Shaw, who was tragically murdered a mere five days after the announcement. Requests for a statement from Avery in the wake of his death were denied. It seems Avery has moved on very quickly judging by the photos which surfaced online at around midnight last night.

I scrolled down finding several photos of us. We were holding hands as we left the Ritz. One of them showed me kissing the top of her head as I helped her into the car. What the actual fuck? Who the hell had photographed us? Shit. What the fuck were we going to do?

I sat down on the bed, checking other articles and social media. It was everywhere. Fuck. I realised now just how much of an invasion of privacy it was to have our faces plastered over the internet. I'd known Avery hated it, but this was the first fucking time I was experiencing it myself. They didn't know who I was, which I suppose was a saving grace, but it still didn't make it better.

Avery stirred. I felt the bed shift as she moved and sat behind me, wrapping her hands around my stomach. She kissed my shoulder, leaning her head against my back.

"Morning," she said with a voice still full of sleep.

I didn't want to tell her about this, but I had to. I ran my hand over hers.

"Princess."

"Mmm, you smell so good."

I smiled. Fuck. My heart hammered against my chest. The urge to pin her down on the bed and tear her shorts off threatened to overcome my self-control. Instead, I handed her my phone wordlessly. She took it. I felt her pull back from me followed by the sharp intake of her breath.

"What the fuck?" she said.

"Yeah… another shitstorm for us to deal with."

"Are they for real right now? Fuck. Do people not have anything better to do than gossip about who I'm with?"

"Apparently not."

She handed the phone back to me and rested her forehead between my shoulder blades. I heard her let out a long sigh. I popped the phone on the bed next to me.

"Are you okay?" I asked.

"No. We haven't even had a chance to talk to my uncle since he found out and now this. No doubt they'll be fucking camped outside the office when I get there. Fuck. Just what we fucking needed."

"Come here."

She shifted around and crawled into my lap. I held her to my chest, stroking her hair.

"I'm so fed up, Aiden. It's like a never ending carousel. One problem gets solved and another turns up. When the hell is all of this going to end?"

I tipped her chin up towards me, staring down into her doe eyes.

"Soon. It'll be over soon. We're not letting this go on forever. Trust me, princess, I want it to be over just as much as you. I want to wake up and not worry about whether we're going to survive this war or not."

She reached up, cupping my face with her small hand. Fuck. She looked so tiny and fragile. The past weeks since her birthday had left her exhausted and worn down. I could see it in her eyes.

"I want that too. Is a quiet life together too much to ask for?"

I shook my head.

"No. I promise we'll have that. Just you and I. Don't forget we vowed to be there for each other for the rest of our days."

She smiled. So fucking radiant.

"Shit, you're so fucking soppy when you want to be."

I pulled her face towards me and devoured her mouth. I nibbled her bottom lip causing her to squirm in my lap. My cock stood to attention immediately. Fuck. My hand disappeared under her t-shirt, finding one of her perfect tits. I rolled her nipple between my thumb and forefinger. She moaned in my mouth.

I pulled away, whipping her t-shirt off her and replacing my mouth with my fingers. I bit down on her nipple. My hand trailed down her stomach, dipping below her shorts and finding her sweet spot.

"Aiden," she groaned, her fingers curling into my hair.

It didn't take long for her to buck against my fingers, her arousal coating them. I pulled my hand from her shorts and picked her up. Placing her on the bed with her legs dangling down, I pulled off her shorts and underwear, leaving her naked before me. I knelt on the floor and buried my face in her sweet pussy, holding her legs open wide for me.

She bucked and writhed on the bed, moaning and calling out my name as my tongue lashed against her clit. I watched her, loving the way she lost all control when I plunged my fingers inside her, hooking them upwards and pressing on just the right spot.

"Fuck, Aiden, please don't stop. Please, oh fuck."

She tasted so fucking sweet. Hell, I loved tasting her. I loved this girl so fucking much. My desire for her was fucking relentless. She utterly consumed every waking moment. When I wasn't with her, I thought about her. Desired her. Craved her. Needed her.

She cried out, her body convulsing as her climax washed over her. Fuck. So beautiful. So fucking perfect. She'd barely come down from her high when I released her. I stood up, flipped her over onto her front and pulled off my boxers. Gripping her hips, I thrust inside her. Fuck. She felt so fucking good. So deliciously wet after she'd come all over my tongue.

Her moans spurred me on as I fucked her harder. Her fingers curled around the sheets as she looked back at me. Doe eyes wide with heat and lust burning in their depths. Fuck. Such a beautiful sight.

Her phone started beeping, signalling her alarm going off but we both ignored it. I slammed into her over and over until she cried out again, her second orgasm rushing through her. I cursed, feeling her clenching around my cock like a fucking vice. I put a hand on her back, keeping her pinned to the bed. I was so close. I couldn't fucking stop even though the fucking beeping from her phone was doing my head in.

"Let me turn it off," she murmured.

"Fuck, no, stay there," I grunted.

I lost it. I shuddered above her, my cock spurting wildly inside her. Fuck. Fuck. I hammered into her until the last pulses faded. My hands fell on the bed, stopping me from collapsing on top of her.

"That's one way to wake up," she said.

I grinned. If it made her relax after finding out pictures of us were plastered all over the media, then I was fucking happy. I didn't want her to worry about it. We'd work it out somehow. We had to.

I helped Avery out of the car. John came around and stood with us, eying the press who instantly surrounded us, shouting, "Miss Daniels. Miss Daniels."

I wrapped an arm around her waist, shielding her as we pushed through the crowd.

"Miss Daniels, who is the man you're with?"

"Miss Daniels, care to comment how you've moved on since Tristan's death?"

We were almost at the door when Avery stopped in her tracks, turning to the press. They started shouting louder, but she put her hand up. They all fell silent, cameras and microphones poised.

"I'm only going to say this once. My engagement to Tristan Shaw wasn't real," she said. "I am saddened by Frazier and Tristan's deaths, but I will say nothing further on the subject."

She reached out for me with her hand. I took it, holding it tightly in mine, knowing she needed me as her anchor.

"I will confirm that I have been in a relationship with the man next to me for quite some time. We got married five weeks ago. I will not confirm my married name nor will I take any requests for interviews on the subject. Please respect our request for privacy at this time."

Squeezing my hand, she gave the press one last look before turning away towards the door, tugging me along with her. I could hear the shouts behind us, but we ignored them. John followed us through the doors.

"Well, that will set tongues wagging," he said as we stepped into the lifts.

I'd come to work with her to make sure Chuck didn't give her any shit.

"They were pissing me off," Avery said, leaning into my side.

I kissed the top of her head. She looked up at me.

"You're not mad, right?"

I shook my head, wrapping an arm around her.

"You know they're going to go digging to find out who you are."

"I know, princess. It doesn't matter. We're not hiding in the shadows any longer."

"Chuck won't be happy," John said.

"Fuck Chuck. Whatever he says, we'll deal with it."

We all stepped out of the lift together, making a beeline for Avery's office. She waved a hand at Saskia, indicating she come with us. The blonde haired girl got up from her desk and followed along behind us. Avery shut the door when we all piled in. Saskia fidgeted nervously, looking between the three of us.

"I know you sort of met yesterday," Avery said. "But this is my husband, Aiden. Going forward, I wish to be known as Mrs Lockhart. Please make sure to send a memo to the staff."

Saskia bobbed her head. Fuck. I didn't often hear her refer to herself as that and it made my heartrate spike. Mine. My wife.

"Yes, of course, Mrs Lockhart. Um… it's nice to meet you."

I nodded at her.

"If you can make tea for all three of us, I'd be grateful and also we're going to have lunch in the conference room about oneish if you can set that up too."

"Of course, I'll see to it now."

Saskia walked out of the room, leaving the three of us alone. John and I got settled by the sofas whilst Avery sat at her desk.

A few minutes later, she let out a squeak of surprise. I looked up, frowning.

"What's wrong?"

She looked over at me, eyes wide.

"They didn't beat around the bush. Listen to this… 'The heiress herself confirms rumours. The twenty one year old owner of Daniels Holdings announced in front of her building today she is a married woman. The mystery man himself was stood beside her as she spoke to the press. Who is this man? Nobody knows. Avery refused to tell us his name, but she did let us know she has a new one.' Who wants to bet how long it takes my uncle to storm in here?"

And as if he knew we were talking about him, her office door was flung open and Chuck strode in.

"What the actual fuck did you do?"

"Good morning Uncle Charlie.

"Don't you good morning me, Avery. You have some explaining to do."

He stopped, catching sight of me and John. Avery got up from her desk and walked over to him, putting a hand on his arm.

"Come on and sit down, you look like you're about to keel over."

He scowled, batting her hand away.

"Firstly, why on earth were you at the Ritz last night and secondly, what the fuck do you think you're doing telling the press you and Aiden are married?"

She sighed, rubbing one of her arms.

"Rick wanted to have dinner with us. And I told the press because it's the truth. Do you want proof or something?"

"No, I don't fucking well want proof. Honestly, when will you stop running headlong into things without fucking well discussing them with me first?"

She crossed her arms over her chest and levelled him with one of those intense gazes of hers.

"I don't recall my private life being any of your business."

"It is my business when you fucking well go ahead and get married to an employee of the company."

Her expression didn't change.

"We were already together before I took over the company. Also, it's still none of your business. I don't have to tell you if I'm in a relationship or not. I don't answer to you. You answer to me. So get off your high horse and stop acting like I'm a spoilt brat who doesn't understand the consequences of her actions."

His mouth dropped open and he stared at her like she'd grown two heads. I tried not to smile at their verbal sparring.

"Excuse me?"

"You heard me. Unless you want me to fire you, I suggest you start treating me with the respect I deserve."

I bit my lip. Fuck. I glanced at John who was trying desperately not to laugh. He had a hand over his mouth and I could see the amusement in his eyes. I don't think he'd ever seen anyone speak to Chuck like that. To be honest, neither had I. I had no idea what had gotten into Avery, but it was hot. Seriously fucking hot. That was my wife having a go at the man she despised.

"Fire me? You have the audacity to threaten me with that?"

"Yes, yes I do."

I was relatively sure Avery wouldn't go through with her threat to fire Chuck, but it was amusing to watch him stand there in complete disbelief. Seconds ticked by. His face contorted into a snarl, rage painting his features. His hand came up so fast, it barely registered until we all heard the resounding slap across Avery's face.

I practically vaulted over the sofa in my effort to get to them. How fucking dare he slap her? I reached Chuck and shoved him away from her. He looked at me, startled out of his anger. I wrapped a hand around his neck, pushing him back towards the open door.

"If you fucking touch my wife again, I'll fucking dismember you. Make no fucking mistake, Chuck. Go calm the fuck down."

I pushed him out the door, releasing him. He put a hand up to his throat, staring at me with wide eyes. I wanted to beat the shit out of him. Tear him limb from limb. Anger simmered

212

in my veins but I kept a lid on it. Making a huge scene in her office wouldn't end well.

"Go before I change my fucking mind."

I pointed towards his office. Beyond him, Saskia was staring at us with a tray in her hand. Chuck scowled at me, turned on his heel and strode off.

"Let me take that," I said to Saskia.

She handed me the tray of teas wordlessly. I nodded at her, turning and going back into Avery's office. I set the tray down on her desk. She was still standing in the same place, her hand on her cheek with tears pricking in her eyes. John was standing next to her, rubbing her back. I indicated the door with my head to him. He left her side to go close it.

I put both my hands on Avery's shoulders, giving them a squeeze.

"Let me see," I said, keeping my voice soft.

She lowered her hand, tipping her head up towards me. The red mark on her cheek was stark against her pale skin. It took every ounce of self-control not to storm into Chuck's office and smash his face into the floor. Repeatedly.

I leant down, placing a gentle kiss on her red cheek. She shuddered, tears spilling out onto her cheeks.

"Shh, princess, don't cry."

Next thing I knew, she'd thrown herself into my chest, her arms banding around my back. I held her, letting her cry on my chest until her quiet sobs abated.

"I hate him," she whispered.

"Am I allowed to say it was really hot watching you stand up to him like that?"

She pulled away, staring up at me with bloodshot eyes. She bit her lip. I wanted to be the one biting it. Fuck. All I could think about was her splayed out over the bed earlier with my head between her legs. Those delicious breathy moans emitting from her throat. How sweet she'd tasted on my tongue. And I was pretty sure she could feel my cock pressed against her stomach.

"His face was kind of funny. He looked like he was about to have a fit."

She looked down between us and then back up at me, raising an eyebrow. I shrugged. When it came to her, it couldn't be helped.

"I have work to do," she said.

"I wasn't asking for anything."

I heard a slight cough from next to us and remembered John was here. I let go of Avery, turning away and readjusting myself. Fuck. Just what I needed. A raging hardon for my wife in her office with her bodyguard next to us.

When I glanced back at Avery, she was rubbing her cheek and giving me a half smile, mischief in her doe eyes. At least she was amused. I wouldn't want her getting upset after what Chuck just did. Fuck. I was still fucking pissed off with him for slapping her.

Avery moved in between me and the desk, collecting one of the cups of tea and handing it to John before she set the other two cups on the desk and put the tray just outside the door for Saskia. She leant back against the door, sighing heavily.

"I thought I'd feel better having it out in the open, but I don't. At least, not after that reaction."

I put my hand out to her. She came over and took it. I smiled at her.

"We don't have to hide any more. That's a good thing. It'll be fine."

Except I wasn't sure it would be fine at all. I'd seen the way Chuck had looked at me yesterday. Like I'd broken every single ounce of his trust by going behind his back and having a relationship with his niece. I didn't care what he thought of me. I did care what he would do with this knowledge. And whether he'd hurt Avery for it or not.

It was that thought that had me pulling her back into my chest and holding her tightly. I was fucking terrified of him taking it out on her.

Because if he did… I was pretty sure I'd go back on my word to Avery about trying to make sure there was no more bloodshed. I'd put a bullet in his head. And I wouldn't regret it as the life drained out of his eyes.

Not one bit.

SEVENTEEN

Avery

The past week had worn me down so much, I just wanted to curl up in a ball and cry my eyes out. My uncle wasn't talking to me. He hadn't apologised for slapping me. In fact, I think he was avoiding me completely. It should be fine by me, but it wasn't. I still had to work with him. He was sending me messages via Clara and Saskia like we were in fucking preschool. It was ridiculous. He was a grown man in his late forties for fuck's sake.

We'd had constant requests for a statement about my marriage. They still hadn't managed to work out who Aiden was, but I was sure it wouldn't stay that way. I imagined our public relations department was getting hounded every five minutes. Not that they could complain. It was their job to manage this sort of thing.

I should be happy to be moving into my new office as the refurbishment was finally complete, but I wasn't. I wanted this nightmare to be over. Except I wasn't even going to get to go home. We had a stupid dinner with Rick. I didn't want to go.

Not one bit. I wasn't sure I could handle being stuck making small talk with him all over again.

As I threw stuff into a box, Ed poked his head around the door.

"Hello, little cousin."

"Hey… What's up?"

Things were a little weird between us since the whole finding out I was married business. I still didn't know what he and Chuck had wanted to talk to me about. Everything around here had kind of gone up in flames. Nothing felt right any longer. And I was growing tired of being the owner of a company I hated.

"Thought you might want some help since John is with Chuck."

Saskia had been helping me, but I told her to go man the phones because it wasn't like I had much stuff anyway.

"Uh, well you can if you want."

He came into the room, giving it the once over before coming to a halt in front of my desk.

"Listen… I wanted to tell you congratulations on your marriage. I know things have been strained this week, but I wanted you to know I'm happy for you."

"Oh… well, thank you."

I looked down at my hands, unsure what else to say to that.

"Is that the only box?"

When I looked up again, he was pointing at the box in front of me.

"Yes, I don't really have much. It wasn't like I could bring in a framed photo of Aiden or anything…"

Not that I would've anyway. It was weird that people still did stuff like that, but I'd seen some of our employee's desks. Family photos everywhere.

Ed gave me a tight smile.

"Is that everything? I'll take it for you."

I popped the last pile of paperwork into the box and nodded. He drew the box towards him and picked it up. I came around the desk and we walked out together along the corridor towards where our new offices were situated.

"So… What was the wedding like?"

"Small. We only had six guests, which was nice. I've been in the public eye all my life, so having a quiet affair felt right. Oh, the photographer sent us our photos, but I haven't had a chance to go through them. I mean, I can show you if you want."

I looked over at him. He was smiling.

"I'd like that."

We reached my new office. I pointed towards the conference table situated on one side. Ed popped the box down on there before coming around to my desk with me. I'd already logged on so I signed into my emails and found the link to the album.

We sat together for about ten minutes, going through the photos from the day. It almost made me get a little teary eyed seeing Aiden and I so fucking happy together. That day meant everything to me.

"You looked so beautiful," Ed said. "I'm kind of jealous I didn't get to go."

"Yeah… I guess it was different not to have family there."

"So, he's who's been making you so happy."

I fidgeted in my seat. It reminded me of the conversation we'd had where he'd questioned me about guys.

"Yeah, look, I'm sorry I had to keep it from you. It was a difficult situation for us."

He put a hand on my shoulder, giving it a squeeze.

"It's cool. It's not like we're super close, so I get it. So… Charlie still isn't talking to you."

I shook my head.

"No, but that's kind of his fault. We had a fight and well, he slapped me. Aiden wasn't happy about that."

"Saskia may have told me she witnessed him tossing Charlie out of your office."

Seeing Aiden come to my rescue had made my heart thunder in my ears. My avenging angel. My toes curled in my high heels at the memory of that night. Aiden and I had acted out his little fantasy in his office. He'd put me across his desk and fucked me hard until I begged him to let me come. His office wouldn't exist for much longer. He'd been speaking to contractors about the conversion. I was looking forward to us having a second bedroom.

"Yeah. He hasn't spoken to me since. I suppose I did kind of threaten his job."

I looked up at Ed, who's eyebrows had shot up.

"You did what?"

"I told him if he didn't start respecting me, then I'd fire him. It was a heat of the moment thing, but he keeps acting like I'm completely clueless. I'm a grown woman, so I don't know what his problem is."

Ed shook his head, obvious disbelief pasted across his features.

"Perhaps he just never thought he'd reach a stage where his niece was his boss."

I grinned.

"I guess that could be a little… emasculating."

Ed shifted, leaning against my desk with his arms crossed.

"Right? All these years he's worked under your dad and then suddenly, he has to answer to a twenty one year old girl. Think that'd grate on most men his age."

He was right. I imagined it did go against the grain a little. Obviously, he never expected me to take over the company so soon.

"Does it grate on you?"

"Me? No. I respect you. Also, I'm not too proud to admit that having a woman in charge is a good thing."

He respects me?

I didn't realise Ed felt that way unless he was lying. I looked up at his face. There was absolutely nothing in his expression that indicated he was speaking anything but the truth. I kept flittering between trusting him and not. I knew it was dangerous. I couldn't trust anyone in my family. Aiden had told me that on numerous occasions.

"Oh yeah? Are you like a hardcore feminist or something?"

Ed threw back his head and laughed.

"Oh wow, I wouldn't go that far."

I swivelled my chair towards him.

"So you know about my love life… what about yours? Who's that blonde girl I've seen you with?"

Ed looked away, his eyes suddenly turning dark for a moment.

"No one really."

"Come on, don't be coy."

"It's nothing, I promise. Don't have time for that really."

I raised an eyebrow.

"Not got time for girls?"

He laughed, but it was hollow.

"Oh no, I have plenty of time for girls, but not girlfriends."

Something about the way he said it made me frown. Time for girls but not a girlfriend? What the hell was that supposed to mean? Was my cousin some kind of man whore? Ed didn't seem like the type.

"Oh really? So what, do you just go for the 'wham bam thank you mam' approach?"

He turned back to me. His eyes glittered with amusement, a far cry from his expression when I'd asked about that blonde girl. I was pretty sure she was someone to him, but if not a girlfriend, then what?

"Don't make it sound so crude."

"It is crude. My cousin, the man whore."

He shook his head, smiling at me.

"I'm not that bad. I promise."

"Well… everyone has got to get their kicks somehow."

I winked at him even as my stomach dropped at my words. Some people got their kicks in disgusting and horrifying ways. Ones I didn't much want to think about at that moment. I suppressed a shudder.

"Quite… Some more than others. Say… I hope you're getting your kicks."

I felt my face heating up.

"Um, well… I mean…"

He bit his lip, obviously trying not to smile.

"Is my little cousin into a little bit more than just plain old vanilla then?"

I turned my chair back to my computer.

"None of your business."

He leant towards me and prodded my arm.

"Oh, I think that means yes. Go on, tell me what floats your boat."

"What? No. Gross, Ed. I'm not going to talk to you about my sex life, you're my cousin."

He barked with laughter.

"I'm only pulling your leg."

I gave him a slight smile.

"Yeah okay, you got me."

I couldn't get the sickening feeling to leave my stomach. I wasn't sure if he really was joking or why he'd even brought up that topic. It felt wrong. In fact, the whole conversation with him felt off. I just wasn't sure why.

"Right, well, I should really get back to it… I mean… I heard the boss is a hard arse and all."

He winked at me before shoving off my desk and strolling out of the room without a backwards glance. And I was left wondering what the fuck had just happened.

I sat staring at my screen and feeling like so many people knew things I didn't. What the hell was with my cousin? I needed to find out who that blonde girl was. I felt like it was important. He'd been too cagey about it.

Sighing, I realised John hadn't come back yet. I tapped my fingers against the desk and looked at the clock. It was three in the afternoon. It was the first time I'd been truly alone for weeks. And I really wanted to take advantage of that fact.

Standing up, I got my coat and bag. I slipped out of the office, making a beeline for the stairwell. Saskia didn't see me leave and I didn't run into anyone else. I walked down two

flights of stairs before I walked out into the lobby of the forty
eighth floor and took the lift down the rest of the way. I knew
the press would be outside the front, so I decided I'd slip out
the back.

I got out on the street and walked towards the nearest tube
station. In the midst of the crowded streets, no one noticed
me. I had to change tubes a couple of times, but I finally
reached the one nearest to my own house and walked the rest
of the way.

I let myself in and slumped on the sofa in the living room.
Aiden was going to be pissed at me for leaving the office
without John and not going home, but I just wanted a minute
alone to process everything. And there was something else I
needed to do here.

I didn't bother shrugging off my coat or taking my shoes
off as I went into my studio. Sitting there on my easel was the
half-finished painting of my dad. The one I really needed to
get rid of.

I picked it up and turned it over. Using one of my tools, I
separated the canvas from the wood, rolled it up and threw it
in the bin. As I was walking back into the hallway, I heard the
front door rattling, before it opened.

What?

My tenant hadn't moved back in yet so it couldn't be them.
The only other person who had the keys was Aiden and it
definitely wasn't him.

When the person stopped outside my flat door and the
locks started to turn, I darted into the hall cupboard. I fumbled
for a moment before I found the panel. I put my hand on it
and within thirty seconds, it registered who I was and the false
door opened. I hurried through the doorway and down the

stairs. The automatic lights had come on so I could see. The door at the top swung shut silently. I reached the bottom where a huge door lay. I placed my hand on the panel and that door opened too.

I walked into the bunker and pushed the door closed, sealing me inside the room. I tried not to panic, but someone was in my fucking house. I strode towards where the monitors were and turned them on. The display came on and showed me several angles of my flat.

I sat down in the chair and stared at the monitors. I couldn't see the person properly. Tugging my phone out of my bag, I dialled a number. It was fucking lucky I still got signal down here.

"Princess."

"Aiden… There's someone in my house."

There was silence for a moment.

"What? Why are you at the house? Where's John?"

I knew he wouldn't be happy about this, but I didn't have time for explanations.

"He was speaking to Chuck. I left work because I wanted to deal with something here and I needed space. That's not the point. Someone is in my flat. They had the key. No one has the key except you and me."

"Avery… why the fuck would you leave the office without him?"

"Now isn't the time. There is a man in my bedroom right now."

"What the fuck? Are you safe?"

I watched the man on the camera walk over to my chest of drawers and climb up on top of it.

"I'm in the panic room. You know there's cameras everywhere so I can see him… Oh… Oh my god!"

"What? What is it?"

I recognised the man. He was pulling something down from next to where my camera was situated. I leant towards the screen and then I could see exactly what it was.

"Seriously? He put fucking cameras in my fucking flat."

"Who? Princess, what the fuck is going on?"

"Kurt. It's Kurt. That's Rick's man. The one who helped take me. He put cameras up in my flat, Aiden. Oh my god… That's how he knew about our sex life. Oh my fucking god, he recorded what you did to me. Oh, oh, oh god, no."

My whole fucking world crumbled before my eyes. Rick had a fucking sex tape of me and Aiden. And it wasn't just any old sex, it was the night he'd put me in that harness and punished me.

I watched Kurt walk around the rest of the flat and take more cameras down. They must not fucking know I already had cameras everywhere. The footage it recorded was stored in the panic room and I'd deleted the evidence of all our sexcapades from it already.

"What do you mean Rick's man?"

"Kurt, the bald head guy. He's Rick's man. This makes so much sense now. Everything he said to me that day. That's how come he knew so much. Those cameras, that means he saw us… together."

I felt sick to my stomach. My husband's father had seen everything. All of me at one of the most vulnerable moments I shared with Aiden. I'd been completely at his mercy. I didn't want anyone intruding on that memory. Now it just felt tainted.

"Fuck. Fuck. That cunt. I'm going to fucking kill him."

I was glad he was just as angry about it as I was, but we couldn't afford to take out Rick. Not when he was the only one who could tell us who murdered Lizzie. Unless he was lying. He could be. Except I had a feeling he wasn't.

I watched Kurt carefully put everything back in place which he'd moved, stuff all the cameras into the bag he'd brought with him and slip out of the flat.

"He's gone. Aiden… I… I need you here."

I heard a door slam through the phone.

"I'm coming right now. Stay in the panic room until I get there, okay? I'll text you. Fuck. This is a fucking nightmare."

"I can't believe it. I wouldn't have cared if it had been any other time, well I would've, but that was…"

"I know, princess. Fuck. I warned you he was dangerous. Fuck and now we fucking well have to see him this evening."

That was the absolute worst part. How the fuck were we going to get through this dinner without Aiden going off the deep end at him over this? And I wanted to have a go at him too.

"I was dreading it earlier and now I definitely don't want to go."

"We'll talk about it when I get there, okay? I've got to get in the car."

"Okay. I love you."

"Me too."

He hung up. I sat back, staring at the screens. What a fucking mess we were in. This changed a heck of a lot of things. I'd already been suspicious of what Rick knew and now I was sure. He had to know it was Aiden who killed my parents. What I didn't know was why he hadn't said anything about it.

Why had he kept this a secret? Surely if he was friends with my granddad and perhaps my father, then he'd have a reason to turn Aiden in. Except I wasn't so sure he was a fan of my father. And it couldn't just be fatherly love he felt towards Aiden either.

I wasn't certain of anything at all when it came to Rick Morgan and his motivations. I was dreading finding out what he meant by telling us everything.

There was no doubt in my mind.

This would shake up the foundations of everything Aiden and I thought we knew.

And we weren't prepared for it.

Not one bit.

Not at all.

EIGHTEEN

Aiden

W hen I reached Avery's house, I texted her to let her know I was there. I found her coming out of the cupboard when I unlocked the front door of her flat. She paused in the hallway, staring at me for a moment before she barrelled her way into my arms. I held her, knowing she needed me to comfort her.

Fuck. I was so fucking pissed off. Rick really was a fucking piece of work. Who knew how long those fucking cameras had been in her house. Too long. And why would Rick have a fucking key to Avery's house?

"This doesn't make any sense," she said, pulling away and staring up at me.

"No, it fucking well doesn't."

"You know we can't say anything to him yet, right?"

I gripped her coat with my fists, trying not to lose my shit completely. I knew she was right, but I was too fucking angry.

"How the fuck do you expect me to sit there with him knowing he saw that and fuck knows how many other times?"

"I could say the same thing."

She reached up, stroking my cheek with the gentlest of touches. The tension in me started to fade at her expression. She looked so miserable. Fuck. I thought I couldn't hate that fucking bastard any more than I already did.

"I'm sorry, princess. I'm so fucking sorry that my piece of shit father stole that fucking moment from us."

"It's not your fault. Neither of us knew. How could we?"

I shook my head. It wasn't either of our faults. It was all fucking Rick's fault for interfering in my fucking life. In our lives. Hers and mine. I wanted to kill him. Smash his stupid face in. I wanted him gone forever so I never had to think about what he'd done to my mother. Never had to think about how he'd dragged her into this sorry mess. It wouldn't have even fucking mattered if I'd never been born. At least my mother would still be alive. She'd have lived a full life without all this bullshit.

I took a breath. I couldn't think like that. The past couldn't be changed. What I had right in front of me was more important. My wife was my world and I had to be there for her. I promised myself I'd quit this shit. Wallowing in self-misery wasn't going to help anyone. I had to be strong for Avery.

Besides, what the fuck would she think if she knew I'd even considered giving up my own fucking life in place of my mother's. I knew how much Avery loved me, needed me, craved me. I was hers and I couldn't afford to forget that even though I'd give up my own life in place of hers if it came down to it. That's how much this girl meant to me. She was the fucking world. My brightest star. My girl. My wife.

I leant down and captured her mouth, clutching her to me. She responded, arching into me when I deepened the kiss. She was breathless when I pulled away and leant my forehead against hers.

"We'll deal with it, princess. I promise. We'll make new memories together. Ones he can't take away or ruin."

No matter how angry I was, I could see the agony in her eyes and I had to fix it for her.

"We already have one he can't take away from us."

"Remind me again which one that is?" I replied with a smile.

"Our wedding day," she whispered.

The most perfect fucking day of our lives. No one was going to fucking ruin that shit for me. She'd looked so stunning. The perfect dress which hugged her figure in the right places. Hell, she'd never looked more beautiful. Those moments we'd said our vows were the most precious ones. And when I'd got all fucking emotional when we were alone and she told me how much I meant to her and made love to me.

Fuck. No. Rick could never take that away from us.

"Will you do a painting of us from that day?"

She nodded.

"Yes… I'll do anything you want."

I kissed her again. Having her close made my heart thump. She soothed me. Calmed me. My fucking girl. Mine. No one else would get their hands on her. No one. Especially not after what happened with the Shaws. I still wish I could've fucking spared her that pain. I knew the guilt still tore at her pure soul. She felt tainted, but to me, she was perfect in every single fucking way. No matter what she'd done.

This war had taken no fucking prisoners, but I was determined to bring us out the other side. So we could have a life together. Me and her.

For now, we were going to deal with this new fucking bullshit situation.

"Take me down there. I want to see for myself."

The doors only opened for her. She nodded, pulling away. I followed her into the cupboard and down the stairs into the bunker. I sat down in front of the bank of monitors as she pulled up another chair.

We spent the next hour fast forwarding through the footage to see if we could find out when Rick had the cameras installed, but we had to leave to get ready before we could finish it. It didn't matter anyway. I was fucked off enough with the fact that he had them in here in the first place. Fucking scumbag thought that was appropriate. He had another fucking thing coming.

Avery clutched my arm as we walked into the restaurant Rick had picked for this evening.

"We have to be careful," she whispered.

"I know, princess."

This was only the first fucking week of dinners we had to have with him. I wasn't sure how we would cope with two more. Fuck. I didn't want to spend any more time with him than I had to.

The host led us over to the table he was seated at after taking our coats. Today, he was looking rather more casual in a polo shirt and chinos with loafers. He still looked like a jumped up fuck to me, but I chose not to say anything. He stood, giving us both a bright smile.

"Evening little darlin'," he said.

He didn't try to touch her. I think he knew if he did, I'd fucking have him in a headlock so fast, he wouldn't know what hit him.

"Hello, Rick," she said as I pulled out her chair and she sat down.

I rested my arm across the back of her chair as I sat in my own seat, my fingers brushing over her shoulder. He sat, giving us a bright smile.

"How are you both?"

"Okay… I suppose you saw the news."

I was fucking glad he knew I wasn't interested in making small talk with him.

"Oh yes, can't see your uncle being too pleased."

"Well no."

I looked at the menu, stroking Avery's shoulder. I needed the physical contact just to keep myself from doing or saying something stupid. Since Rick was footing the bill, might as well pick the most expensive item on here. Not that I couldn't afford it anyway. Wasn't sure why he insisted on taking us to a bunch of expensive restaurants. Avery and I would've been just as happy going to Nando's.

When the waiter came over and I ordered the prime Wagyu beef steak, Rick raised an eyebrow at me but said nothing. He probably knew what I was doing and I really didn't give a fuck. Avery ordered a sirloin whilst Rick picked out the rib-eye.

He sat back and eyed me warily when the waiter left us to it. He'd ordered some expensive sounding red wine, but I wasn't going to fucking drink it so I told the waiter to bring water for the table. I had to keep a clear head.

"Are you two planning on creating any more scandals?"

Avery stiffened. I gave him a dark look. We hadn't meant to create any in the first place. It wasn't our fault we'd been photographed.

"If you hadn't insisted on us going to dinner with you, we'd never have been splashed over social media," I said, trying to keep the venom out of my voice.

He smiled. *Prick*.

"Oh well, would've come out sooner or later."

We always knew our relationship would be out in the open one day. I was fucking glad of it. Hiding it from everyone was taking a toll on both of us. Avery especially.

"No, we're not planning on creating any more shit for the press."

"Come now, Aiden, you and I both know what you want."

I glared at him. I didn't want to talk about this. Avery put a hand on my thigh, giving it a squeeze.

"And whatever might that be… Rick?"

His eyes darkened at the way I'd overly enunciated the word. I was never calling him dad or father. He could quite frankly wait until hell froze over.

"Your little darlin's family… gone… for good."

"Stop calling her that."

Fuck, he was really getting on my fucking last nerve. I knew she hated it.

"Aiden…" she started.

"No, he doesn't get to call you shit like that." I grabbed her hand on my thigh and held it. "She has a fucking name. Use it."

"Aiden, don't, please," Avery whispered. "It's okay."

I turned to her.

"It's not fucking okay," I said, keeping my voice low so as not to make a scene.

The only person who was allowed to fucking call her any sort of term of endearment was me. I was her fucking husband.

Her doe eyes were wide with concern and her face told me to chill the fuck out. How could I fucking calm down with him provoking me so fucking much? Fuck. I wanted to strangle the fuck.

I took a breath, trying to keep my temper in check. I'd say something stupid as shit if I didn't. She shifted closer, leaning her forehead against mine as she cupped my cheek.

"Please, just get through this for me," she whispered. "Later… I'll make it better. I promise."

I tried not to tremble under her touch. Fuck. Her eyes told me exactly how she'd make it better. She'd let me tie her to the bed and fuck her without mercy. Take out all my fucking frustrations on her if I wanted to. What the hell did I ever do to deserve this fucking goddess in front of me?

I nodded, squeezing her hand. She gave me the briefest of kisses which only left me wanting so much more. It was bad enough Rick was fucking sitting there intruding on this moment, so I let it go.

I turned to him when she sat back in her chair properly.

"She has a name."

He inclined his head.

"I'm aware of it."

Yeah, well, he better start fucking well using it then.

"How is your wife?" Avery asked, interrupting the both of us.

Rick's eyes flashed with pain for a moment before his expression cleared. I wondered what the fuck that was all about. Why would the mention of her make him react like that? Did it have anything to do with the fact that I was his son and he'd lied to her about it every day since I was born?

"Well enough. Used to me being away for work."

"Do you work away often then?"

"Well, our head offices are in New York, but the family home is in Washington DC."

Avery nodded.

"I suppose the distance makes it difficult."

He shrugged.

"Annabelle has her family to keep her occupied. Her sister lives close by. She takes care of our nieces and nephews."

I knew what she was going to ask him next and I almost stopped her, except I wanted to know the answer too.

"You never had kids?"

His expression faltered, eyes flicking over to me momentarily. I wasn't sure if I was seeing things or not but they were filled with regret.

"Annabelle had trouble conceiving. We tried everything, but it wasn't meant to be."

A part of me felt sorry for his wife, but I didn't feel any sort of sympathy for him. He was a dangerous piece of work.

"I'm sorry. That must've been difficult."

I glanced at her. She didn't look very sympathetic or sorry. Trying to be diplomatic despite what we'd discovered earlier today.

The waiters arrived with our food, saving him from saying anything. I didn't give a fuck that I was his only offspring. Still didn't make me want to have a relationship with the man.

These dinners had nothing to do with me actually wanting to get to know him. All I needed was the information he was keeping from us.

At least this meal sort of made up for having to sit with him for an evening. I cut a piece off for Avery and fed it to her because I couldn't not share it. Her eyes lit up. She leant closer when she swallowed.

"Can we have this at home one day?" she asked, her voice low.

I nodded. I'd make her whatever the fuck she wanted if it made her smile like that.

"Have I told you how good you are to me?"

"On a few occasions," I replied, smiling at her.

I brushed her hair out of her face before kissing her forehead. Turning back to my meal, I noticed Rick assessing us. I wondered what he made of my relationship with her. Not sure why I cared. I hated the man. Except a part of me would always feel conflicted when it came to him. He was my only flesh and blood.

My mother's parents died when she was young and she'd gone into foster care. It was when she'd run away at sixteen that she'd got involved with the Daniels and Rick. A sorry fate. I only found this out from Tina when she deemed me old enough to know the truth. That's when I started digging and I never stopped.

The rest of the meal continued in relative silence. Avery excused herself to the bathroom when the waiters removed our plates. Rick sat back, eying me warily.

"Not going to follow her in there like last time?"

I clenched my fists under the table. What a fucking surprise that he'd worked it out. *Not.*

"What I do with my wife is none of your fucking business."

"Come now, Aiden, she's a pretty girl. I can see the attraction. She gives you what you need, doesn't she?"

He was fucking baiting me. Despite what I'd promised Avery, I couldn't fucking help myself.

"You'd fucking well know all about that. Bugging her fucking house and all. You better not have kept that shit."

His eyebrows shot up.

"You know about that."

"Yes and believe me, it's taking a fucking supreme effort not to punch your fucking lights out right now."

He drummed his fingers on the table, his expression turning dark.

"Yes, well, I suppose it was an invasion of her privacy."

"Our fucking privacy. You've got some fucking nerve."

"You seem to think she's not an important part of this, but she is. I must admit I was rather surprised by this little development between the two of you, but it's neither here nor there."

He could be surprised all he fucking wanted. I was done with his bullshit.

"Why the fuck are you dragging this shit out? You know what I want to know."

He sighed, settling his hand on the table.

"It's not the right time."

"What the fuck is that supposed to mean?"

His eyes flicked towards where Avery had disappeared to.

"It means I'll tell you the truth when I'm good and ready to."

"Tell me why the fuck you need all this fucking time."

His eyes fell on me again. They were almost calculating.

"You're my son, Aiden. It ain't easy for me to know you hate me so much. It won't matter to you, but I'm sorry for what happened to Lizzie. I cared about her. She wasn't supposed to die."

It took every ounce of self-control to stay seated. I didn't want to hear him talk about my mother even though I knew he would eventually have to since he knew who'd murdered her.

"If you cared about her so much, you would've stopped all this shit long before it resulted in her fucking death."

He sighed, looking down at his hands.

"Lizzie got pregnant just after the doctors told Annabelle she would likely never conceive a child. The deep seated sadness I felt was outweighed by the knowledge I would have you. It was the only good thing I did for your mother, giving her you even though she hated me for it. I was there the day you were born. I held you in my arms and you were the tiniest little thing. I ain't telling you this to make you feel anything for me. I know that ship has sailed."

I said nothing. I didn't know he'd been there. My mother never told me. In fact, the only thing she ever said about Rick was that he'd made sure we were comfortable. I hadn't realised what that meant. Until now.

"I paid for everything. After Lizzie died, I gave all the money to Tina. She loves you, that woman. She thinks of you as the son she never had. Lizzie's death is my only regret. That I couldn't take her away from the Daniels soon enough. I knew what was happening. I knew about Mitchell's obsession with her."

Why the fuck was he telling me all this shit?

"If you knew, then why the fuck did you let it happen?"

239

"I wasn't here to stop it."

He fucking well should've been. Fuck.

"I know you were there that day. Tina told me. I'm sorry."

"Sorry isn't fucking good enough. Sorry doesn't bring her back or change what's happened since. You know she called me her angel. Said I was the only good thing in her world."

I laughed, but it was hollow.

"The fucking irony is that Avery calls me the same thing. Her avenging angel. That's what she thought of me the first time she saw me."

"I know what you did."

It didn't shock or surprise me in the slightest. I'd been aware he knew what I'd done to Avery's parents since the day he'd returned her to me after he took her.

"And? You've not turned me in."

I looked up, finding Avery striding towards us, a concerned look on her face. She must've seen my expression. I didn't try to hide it. This conversation had completely thrown me. I didn't know what to fucking say any longer.

She sat down, putting a hand on my arm. Rick looked at her for a moment, as if he was trying to decide whether to continue our conversation or not.

"I don't intend to. Do you think I wasn't aware you'd take revenge on them? I counted on it happening."

I heard Avery's sharp intake of breath, but I didn't look at her.

"You what?"

"Tina told me how you were doing. Told me about the trouble you got into. It was my stipulation regarding the money. So I knew when you found out about… Avery's family and what they'd done, that you'd want to take them out. I didn't count on what happened afterwards nor that you'd take it as far as you have done now."

Avery's hand on my arm tightened. I looked over at her. Her eyes were wide and she'd gone as white as a sheet.

I should've known he'd manipulate Tina in that way. I didn't blame her. All she wanted was to provide for me. Give me a life because she loved me. She'd had to take Rick's money because I knew the Daniels had cut her off after what happened to my mother. And they'd made it impossible for her to be employed as a nanny for anyone else. She hadn't told me where the money had come from, only that she had no other choice.

"What do you mean take it as far as I have done?"

"The Shaws."

I wasn't going to fucking apologise for that. They deserved it. Especially after what they'd tried to do to my wife. Fucking pricks.

"That wasn't supposed to happen."

It was the truth. We were supposed to take them down without the need for their deaths. At least, Avery wasn't meant to be involved in that side of things.

"Quite."

"You knew?" Avery piped up. "You knew he would do that to them?"

Rick nodded. Her expression turned venomous. Her doe eyes glowing with hatred.

"Why the hell did you let that happen? Huh? Did you think for one second what it would do to everyone around them? What it did to me?"

"It was necessary."

"Necessary?" she hissed. "It wasn't fucking necessary."

241

I tried to put an arm around her, just to calm her down a bit, but she shoved me away from her.

"Do you have any idea what shit you've caused? You could've fucking stopped it."

Fuck. I had no idea she'd react like this. I wanted to soothe her. She looked so enraged, like she couldn't comprehend why anyone would allow their own son to go on a killing spree. It wasn't like Rick could've stopped me. I hated the man.

"Avery," I said. "It was my choice."

She turned on me.

"Stay out of this."

"Princess…"

"No. You and I will have words later. Right now, I'm talking to him and you're going to shut up before I make a scene in this fucking restaurant. Do you understand?"

I stared at her. She rarely spoke to me like that. When I didn't respond, she turned back to Rick.

"Do you know what it felt like to see that? No, because you don't give a shit about anyone but yourself. I see that now. You claim to care about him, but you don't. This is all just some kind of joke to you. A means to an end. Well, let me tell you something. This isn't a fucking joke. This is real life. And by not being an actual father to Aiden, you've just let everything go up in flames."

She stood up, throwing her napkin on the table.

"You can kiss your dinners goodbye." She looked at me. "We're leaving."

Rick didn't try to stop me as I got up. There were people staring at us, but I ignored them, letting Avery lead me through the tables. We collected our coats and walked out onto the street. She didn't say anything to me as we made our way to the carpark nearby.

When we got in the car, she turned away from me and sat staring out the car window. I didn't know what to say to her. How to calm her down.

"Princess…"

"Don't. Just don't."

"Avery, I know you're upset, but I'm not letting you get out of talking to me about this."

She sighed. I glanced at her. She was fiddling with her coat pocket.

"I'm sorry I spoke to you like that."

"You're forgiven. Now what the fuck is going on with you?"

She didn't respond. When I looked at her again, I could see the pain in her expression. I turned my hand on the gear stick, leaving my palm facing upwards. After a moment, she placed hers in it, clutching my fingers tightly.

Then I knew exactly what had happened. She'd remembered both the nights which had completely changed her world. The nights which destroyed everything for her.

And I couldn't do anything about it because those memories would probably haunt her for the rest of her life.

NINETEEN

Avery

I hated him. I fucking hated him. Rick fucking Morgan could go to fucking hell. I was so angry and yet, Aiden just held onto my hand and stroked his thumb along the back of it most of the way home. His touch soothed me somewhat. It reminded me he was there for me.

I felt like such an idiot for getting so worked up in a public place, but what Rick said made me see red. He'd known that Aiden would go after my parents. Probably long before it ever even occurred to Aiden himself. That's what made me sick. That he'd counted on his own son becoming a murderer. It horrified me that anyone could ever think their child was capable of that. That they wanted their kid to turn into a cold hearted killer.

And now I was dreading getting home because I was pretty sure Aiden didn't know why I was so pissed off.

We reached the flat long before I wanted to. I trudged into the lift with him, feeling completely exhausted all of a sudden. It felt like every day of my life had become a nightmare. There was always something lurking around the corner to catch me off guard just when I thought we had things under control.

Aiden unlocked the front door and we stepped in. He took my coat off me and hung both of ours up. He followed me into the bedroom, watching me strip down to my underwear. I took off my bra. He didn't say anything when I stole one of his t-shirts out of his cupboard and put it on. It was huge on me but being wrapped up in something of his comforted me. The smell of cedarwood and pine filled my nostrils. Perfectly Aiden. He was right there and could comfort me himself, but I needed something more. Something to settle my racing heart.

I sat on the edge of the bed and waited. He teetered on his feet for a moment before he stripped out of his own clothes and sat next to me in just his boxers. He put his hand out to me and I took it.

"What's wrong, princess?"

"He's a bastard."

"Well, that's not news to me."

"I hate him. I hate everything about him."

He watched me carefully as if waiting for me to elaborate.

"I know you don't think of him as your dad, but he is. And it makes me sick. Sick to think he wanted you to… to…"

I couldn't get the words out. I couldn't call him a killer even though that's what he was. Heck, that was now what I was even though I hadn't meant to kill Tristan. Not really.

"He knew you'd kill," I whispered. "He expected it of you. How can a parent want that for their child?"

Aiden let out a long breath as if he'd been holding it in for a lifetime.

"That's why you're upset?"

I nodded, feeling tears pricking at the corners of my eyes.

"Not because it reminded you of that night?"

I shook my head. It had reminded me, but I dealt with it. I was done crying over what happened. Done feeling like my world was collapsing before my eyes every time I thought of my parents dying in front of me. I'd faced that the day I went to the penthouse. I'd relived it over and over again. I couldn't stay stuck in the past.

"I told you Rick was a psychotic cunt. He doesn't know the first thing about being a parent."

He let go of my hand, reaching up and cupping my face in both his hands.

"You're too fucking good for this world, princess. That you would even care so much about this… fuck. I don't need him and neither do you. He might be the man who brought me into the world, but he's never going to be my parent. Even if he paid for everything, he's not my mother and he's not Tina."

"He paid for everything?"

He nodded.

"He told me that. He also said he regretted that my mother ever died. That he wasn't there to stop it happening. I don't know how I feel about any of that shit. I'm sorry you had to hear it though. I knew what kind of man he was, but you didn't."

I looked into his grey eyes. They were so full of compassion for me. How could I ever have thought that Aiden was a monster? How could I ever have seen anything but the man in front of me who loved me without any conditions? Who saw me for me and who cared for me the way he did.

"How did you know?"

He shook his head, dropping his hands from my face.

"Like father, like son, princess."

"What's that supposed to mean? You're nothing like him."

"No? Do you think what I want from you is normal?"

It was my turn to take his face in my hands. I didn't see him as anything but the man I loved. Who gave a shit if he was normal or not. I didn't want fucking normal. I wanted him. Aiden. Just the way he was.

"Normal is overrated."

He looked down, not meeting my eyes.

"You know, it kills me to admit this… but I saw him once… with her."

"With your mother?"

He nodded slowly.

"That's when I first knew he was my father. I mean I didn't know his name. I just saw him from behind. Saw him…"

He peeled my hands off his face, shaking his head.

"Saw him what?"

"He was fucking her. I mean I was only six at the time, but I knew what sex was back then because I'd seen it. Except I was confused because he was… Fuck. He was giving it to her up her arse and I didn't know what the hell that meant at the time, only that it fascinated me, you know, that anyone would want to stick their dick there. Because he was clearly enjoying it even if she wasn't."

I stared at him, trying to comprehend why he was telling me this.

"You think that's why you want…"

"No… I mean I don't know. I guess I wanted to know why and when I did finally… I understood. It makes me a little sick to think he's the reason I ever wanted to do that in the first place. It has nothing to do with my mother. I don't think of her like that."

I took his hand. I could feel the self-hatred radiating off him in waves. No wonder he was so messed up about this shit. The things he'd had to witness. The shit he'd had to go through as a child. It broke my heart all over again. I'd known he had a fucking tough time growing up, but he kept landing me with further bombshells.

"Aiden… there's nothing wrong with you," I told him. "Wanting that doesn't make you sick or wrong."

"Doesn't it? I made you give that to me even though I don't think you ever really wanted it in the first place."

So fucking what if I hadn't ever thought about it before I met him. I'd tried it and I liked it. No… I loved it. I loved everything about our sex life. Even if I'd been completely unprepared for Aiden's desires, I found myself adoring them just as much as he did. I loved what he did to me. I craved it. I wanted to be at his mercy. To have him take me ruthlessly. Tie me up. Fuck me every which way he could.

"Hey, enough. You've never made me do anything sexually that I didn't want or agree to so don't start. Don't forget who got drunk and asked you to take her virginity in the first place."

I saw a small smile play on his lips before he looked up at me.

"You were spectacularly drunk that night. You stomped off like a little kitten who was denied her cream. I was trying not to smile because you looked so fucking cute."

"Excuse me? I was really upset with you. And embarrassed."

He reached for me, pulling me into his lap and holding me to his chest as he stroked my back. I curled my arms around his neck, burying my face in his shoulder. Hell, he smelt so good. He felt so fucking wonderful. Aiden had always made me feel so safe. Even when I'd known it was a bad idea to let him in.

"I didn't want you to do something you later regretted because you were drunk."

"I only got that drunk so I had the courage to ask you to."

It was true. I'd never really admitted it to myself at the time, but I was terrified of the whole thing. A part of me knew I wanted it with Aiden, wanted to know what it felt like, but the other half was scared shitless. I felt so vulnerable. Even though he'd had me at his mercy several times over, giving him that seemed like far more of a big deal than letting him tie me up.

Now I felt stupid that I'd made such a huge deal out of the whole thing because having Aiden fuck me there was the sweetest ecstasy. There was something so primal and unforgiving about it all.

"Is it so fucking terrible that I can't get the image of you splayed out for me so I can fuck you there out of my head despite what's happened this evening?"

I shook my head. Hell, whenever something shit happened to us, sex was always the balm. I didn't care if that was messed up or not. I didn't even care what that meant. It was just us. Me and him. It's what worked. It's what brought us together.

But there was still something we had to deal with first.

"I know what I said to him about no more dinners, but… if we don't keep going, he won't tell us what you need to know."

"It's okay, princess. It was the heat of the moment. I'll tell him we'll still go, but only if you're okay about that."

"I don't want to see him, but we've never really had a choice in the matter."

"He keeps telling me you're important to all of this, but fuck knows what it means. We need answers and the only way we get them is by playing his fucking game. Then, we never have to see him again. He'll hopefully fuck off back to America and we can go back to living our lives without all of this shit. Just you and me."

I pressed closer to him, running my fingers up his neck and curling them in the hair at the back of his head.

"Just you and me sounds like heaven."

"And it will be heaven. When this is all over, I'm going to take you away. We never got to have a honeymoon."

"Did you have anywhere in mind?"

"Somewhere hot so I can watch you strut about in a tiny little bikini that barely covers your tits because you know how much I fucking love them."

To reiterate his point, he cupped one of my breasts through his t-shirt, running his thumb over the rapidly hardening nub. I laughed.

"Mmm, somewhere private and secluded so you can fuck me on a sun lounger?"

He nuzzled my neck.

"Fuck yes… our own private villa where no one can see me ravage you until you're begging me to stop."

"You know I'd never tell you to stop."

He growled. The sound vibrated across his chest, causing me to squirm in his lap as his thumb continued to brush over my nipple. I was getting wet already, thinking about him laying me on the bed and preparing me with his fingers so I could take his cock.

"Princess," he grunted, grinding me into him. "Fuck, I want you so much."

"Fuck me," I whispered against his skin. "Fuck me until I'm crying out your name in ecstasy."

He picked me up and put me back on the bed. I pulled off his t-shirt and lay back as he tugged off my underwear. He stared down at me, grey eyes blazing with heat.

"You're the sexiest girl I've ever seen. Look at you, so fucking perfect in every single way. All your curves and edges. All that fucking beautiful ink. Your skin fucking glows. Everything about you is amazing."

I smiled at him. I loved the way he adored me. It didn't make me feel embarrassed when he said those things. I believed him when he told me I was beautiful. I saw it in his eyes when he looked at me.

I opened my legs for him, showing him exactly what he did to me. He nipped his bottom lip between his teeth. He was so fucking sexy too. Standing there in all his tattooed glory. His muscles rippling with each breath he took as he watched me. He simply would always be the most beautiful man I'd ever laid eyes on.

"My beautiful tattooed sex god," I whispered.

He released his bottom lip and smirked at my words. His fingers hooked into the waistband of his boxers before he pulled them down slowly. His cock sprang free, slapping against his stomach. Fuck me. He really was a fucking sight for sore eyes. I tried not to drool because Aiden was like looking at a perfectly sculpted Adonis. And he felt like one when I had my hands on him. All that hard muscle pounding into me. Making me feel the sweetest fucking bliss.

The anticipation was killing me. I needed him in me. I wanted his skin against mine. His hands running over my body in that possessive way of his. I was his. His girl. His wife. And he was mine.

He knelt on the bed, his fingers running up my calf as he crawled towards me. They brushed up my side when he leant down and captured my mouth in his. His kiss was demanding. I gave in, letting him devour me whole.

When he pulled away, his grey eyes were wild with desire. They scorched my skin. He shifted back, reaching over to the bedside table and grabbing the lube off it. We both knew exactly what was going to happen. He was gentle as he prepared me, making sure I was ready to take his cock. I arched up against him, groaning as his fingers thrust inside me.

Usually, Aiden had me bent over the bed or laying on my side when he fucked me there, but it seemed tonight he didn't want that. He wanted to be looking into my eyes.

Pushing my legs up slightly, he pressed his cock inside my pussy first, knowing I was dripping wet for him. He grunted as he thrust into me. Fuck, he felt so good. Then he pulled out and spread lube all over his cock.

The initial thrust gave me a slight amount of discomfort, but he took it slow, letting me set the pace in which he fed me his cock. I squeezed his arm every time I was ready to take more. His grey eyes bored holes into mine as he sunk ever deeper inside me. I felt like I was burning up under the intensity of it and the sensation of his cock inside me.

"Aiden," I whispered. "No one has ever made me feel the way you do. I love it when you're inside me like this."

I reached up, tangling my fingers in his hair as I brought him closer to me until our lips were almost touching.

"I love you to the stars and back."

"Princess… you're so perfect."

He kissed me. It was gentle like his thrusts as he began a steady rhythm. I hooked a leg around his waist, allowing him deeper access to me. He didn't fuck me hard. He fucked me slow and deep.

It occurred to me this wasn't fucking. This was making love. The first time we'd actually had slow and sensual anal. It wasn't rough and hard in the way he usually took me. I wrapped my arms around him, holding him close as he thrust into me.

"I love you," he whispered against my lips. "I love you forever, Avery. You're my world. You ground me. Keep me sane. I don't know what I'd do without you."

My heart thundered in my chest. His words made me feel so alive. So wanted. So precious to him. The way his fingers brushed over my sides, stroking my skin as he took me. All of it reminded me of how much I meant to him.

I cried out as he took me higher with each thrust. His lips trailed along my neck. Fuck. He always knew how to make it feel so good. Sex with him was utter bliss. I couldn't get enough of him.

"Please," I whimpered. "Harder, Aiden, please."

One of his hands gripped my hip as he pounded into me.

"Princess, fuck, you're so tight, fuck."

I could feel the tension inside him as he held back from erupting inside me. I hooked my other leg around him, holding him to me. The angle had him brushing up against just the right spot. I panted, feeling so close to the edge I almost couldn't handle it.

"Please," I begged. "Please, fuck, don't stop."

He peeled one of my hands off his back and pressed it down on the bed, holding it there as he kissed my neck. His tongue found my earlobe, circling it before he bit down. I cried out, completely coming undone. Tingles shot down my stomach, erupting in my core.

My head rolled back, loud cries of pleasure emitting from my throat as my climax waged war through my body. I pulsed around his cock, causing him to curse and his grip on me tightened.

"Fuck, princess. Fuck. I can't…"

I felt it. Him. Coating me with his cum. Giving me everything he had. The utter blissful feeling which we both gave into. That's what we sought out. What we needed. Craved. Desired.

Both of us were a panting, sweaty mess when the last pulses faded. He stared down at me with those beautiful grey eyes of his.

"You know what I've just remembered?"

I cocked an eyebrow.

"Hmm?"

"Lunch with your friends tomorrow."

I almost slapped a hand over my forehead. Aiden was right. We were meant to be meeting James and Gert along with her new girlfriend. I wasn't entirely sure how James would be around Tilly. It would be the first time we'd all met. I just hoped he wouldn't be sullen.

"Did you have to remind me now?"

He grinned, rolling off me and propping himself up on his elbow.

"I thought you were looking forward to it."

"I am, it's just… Well, you see, I don't know if James is going to be on his best behaviour or not."

"No?"

"Gert doesn't exactly have the best track record with relationships. He's just worried about her. You know, she legit cried on our shoulders for a month after the last one."

"Was it that bad?"

I turned over on my side, looking up at him.

"I think finding your girlfriend in bed with two other women constitutes the worst way to find out you're being cheated on."

His eyebrows drew down.

"Shit."

"Yeah." I rubbed the back of my neck. "I think part of the reason why I never really got involved with anyone was because of what I saw her go through. I guess you could say I distrusted a lot of people."

He gave me a smile, brushing my hair from my face.

"You trust me though, right?"

I knew he was teasing me, but I didn't want him to think I didn't take our trust in each other seriously.

"With my life. Besides… I know you wouldn't stray."

He gave me a semi wounded look.

"Did you ever think I might at any point?"

"What? No."

I reached over, stroking my hand down his chest.

"I don't think anyone could think that given how much sex you demand from me."

I held back a smile when I saw him rolling his eyes.

"I don't hear you complaining."

I winked at him before jumping off the bed. I cocked my hip out to the side.

"Also why would you go elsewhere when you have this all to yourself?"

I pointed at my chest. He bit his lip.

"Where are you going?"

I didn't reply, strolling away towards the door. I turned back to look at him.

"I won't be long."

"Avery…"

"I have a surprise for you."

I ducked out of the door before he could ask me what it was. I made my way to the bathroom, cleaning myself up before walking into the kitchen. Pulling open the freezer, I deposited some ice from the tray in a bowl. Aiden might not remember how much it drove me crazy when he'd used ice on my body during sex before, but I certainly did.

I brought it back into the bedroom with me, jingling the ice in the bowl as I approached the bed.

"And what do you have there?" he asked, raising an eyebrow.

I crawled on the bed, shoving him on his back as I straddled his waist. I picked out one of the ice cubes from the bowl, placing the rest on the bedside table.

"Just something a little… cold."

Popping it in my mouth, I leant down towards his chest, watching him the entire time. His pupils dilated, a smirk appearing on his face.

"Princess…"

Two could play at this game.

And the only sounds he made after that were curses and moans as I showed him exactly how much ice play could be pleasurable for him too.

TWENTY

Aiden

*A*very looked back from the front seat at James who was sat in the back. We'd picked him up on the way to lunch.

"Why do you look so miserable?" she asked.

"It's nothing."

I looked in the rear view mirror. His arms were crossed over his chest, expression sullen as he stared off out the window.

"Don't be such a big fat baby. Is it because we're meeting Tilly?"

"No, it's not that."

"James…"

He turned, looking at me directly before his eyes fell onto his lap. Avery twisted back around in her seat. She reached out and put a hand on mine. I wondered what that look he gave me meant.

"He already knows about the shit with your family, James," Avery said after a long minute.

"Oh well thanks, now the whole fucking world knows."

"Hey, don't be like that." She turned back to him. "He's my husband, what do you expect me to do? Lie?"

She hadn't told me much about them. Just heavily implied that James' father, Zachary Benson, abused his kids. I should've been surprised but living in the world of the super-rich had tainted my view of them. Too many people with skeletons living in their cupboards.

"No… I just… never mind."

"Seriously, what's wrong? Did they do something?"

"You know I mentioned they were having a weird conversation about a girl? I overheard more shit last night. Then Dad found me outside his office and well…"

"What did he do?"

"I think he would've beat me if Dante hadn't intervened."

I stiffened. A grown man beating on his own fucking kids sickened me. Especially since his kids were adults.

"Fuck," I muttered.

Avery gave me a sharp look before turning back to James. "What did you overhear?"

"Just a name. They kept mentioning the girl in relation to the name Stewart. Like I think he's talking about one of his clients. It might well be the guy he sources tartan from in Scotland. I mean he's called Mr Stewart."

"What girl?" I asked without thinking.

Avery turned to me.

"James overheard them talking about some preparations being made for a girl, but that it was still a year away."

"Sounds a bit sketchy."

"It is," James said. "Fuck knows what they're involved in. I just don't know why Dante stopped him. Like he's been such a fucking dick to me and yet he still defended me to Dad. I don't get him."

Avery let out a long sigh. She knew all about family drama. So did I. Fucking families were a nightmare.

"I wish you and him hadn't fallen out."

"That's hardly my fault. He was the one who started acting like Dad. Turned into his perfect little heir whereas I'm the big disappointment. Not that I even want to be his fucking prodigal son. I'd rather cut my own fucking balls off."

I winced, resisting the urge to check if mine were still there. Fuck. James really didn't like his dad. I supposed I could hardly blame him after everything. I fucking hated mine too, but for very different reasons.

"I don't think Dante is like Zach… not deep down."

"You don't fucking know what it's been like with him. You haven't seen him in forever."

She was silent at that. She looked over at me, her eyes radiating with sympathy for James. I squeezed her hand before letting go as I shifted gears. I knew she wanted to press him further, but it probably wasn't a good idea.

No one spoke for the rest of the drive. I pulled up in a carpark and we all bundled out onto the street. Avery held my hand tightly in hers, glancing at James every couple of minutes. My poor princess was worried sick about him. I couldn't blame her. He looked downcast and defeated. I felt shit for him too. Having to deal with that kind of crap with your family would make anyone fucking miserable.

Before we reached the café, Avery put her hand on his arm.

"Hey… I know you're feeling shit, but you can't let on to Gert, okay?"

He nodded.

"I know, I know. Don't worry, I know this is important for her."

Avery gave him a sympathetic look before she turned back to me, her doe eyes wide. I wanted to comfort her and tell her he'd be okay, but I wasn't so sure of that myself. As James pushed the door open, I leant down to her.

"Don't worry so much, princess," I whispered.

"I just don't want Gert to think it's because he's unimpressed by her girlfriend," she replied, her voice equally as low as mine.

We walked through into the café. I spied her red haired friend immediately because the girl she was with had bright pink hair. I raised an eyebrow at Avery but she gave me a warning look. I wasn't judging by any stretch of the imagination. If that's what her type was, who was I to say anything about it?

As we approached them, Gert let go of her girlfriend's hand and gave James and Avery a hug. She looked up at me with a raised eyebrow. I was not about to hug her friend after all the times she'd asked Avery inappropriate questions about me. And I was not about to forget what she referred to me as.

"Gert."

She grinned, giving me a lascivious look which had Avery frowning at her.

"Aiden."

"Gert," Avery hissed. "Cut it out."

Her friend's expression turned innocent all of a sudden. "What?"

"You fucking well know what."

I looked over at James who was rolling his eyes, followed by Gert's girlfriend who seemed a little bewildered by what was happening. Well, this was just fucking wonderful.

"Gertie, introduce us to your lady friend," James said.

Gert shifted back, taking the pink haired girl's hand.

"Tilly, this is James, Avery and Aiden." She pointed at each of us in turn. "This is Tilly."

"It's nice to meet you," Avery said, sticking out her hand.

"You too, Gertrude has told me so much about you," Tilly replied, shaking Avery's hand.

Avery raised an eyebrow at her friend. Gert shrugged. James just looked like he wanted to laugh.

We sat down at the table they'd snagged for the five of us. I wrapped an arm around Avery, leaning towards her.

"What the hell just happened?" I asked, voice low.

She turned to me. The others were looking at the menus so weren't paying attention to us.

"Fuck knows. I told Gert to stop objectifying you, but she doesn't listen. I'm getting sick of it."

"You objectify me."

She looked horrified for all of thirty seconds until she realised I was teasing her. She shoved my arm.

"I do not, shut up."

"Trouble in paradise?" Gert piped up.

Avery turned back to the rest of them, giving Gert a 'shut the fuck up' look.

"No… Now, what's good here?"

She grabbed a menu and started perusing it, ignoring the stares from her friends. This lunch was going to end in tears in a minute. Fuck.

"Princess," I whispered in her ear. "What's wrong?"

She put a hand on my thigh, giving it a squeeze. I reached over with my free hand and held it. Something was bothering her and I wasn't sure if it was what James said in the car or if it was because Gert kept making inappropriate comments.

"Nothing," she whispered.

I didn't believe her but I wasn't going to push the subject. James looked over at me, raising his eyebrow and indicating Avery with his head. I shrugged. He sighed, turning back towards Gert and Tilly.

"So… Gertie says you're an artist."

Avery leant into me, resting her head on my shoulder.

"I'm sorry," she whispered. "I just can't stand anyone looking at you like that."

"Like what?"

"Don't tell me you didn't notice. I know she's my best friend, but you're mine."

I tried not to smile. My princess was jealous and it was kind of fucking cute.

"Avery, I love you. I have no interest in anyone else."

"I know that."

I tugged her closer. Perhaps our conversation last night had rattled her a little and having Gert look at me like I was some kind of dessert she wanted to devour had been the icing on the cake.

"Princess, you're jealous and it's cute, but you don't need to be."

"I'm not… Okay, fine. I am. I feel so stupid."

I kissed her forehead, letting go of her hand so I could cup her face.

"You're not stupid. Now, chill out and get to know your friend's girlfriend. That's why we're here." I leant towards her, brushing my lips against hers. "I'm yours, Avery. Forever. This ring on my finger guarantees that and even if we weren't married, it would still be the case."

She smiled and fuck if it didn't make my heart sing.

"Okay."

I dropped my hand and she pulled back, turning to her friends. Gert gave her an 'I'm sorry' look and Avery shrugged it off like it was nothing. Having spent a little time around her friends, I knew this kind of shit was par for the course. The three of them constantly wound each other up and bickered like five year olds.

"So, Aiden, are you planning on ever taking your wife on a honeymoon?" Gert asked, looking at me.

"Soon."

"Really? Somewhere exotic?"

I hadn't honestly decided where we'd go. After I mentioned it to Avery last night, I wanted to make sure it was somewhere special for her. She deserved a break. Hell, she deserved not to have to worry about all this shit we'd gone through. When it was fucking over, we both needed time to rest and recuperate.

"Most likely. Sun, sea, sand. What do you think, princess?"

"I need to work on my tan," she responded, grinning.

The twinkle in her eye returned and I knew things were okay again.

I decided right then and there. As soon as we took her family down, I was taking her away for a month long break, maybe even two. Just the two of us with nothing but good food, booze and a shit ton of sun.

Now, I just had to make sure everything ended. And that fucking well started with sorting this shit out with Chuck, finding out who the fuck killed my mother from Rick and working out who the hell 'The Collector' was.

Two days ago Avery told me about her conversation with Ed last week. It'd slipped her mind after all the shit that went down with Rick. I'd asked John to see if he could find out who this blonde girl that Ed had taken to some family functions was. I couldn't ask Chuck myself because he wasn't fucking speaking to me or Avery. Now, I had a solid lead since Avery was suspicious of who she was. Something about it didn't add up for her, especially the way Ed had reacted to her pressing him about it.

Strip clubs were not my idea of fun, but apparently, this is where she was. John had questioned Chuck who told him her name was Flavia and she was an escort who Ed had passed off as his girlfriend to his mother. I suspected that wasn't her real name. I was also suspicious of why her cousin felt the need to bring an escort to a family function considering he could probably have any girl he wanted. Except Avery told me he said he had no time for girlfriends.

And when I told her I had to go track this girl down at a strip club, Avery hadn't been especially pleased. I didn't want to see a bunch of half-naked chicks gyrating on poles but needs must. I'd reassured my wife that the only person who held any interest for me was her. I wasn't sure why she was so insecure recently. Fuck. I loved that girl to death. She knew that. It was just something else I'd fucking well have to deal with at some point. And I would get to the bottom of it because it concerned me that she felt that way.

I walked in, having fucking had to slap down a tenner to get into this place. It was mid-afternoon, but it was packed with suits and lonely men who weren't quite confident enough to book themselves an escort. I went over to the bar, ignoring the underwear clad women walking around and the ones up on stage shaking their tits at the leering blokes.

The bartender walked over and asked me what I wanted.

"I'm looking for Flavia," I said over the noise of the music.

He looked around the club before pointing over at a blonde haired girl who was serving two guys in a booth drinks. I nodded at him in thanks.

I waited for her to come back over to the bar. She was wearing black underwear which barely covered her clearly fake tits. When she noticed I was staring at her, she looked over at me.

"Can I help you?"

"Yes… Flavia, right?"

"Who wants to know?"

"I need to talk to you."

She cocked an eyebrow.

"I take it you're not looking for a lap dance."

I didn't even want to think about Avery's reaction to a woman asking me that. Hell, she was pissed off enough at Gert for even daring to look at me like she could eat me alive.

"Fuck no. I just have some questions."

She gave me the once over before leaning over the bar.

"Frank, I'm taking my break now," she called to the bartender, who just nodded at her in return.

She curled her finger at me and I followed her through the club. We walked through the door marked 'staff only' and down a long corridor until we reached what looked like a dressing room. She snagged a dressing gown from the sofa and pulled it on before turning to me.

"So, what can I do for you…?"

"Aiden… Look, I'll be straight. You have no reason to be up front with me or even talk to me about this, but you know Ed Daniels, right?"

Her blue eyes flashed with shock for a moment before her expression cleared.

"Yes."

"He took you to some of his family functions."

"That's right… Wait a second, I've seen you in the news. You're Avery Daniel's mystery husband."

I crossed my arms over my chest and stared at her.

"Yes, I am."

"So, why are you here asking me about Ed?"

"Because I think you know something. You see, when Avery asked him about you, he was rather cagey. That made her suspicious."

"And what? She sent her husband to track me down. How did you even find me?"

This wasn't going to be as easy as I thought. Also, her reaction made me suspicious. Why was she being cagey about Ed? What did she know? I had to approach this carefully.

"Chuck Daniels."

Her face dropped and she looked away.

"Look, I don't know what you want me to say. I'm trying my best here with everything but dealing with them is difficult."

"Dealing with who?"

She looked up at me, frowning.

"You don't know?"

"Know what?"

"I take care of them for Ed and Chuck."

What the fuck was she talking about?

I stared at her, not sure if asking her further questions would make her suspicious or not. She fidgeted under my gaze for several moments, playing with the belt of her robe.

"The girls they have… They're really fucked up, some of them. I try my hardest to make sure they don't run off, but what their clients want to do to them… It's not easy."

I almost fucking lost it. She was involved in the shit too. And fucking Ed knows.

"You know who runs them."

"Isn't that why you're here?"

I walked further into the room, uncrossing my arms. She knew who 'The Collector' was. And I was going to make her fucking well tell me.

"Who runs them, Flavia, if that's even your real name."

"You don't know?"

"Listen to me very carefully, I'm not here to play fucking games with you. I want to know who runs them."

She paled, taking a step back. I didn't really give a shit if I was scaring her. She had the exact information I wanted. The information I'd been seeking for months, years even.

"What are you going to do if I don't tell you?"

"You don't want to know the answer to that question."

She took another step back, putting her hands up.

"Okay, okay. Can you tell me one thing?"

I stopped, cocking my head to the side.

269

"What?"

"Are you going to stop them?"

"Yes."

She dropped her hands, looking at the floor for a moment.

"Good. I don't want to be a part of it any more. It's horrible. Those girls don't deserve it."

"Tell me who runs them."

"Ed does… He has done for six years and before that, it was that guy who got murdered, your wife's father."

As if I thought this couldn't get worse, it just did. I expected it to be Troy or Arthur, but no, it was her fucking cousin. The one she worked with so fucking closely. Fuck. I needed to get to her office. I needed to fucking make sure she was safe.

"Do you know where they are, the girls?"

She shook her head.

"No, they blindfold me when they take me back to the house. I couldn't tell you where it is."

"What else do you know?"

"Not much, I promise. I help them when they're unable to perform. I patch them up. I was a nurse before."

It made me sick to think that they were damaged enough that they required medical attention.

"When I leave, you're not going to tell anyone I was here or I will take you down too. Do you understand?"

She nodded, fear in her blue eyes. I wasn't above threatening a woman who was complicit in the sex trafficking Avery's family was involved in. I didn't care if she was coerced or not.

"I want to hear you say it."

"I promise, I won't tell Ed or Chuck. I swear. Shit, please, I just want all of this to be over. I'm so tired of it. I don't want

270

their money. All I wanted was to be a nurse, but they got me hooked on heroin and… well… you can imagine the rest. I need my fix."

I didn't really feel much sympathy for her. It was shit that the fucking Daniels had got her hooked on drugs, but that's where my compassion ended. Anyone who was involved in their sick business was just as bad as them.

"Good. Keep that fucking promise. I'm not a nice guy, Flavia. I don't take kindly to people involved in the Daniels and their shit. I suggest you find some other way to get your fix because the Daniels are going down in flames."

Her blue eyes widened, but she didn't say anything else. I turned and stalked out of the room. I wasn't sure she'd keep that promise, but I didn't have time to waste. I had to get to my wife before she decided to blab. I shoved my way back through the club and got out on the street after I grabbed my helmet from the doorman.

I got on my bike, which was parked in the alley, and made my way into the city centre. Parking the bike up nearby, I walked into Avery's building. The receptionist knew who I was so she waved at me. I nodded and got in the lift, pressing the button for the top floor. I paced the small enclosed space, feeling anxiety coiling in my chest.

I pulled out my phone, firing off a quick text to her.

ME: PRINCESS, I NEED YOU TO BE CAREFUL. I KNOW WHO IT IS.

AVERY: WHAT DO YOU MEAN?

ME: THE COLLECTOR.

AVERY: WHO IS IT?

The lift dinged. I didn't have time to reply to her. I strode out of it and made my way to Ed's office. I threw open the door. He was standing at his desk with his phone to his ear. As soon as he saw me, his face dropped.

"I have to go," he said to the person on the phone.

I was relatively sure it was Flavia.

"You and I need to talk," I said when he dropped his phone on his desk.

"You can't come storming in here," he replied, walking around his desk.

"Oh, I think I can."

Ed stared at me for one long moment before he bolted from the room, not giving me a chance to stop him. I turned and ran after him. He shoved open the door to Avery's office and my stomach dropped out from under me.

What the fuck did he think he was doing going in there?

When I got through the door, I almost fucking died on the spot.

My heart hammered in my chest.

Ed had a knife to her throat.

And Avery's doe eyes were wide with fear and confusion.

Fuck.

TWENTY ONE

Avery

I looked down at my phone, frowning. Why hadn't Aiden texted me back? He knew who The Collector was. How had he found out? Did that escort tell him? Why would she even know? I had too many questions and Aiden wasn't responding.

The door to my office flew open. I looked up. Ed strode in. I was about to ask him what he was doing when he tugged me up out of my chair and pulled me against his chest. The next thing I knew, he was holding his arm across my chest and had a knife to my throat.

What the fuck?

Aiden walked in and stopped dead. His grey eyes were dark with shock and then anger.

"Let her go."

"No. Don't come any closer," Ed said.

"What are you doing?" I asked, fear lacing my tone.

He had a fucking knife against my throat. What the hell was he doing and why?

"Shut the fuck up," he hissed in my ear.

I couldn't stop my limbs trembling. The knife was cold against my skin. Whilst it wasn't digging in, I was still petrified. And worst of all, it brought back all my memories of that night I'd killed Tristan.

"Let her go, Ed," Aiden said.

"You think I'm going to give up the only fucking leverage I have? Don't make me laugh."

My eyes met Aiden's again. The agony in his expression killed me. My life was in danger and there was nothing he could do about it. I wasn't entirely sure Ed would actually hurt me, but we couldn't take that risk.

"She's not a part of this."

"You know. You fucking know."

"Yeah, I do know."

"What were you going to do, huh? I know you hate what we do. I know everything."

Aiden shook his head.

"Put the knife down and we can talk."

Ed pressed the knife into my throat. I almost couldn't breathe.

"Please," I whispered, terrified that speaking would make it dig into my skin.

"I told you to shut up."

His arm around me tightened.

"Let Avery go."

"And risk you coming after me? I don't think so."

"Ed, please, I don't know what's happening," I whispered. "Please."

And then it dawned on me. Aiden had come here for a reason. That reason was my cousin. Ed was The Collector. Ed ran the girls.

Fuck. Fuck. Fuck.

How could I not have known that?

"Let my wife go, Ed. I won't tell you again. Do you really want to murder your own cousin? There are cameras in this room. This is being recorded. Don't be fucking stupid."

It took a moment, but Ed's grip on me loosened a little. He still kept the knife to my throat, but I felt like I could breathe again. I shifted, feeling increasingly uncomfortable pressed up against my cousin.

"I don't want to hurt her," Ed said, his voice a little high pitched.

"Then put the knife down."

"What do you want, Aiden? Are you going to turn me in?"

"I want you to tell me where they are."

I couldn't see Ed's face so I didn't know what he was thinking, but Aiden just looked tense. His grey eyes were fixed on mine. He was pleading with me to stay still. To not aggravate the situation.

"And what, you're going to take them, aren't you?"

"Yes."

"What are you going to do with me?"

Aiden's hands came up.

"Nothing. I just want to shut it down."

Except I knew he was lying. We were going to destroy all of them because we had enough evidence to.

"I don't believe you."

"You tell me where they are, I'll let you walk out of here and you can run. I don't care where you go as long as you don't fucking come back. Just let Avery go, please."

No one moved or said anything for several long moments. All I could hear was my heart pounding my ears. And all I could think about was how I'd killed with a knife. I'd stabbed Tristan in the neck with a knife. That night decimated me. I felt tears pricking at my eyes. I tried to squash the memories, but they blared in my head.

"Am I? Are you sure about that? Too fucking bad for you, isn't it? That I'm Avery Lockhart now."

"You fucking bitch."

There was blood everywhere. So much blood. I choked back a sob. Ed shifted behind me. Tears rolled down my cheeks. The agony in Aiden's expression told me he knew exactly what was happening to me.

"Please," I sobbed. "Let me go."

I couldn't do this. I needed the knife away from me or the memories would ruin me.

"You're just a little whore to him. He could never truly want you."

I felt his hands all over me. I felt it when he slammed me into the floor after I'd tried to run. I felt the knife slicing into his flesh. More tears rolled down my cheeks. I couldn't stop the tidal wave of emotion crashing down on me. And the one person who could make it go away was standing several feet away from me, completely helpless to stop this.

"Please, Ed. Please let me go."

The next moment, the knife left my throat and Ed shoved me away from him. I almost collapsed in a heap on the floor, but I didn't. I took several shaky steps towards Aiden. He met me halfway and bundled me up in his arms.

"Do not fucking move," he said to Ed over my shoulder.

He stroked my back as I sobbed on his chest.

"Shh, princess. It's okay. I've got you."

"What's wrong with her?" Ed asked.

"Nothing you need to concern yourself with. Now write down where they are and don't fucking bullshit me, Ed. I will find you and then you're going down. I want you to ring whoever is in charge of this shit for you and tell them they're not going to stop me taking them. Do you understand?"

"Yes, fuck, yes I do."

"Good."

I clutched Aiden tighter. I couldn't deal with any of this shit. I wasn't prepared to find out my cousin ran the girls. I wasn't prepared to deal with the onslaught of emotions having a knife pressed to my throat brought on either. The images were still there. Haunting me. Tearing me to shreds.

"Princess, shh, shh, it's okay," Aiden murmured. "You're okay. Nothing can hurt you. I'm right here. You're not back there, okay? You're not. I promise."

"Aiden," I sobbed. "I can't stop."

He stroked my hair, his touch soothing.

"Get on with it, Ed, then you can fucking well leave," Aiden said over the top of my head.

"Okay, okay."

I heard the shuffling of paper.

"Their schedule is on my phone, all right? I'll send it to Avery's email. Then you can see who they're with."

"Don't forget to phone their fucking handlers."

I heard Ed talking in low tones a few minutes later whilst Aiden continued to stroke my hair and my back. Having his solid form pressed against mine calmed me. He grounded me.

My breathing slowed. My heart rate subsided to a normal rhythm and my tears dissipated.

"You remembered it, didn't you?" Aiden whispered.

I nodded against his chest.

"He can't hurt you anymore, okay?"

"I know," I whispered.

I really did know that. Tristan and Frazier were dead. We knew where the girls were. We had everything we needed now. All of it. This could finally be over. The nightmare that had encompassed our lives for months. I couldn't believe it. That it was almost done with.

I pulled away, staring up at Aiden. He gently brushed away my tears with his thumb.

"I've got this, okay?" he said.

"Yes," I replied.

He let go of me and stepped towards Ed.

"You, sit and stay."

"What? You said I could go."

"I was lying."

I turned to find Ed's face growing white. He'd put the knife down on my desk. Aiden strode over to it and picked it up off there before Ed had a chance to go for it.

"Sit down," he demanded.

Ed sat at my desk, placing his hands on top of it.

"What are you going to do?"

"End this bullshit once and for all. You and the rest of them are going down for this. So you're going to stay there."

Aiden turned to me.

"Get John in here."

I nodded. I walked away out of the room. I'd sent him off for lunch half an hour ago. I found him in the conference room.

"John… I need you to come back to the office," I said, poking my head around the door.

"Sure thing," he replied, standing up abruptly.

He chucked away his wrappers in the bin before following me back into my office. When he spied Aiden and Ed, he looked at me.

"What's going on?"

"This shit right here is The Collector," Aiden said, pointing at Ed.

"You're kidding."

"No, I'm not. We know where the girls are now. I want you to watch him in case he tries to bolt. I need to speak to Rick."

John nodded. He walked over to my desk and eyed Ed with some distaste.

I went over to Aiden, putting my hand on his arm.

"Why Rick?"

"Because this shit is going to end tonight. I'm done. You're done. It's time for us to live our lives without all of these fuckers ruining it. We have everything now, princess. All the evidence. I told you no more bloodshed and I meant it. These pricks are going to prison."

I moved closer to him, lowering my voice.

"But what if they work out what we've done. Won't they tell the police?"

He shook his head.

"No proof to back it up even if they did."

He was right. The only people who could implicate us were ourselves. I would never turn him in and he'd never tell them what I did. He'd covered it up for me. I trusted Aiden with my life. I don't know why I'd been getting so insecure and worked up about shit between the two of us. Maybe I was just on edge because we were so close to finding out the truth.

The only thing we didn't know was who killed his mother. That was why he had to speak to Rick. And we had to find out why Rick kept saying I was important. What did he want? He must've had his reasons for wanting Aiden to get rid of my father. To destroy all of this shit. Was it because of Aiden's mother? He said he regretted that he wasn't there to save her. Was this his version of revenge?

The only way we'd know is if we spoke to him. Aiden needed this. Needed to have closure. I knew it was the only way he'd move on from his mother's death. The only way he'd let go of all the pain and heartache he'd carried for almost twenty two years. Longer than I'd even been alive. My beautiful tattooed angel. He needed to find peace. Desperately. He'd found some of it with me, but he'd never be free until he knew the truth.

"Call Rick," I said, resting my head against his chest with my hand on his heart.

He wrapped an arm around me as he pulled out his phone. I felt his heart thundering underneath my fingertips. Tension radiated off him in waves. He didn't want to speak to Rick, but this was the only way.

"Come, princess, let's not do this here," he said.

I pulled away from him. He took my hand, nodding at John as he pulled me from the office. We walked into the photocopier room nearby. He shut the door behind us.

"Are you okay?" I asked.

He paced the room, running a hand through his hair.

"No. That fucking prick had a knife to your throat, do you think I'd be okay after that? Fuck, princess, if I lost you…"

My heart broke for him. I knew he hated having to see me like that. To know my life was in someone else's hands. I put my hand on his arm when he came near, stopping him in his tracks.

"Aiden, I'm right here. Look at me."

He stood in front of me, staring down into my eyes with his grey ones. They were full of suppressed anger and fear. I reached up, cupping his face.

"I was so scared he'd hurt me."

"Avery…"

"No, let me finish."

He sighed, stepping closer and wrapping a hand around my waist.

"Ed isn't a killer. Maybe he would've done it if you hadn't been so calm about it. Not everything has to be handled with violence. You understand that, don't you?"

"Yes, of course I do. Why do you think I'm turning your uncle and cousins in rather than taking them out? I told you if we could avoid killing them, then we would."

I didn't think I'd ever hear Aiden say that, but he had a habit of doing the opposite of what I thought he was going to. He had gone and beaten someone up just for daring to help his father take me. Ed held a knife to my throat. All things considered, that was far worse.

"So you don't want to kill Ed for what he did?"

"I didn't say that. I want him dead for ever threatening your life, but I don't want to be that man anymore. The one who kills. You told me once that side of me terrified you. I don't want you scared of me. I want you to love every part of me because I'm deserving of it."

Tears pricked at my eyes. Fuck. Aiden. Sometimes he really gutted me. My insides were like jagged shards of ice, cutting into my organs.

"Aiden… you've always deserved me. Don't you see that? And I do love you. Every single inch of you. Even the dark parts. Even the cold parts. Every single part of your soul. I will never see anything other than the man I love when I look at you. Haven't I told you that enough times? Shown you? Don't you believe me?"

I needed him to believe me. Desperately. I needed him to see what I saw. The man who'd give his own life in place of mine. That man was deserving of me. That man was him.

"Princess," he whispered, his voice sounding a little choked up and hoarse. "I've always believed you. I trust you… I…"

"You just don't see yourself that way," I finished for him.

He nodded.

"Well, you should. You don't have to say it, but I know you. I see it in the way you look at me. You'd give up everything to make me happy, even your own life. Don't you see that's the most selfless thing a person could ever do?"

He stared at me for a long moment.

"I never looked at it like that."

"Well no, you wouldn't. You don't see yourself as a good person, that's why, but I do and I suppose that has to be enough for the both of us."

That made him smile.

"You've got the most perfect soul, princess."

I rolled my eyes. I didn't, but if he saw me that way, then who was I to dissuade him of it. Hell, it made me feel special.

Being Aiden's girl had always made me feel on top of the world even when he'd hurt me. I lived in the darkness with him now. The stain on my soul from my actions guaranteed that, but even before I killed Tristan, I'd already embraced the dark.

He leant down and brushed his lips against mine. Tingles shot down my spine at the briefest of touches. My hands wound into his hair, tugging him closer as our lips melded together. Relief sunk into me. This ordeal was almost at an end. We wouldn't have to be looking over our shoulders any longer. My life wouldn't be in danger and neither would his.

When he pulled back, he just held onto me for the longest time. Savouring each other's warmth and touch.

"You need to call him," I said, knowing we should get back to John and Ed.

He sighed, shifting away from me a little so he could dial Rick's number. He put it on speakerphone and we both listened to it ringing.

"Aiden," came his annoying voice as he answered.

"We need to talk."

"After your wife's little outburst, I didn't expect to hear from you."

"We know everything. We have the evidence to destroy the Daniels and their legacy. We know where the girls are. We have Ed Daniels so he can't run and Chuck has no idea yet. The last piece of the puzzle lies with you. You're going to tell me who killed my mother, why you really took Avery and why you keep telling me she's so important. I'm done with this game now. It ends tonight."

Rick was silent for a long moment. I wondered if he was actually going to agree or not. After all, his stipulation was three weeks of dinners with us and I'd royally fucked that up.

283

"Fine. Bring Ed, I'll deal with the rest. I'll text you when and where."

"You're going to tell me who killed her."

"Yes. I told your little da… Avery, I would. Can't go back on my word now. It is time this ended. Everything is in place."

I wondered what he meant by that. Rick obviously had his own agenda. That much was clear after he told us he knew Aiden would go after my parents.

"No matter what happens tonight, I don't want to see you again afterwards. I'm not interested in a relationship with you. You've caused enough damage, so you're going to stay away from us once we're through, is that understood?"

There was silence for another long moment.

"I want you to hear me out first, Aiden. Hear what I have to say. If you still want me to stay away after that, I'll respect your wishes."

Aiden looked down at me. As much as I didn't want Rick in our lives, I also knew we didn't have the whole picture. I nodded at him.

"Fine."

"See you tonight."

He hung up without saying another word. Aiden slipped his phone back in his pocket.

"I don't know what he expects. He'll never be my father and nothing he can say will ever change that."

"I know," I said, stroking a hand down his arm.

"Time we got back to John."

I nodded. Even though I didn't want to see my cousin again. Not after he held a knife to my throat. I had to do this. I was going to be strong because after tonight, all of this would be over and we'd never have to deal with the shit my family was involved in ever again.

I wish I'd known what kind of revelations were coming.

Because each and every one of them destroyed something inside Aiden and me.

And the only hope we had left in the dust and ashes of the truth…

Was each other.

TWENTY TWO

I held Ed by the scruff of his neck as we waited outside the large townhouse. Avery knew this place. She'd been here before. The place where Rick had his men take her. It was just one of Robert Bassington's residences in the city. He had two in Mayfair alone. Fucking rich prick. He was going down with the rest of them. I'd fucking well make sure of it.

Ed's hands were bound behind him, but he didn't struggle. I think he'd accepted his fate. He didn't try to talk to Avery or apologise to her for what he'd done. He'd just stared at her with remorse in his expression. I didn't think he ever intended to kill her. Avery was right. Ed wasn't a killer. He might have run the girls for Chuck since he was eighteen, but he hadn't crossed the line into the darkness that we had.

I hadn't lied to Avery. I didn't want to be that man any longer. The one who killed. Being with her changed me. Gave me something to hold onto. Something to live for after so many years feeling nothing but hate. The violence I'd grown up with had shaped me in so many ways.

Avery taught me there were other ways to make people pay. She was pure. She was my salvation. And I loved her for it.

I looked over at her. She was tense next to me, her expression dark. I knew she remembered what she'd had to go through in this house. How she'd witnessed so much abuse. I couldn't help but think about how she'd sobbed on my shoulder when she'd come home. How she'd needed me to take her pain away in the only way we knew how. How having her gone had broken something so deep inside me, it'd taken weeks for me to admit how much it had affected me.

In so many ways, seeing Avery in pain and torment had hurt me so much worse than having my mother ripped away from me. My love for my wife was all-encompassing. This beautiful raven haired twenty one year old girl beside me was my entire world. And I was hers. We'd never let each other go.

For a long time, I'd struggled to come to terms with the fact that I loved her more than I'd ever loved anyone. That she was the air I breathed into my lungs. The sun that burnt my skin. The rain which washed away everything. The earth upon which I laid my head.

I could never be the angel my mother really needed to save her, but I could be Avery's. I was Avery's. Her avenging angel. And whilst tonight we would enact our final battle and lay to rest my demons, the only person I was doing this for now was Avery.

My mother was gone. I'd accepted that. I couldn't change it. It had been almost twenty two years and it was time I let go. The last piece of the puzzle was who'd killed her. I hoped that was the only thing I needed to put this behind me.

The door opened, revealing a bald headed man who Avery and I had both seen on the footage from her house. The man who'd taken her. Kurt.

"Good evening," he said, stepping back.

I shoved Ed forward. Kurt had taken my fucking wife and helped Rick put cameras in her house. I held back from punching his fucking face in.

"I'll take him," Kurt continued.

"Good. Little fuck is getting on my fucking nerves."

Kurt took Ed's arm, handing him off to another man that stood in the hallway with him. I took Avery's hand as Kurt indicated with his head that we should follow him.

"Wait, what are you going to do with me?" Ed asked.

"We're under strict instructions to keep you under surveillance until Mr and Mrs Lockhart have finished speaking to my employer," Kurt said. "Then they'll decide what happens to you."

Ed's face went white as a sheet. I'd already told him we were making sure he got sent to prison for his part in the Daniels' dirty business.

"You're not going to hurt me, are you?"

Kurt looked at him like he was a fucking idiot.

"No."

Kurt walked off down a long corridor. Avery and I followed. Her hand tightened in mine. We were both concerned about what Rick might tell us, but we had no choice. It was time for the truth to come out.

The room Kurt brought us into looked like a salon straight out of the fucking 1700s. Gilded furniture with floral patterned fabric covering the cushioned seats. Ornate wallpaper and paintings lined the walls. Avery was looking around with a confused expression, but I was staring at Rick seated in a highbacked armchair by the fire. He was wearing a three piece navy suit with brown brogues. He looked like a jumped up fuck yet again. I mean he had a fucking necktie and a handkerchief in his pocket.

Avery and I, by contrast, were in jeans and trainers with matching leather jackets on. We looked so out of place in this room but I didn't care. We'd gone home to change whilst John had kept an eye on Ed in the car for us. I had to drop the bike back home anyway.

Kurt took our coats from us and indicated we should sit down on one of the uncomfortable looking sofas near Rick. I took Avery over to one of them and sat with her, feeling like I was about to have high fucking tea in some posh rich fuck's house.

Kurt shut the door behind him, leaving the three of us alone.

"Scotch?" Rick asked, indicating the decanter on the side table next to him.

"No thanks."

I wasn't going to have a drink tonight. I wanted a clear head. Rick poured himself a glass and sat back, twirling the amber liquid in the glass.

"Has to be said, the Scots do make damn fine whisky."

Avery and I were silent. Our entwined fingers were resting on my thigh as she sat right next to me, our bodies touching. I needed her to get through this evening. Her touch was the only thing grounding me. Stopping me from ripping Rick to pieces for everything he'd done.

Rick placed his glass back on the side table after he sipped at it. His dark eyes appraised me for a long moment.

"Most of what I am going to tell you is going to remain between these four walls. Is that understood?"

"Yes," I replied.

I'd always known Rick was the one man I'd never destroy or take down. He had too much power and in all honesty, I didn't really have it in me to kill my own father. Even though I'd killed my wife's parents, that was before I'd known her. Before I'd come to love her more than life itself. If I could go back and spare her that pain, I would. No matter how much I hated Mitchell and Kathleen, I would spare Avery that because I loved her to fucking death.

"Good. Let me start at the beginning. You won't want to hear this, but it's important."

My hand in Avery's tightened. I really didn't want to hear about how he'd raped my mother, but I wasn't going to stop him. As long as he told me the truth, I could get through this. I could do it because I needed to know everything. To finally understand what had happened to her and why.

"The day I set eyes on Lizzie was the day which changed everything. Before then, I hadn't cared much what women Nick took. They were just playthings. Lizzie was different. She was special. There was something in her eyes. A darkness perhaps as if she'd lived a life full of pain and suffering. I suppose she had."

He didn't take his eyes off me. Avery shifted in her seat next to me. I looked over at her pained expression. This conversation was already making her uncomfortable, but I needed her here. I couldn't fucking sit here and listen to all this shit without her.

"I realise it was wrong of me to want her. I was almost twice her age, but she was beautiful inside and out. Nick always

291

allowed me first pick of the new girls. I didn't want to share her with anyone, but, of course, I didn't have a say in who she was with when I was back home."

It was fucking wrong. She was a sixteen year old girl and he had no fucking business lusting after her. No fucking business at all.

"I was her first in every sense of the word. Y'all seem to think I'm a complete monster, but whilst I might have… forced her, I never hurt her or beat her into submission. That holds no interest for me, unlike my counterparts."

My fist clenched at my side. Avery wrapped her free hand around my arm, leaning into me. I could feel her trembling, but I didn't look at her again. All my focus was on the man who'd give me the fucking truth.

"Just fucking say it for what it is, you raped her," I muttered.

Rick's eyes flashed for a moment. He picked up his tumbler and took a long draw from it before placing the glass back down.

"You want me to admit I'm a rapist, fine. She never gave consent. Not once in all the years I knew her. The truth is not going to be easy for you to hear, Aiden. I never wanted to tell you like this, but there we have it."

Nausea coiled in my stomach. I'd known he'd forced her, but to know that she never once wanted him, that was the worst thing he could've told me. Listening to him admit he raped her fucking gutted me. Fucking cunt. I had to lock down all my instincts to lunge at him. Only the fact that Avery was next to me, holding onto me and reminding me I'd agreed to sit here and listen to him kept me from losing my shit. I had to stay in control.

I felt her chin on my shoulder. I glanced over at her. Her doe eyes were wide with unshed tears. My heart was fucking shattering in my chest and I knew hers was too. She hurt for me.

Rick's voice made me turn back to him.

"As I told you before, when we discovered she was with child, it was the best and worst moment of my life. I'll repeat this for Avery's benefit. Annabelle just discovered she was unable to conceive. The very next day, I received the phone call from Nick about Lizzie. She was refusing to give you up. He was furious. The whole thing was a mess and, in all honesty, I wanted her to keep you so I couldn't find it in me to tell Nick to make her abort you."

I wasn't sure how to feel about knowing I was wanted by both of them. My mother called me her angel. The only good thing in her life and now I could see why.

"I wanted to bring Lizzie to the US, but I couldn't. Not with Annabelle to think of. So, I paid for her instead. Just to make sure Nick wouldn't cast her out on the streets. I wish now I'd taken her away from him completely, but Nick and I were still close and I trusted him."

A sick feeling dug its way into my stomach. I wasn't sure I wanted to hear any more of what Rick had to say. Not if it was going the way I thought it might be. Fuck. What the hell was Avery going to think when she learnt the truth? I looked over at her again. She was in tears now. They fell down her face, making tear tracks in her makeup.

I felt the urge to comfort her, but my limbs stayed locked in place. I was so close to losing my shit and I could not afford to take any of it out on her. The person I was angry with was Rick. Rick and her family.

I think she knew from my expression I was struggling. She let go of my hand and tugged my arm around her instead, resting her face on my chest as she wrapped both her arms around my waist. She held me to her as she cried on my jumper.

"I'm here," she whispered. "I've got you."

Fuck. I'd said that to her so many times when she was falling apart. Now she was the one holding me up. Keeping me from drowning. I curled my hand around her waist, keeping her pressed against my side as I turned back to Rick.

"Go on," I said, my voice hoarse.

"I was there the day you were born. Lizzie didn't really want me there, but she couldn't stop me. The midwife placed you in my arms and I was lost. Even now when I look at you, I still remember that day as clearly as if it was yesterday. I regret much in my life but having you is not one of those things even if I never got to raise you as my son."

I didn't want to hear this shit from him. I didn't care about his feelings. Fuck. I wanted him to hurry up and tell me who the fuck killed my mother. Why she even had to die.

I reached up with my free hand and stroked Avery's hair. She was still crying silently on me and I couldn't fucking do a thing to stop it. Fuck. This was bringing up too many painful emotions for both of us. My heart burnt. My chest felt tight. My head started to pound, but I couldn't walk out of here.

"As you started to grow, I tried to see you and Lizzie as much as I could, but work kept me away from the UK. When I learnt that Mitchell had taken an interest in her, I wasn't happy. I knew what he liked to do to women. There was nothing I could do because Nick didn't know, at least not at first. Mitchell kept his tracks well covered. He had taken over running the girls so there was no reason for Nick to know."

Avery trembled next to me. I was sure she didn't want to hear that shit about her father.

"It was only when Nick found out, that everything was ruined. I was at home, so I only heard about it afterwards. It was too late for me to save her even though I knew she was in danger. I knew Mitchell could only keep it a secret for so long."

I clutched Avery tighter, pushing her face into my chest as she could no longer hold back her sobs.

"Shh, shh, princess," I murmured.

I knew what was coming. I fucking knew it and it killed me all the same. Broke something so fucking deep inside me.

"The man you saw slit her throat… that wasn't Mitchell. It was Nick. He murdered her."

I swallowed back bile rising in my throat. Avery let out an agonising gasp of abject horror. That was why I recognised his voice. Nick sounded very much like Mitchell. Hell, they'd even looked like carbon fucking copies of each other except Nick was obviously older.

"Why?" I choked out.

"He saw her as the reason Mitchell wasn't focused on anything. That she was tearing apart his family and he hated my interference in his business because of you. So when Tina called me and told me what happened and that she'd taken you, I told her to keep you safe so Nick wouldn't come after you too."

"Then what happened?" I forced myself to ask.

"He covered it up. He wouldn't tell me how they got rid of her body or what they did with her, but no one would care if a girl who'd run away from her foster home died. Not really."

The memory of that day slammed into me, reminding me of how I'd watched him slit her throat. How I'd cried out her name when he left and watched her bleed to death. It tore me to shreds. I couldn't breathe properly.

Avery's tears had left a damp patch on my jumper which had seeped into my t-shirt, but I hardly noticed. I held her, trying to fight against the waves of emotions crashing over me. Absolute despair wracked through my body, like shards of glass digging into my skin.

"Do I need to give you two a moment?" Rick asked.

"Is there more?"

"Yes."

"Then tell me the rest."

I needed this to be over. I couldn't stand having to wait to hear what else he had to say, but what the fuck could it possibly be?

"I wanted to destroy him for what he'd done. Killing the mother of my son wasn't acceptable. We'd been friends for so long, but that day was the beginning of the end. He knew how I felt about Lizzie. I loved her in my own way."

He paused, taking another sip of whisky before continuing.

"It was only when Tina told me about the trouble she was having with you. The violent outbursts and your refusal to get help that I knew if you found out what happened to Lizzie, you'd want to avenge her. It took me years to exact my own revenge on Nick. I still am even though he's dead. You see, this is the final nail in the coffin, but we'll get to that later."

I didn't know what the fuck he meant by that but I wished he would fucking well hurry up. Avery was sobbing in earnest on my chest and I didn't know how much more she could take. Hell, I didn't know how much more I could at this rate.

"Everyone thinks Nick died of natural causes. It's true he had lung cancer, but I wasn't satisfied with him dying that way. I was there the night he passed away. I told him exactly what was going to happen. He was so weak by that stage; he couldn't do anything to stop me. I told him what I thought you would do when you learnt about Mitchell, that you would stop at nothing to destroy his entire family. And that I would ultimately help you do so. I'd make sure you had the final pieces of evidence which would see everyone involved in his operation burn. He tried to reason with me, but I told him he betrayed me when he killed Lizzie. I couldn't forgive him for it.

"And then I placed a pillow over his face and suffocated him. I paid the coroner to say he died of natural causes. It was simple really. Some people will do anything for money. There was no need for a post mortem because of his cancer. No one suspected anything. It was terminal, they all knew he would die."

Avery pulled away from me abruptly. Her makeup was streaked across her face and had probably got all over my jumper. Her eyes were bloodshot and she looked completely shell-shocked. She turned to Rick; doe eyes wide with sadness.

"If it's any consolation, I'm sorry your granddaddy did what he did, Avery, but I'm not sorry he died that way. He deserved worse, but I couldn't allow it to look like he'd been murdered."

"You… you… I hate you," she whispered. "You manipulated all of us."

Rick shrugged, rubbing a hand across his face.

"I never said I was a nice man, darlin'."

I stiffened and watched her fist clench in my t-shirt.

"Do not call me that."

He put his hands up.

"You know the truth now. At least the truth of how Lizzie died and what I did about it."

His eyes told me there was more. He'd said Avery was important, but he hadn't mentioned her involvement yet.

"Why did you keep this from me?" I asked. "I could've made my own fucking mind up about what to do if you'd just fucking told me. Maybe none of this fucking shit would've happened. Maybe Avery wouldn't have had to suffer like this, had to witness what she did. You could've fucking stopped it."

He seemed to contemplate my words for a long moment. He steepled his fingers, looking at me with a grave expression.

"Who said you would've believed me if I had. You hated me, Aiden. There were only a few people who knew what Nick did."

It dawned on me all of a sudden. The memory of what happened after she died sucker punched me in the gut. Tina's words rang in my ears.

"Of course, I know it was him. Who else would it have been?"

Could she have known all this time? Then why the fuck did she help me plan Mitchell and Kathleen's murders when she knew it was Nick who'd done it.

"Did Tina know?"

Rick's expression became pained. I had my answer before he said the words.

"Yes. She knew."

I pried Avery off me and stood up, pacing away as my heart fractured in my chest. She knew. She fucking knew and she didn't tell me the truth.

"I told her she had to keep silent. Don't blame her, Aiden. You can blame me for everything, but don't do that to her."

I didn't want to listen to him. I felt two arms band around my stomach and a face press into my back.

"Avery, let go of me," I said, trying to keep the anger out of my voice.

"No."

"Avery…"

"No. Rick is right. You can't blame Tina for that. You know how much she loves you. It's not her fault."

She clutched me tighter.

"Please, Aiden, I know you're angry, but if you start down this road, it's only going to lead to more pain. Haven't we already suffered enough this evening? Haven't we been through enough in our lives? You know the truth now. Isn't that enough?"

I didn't know if it was. Even though Nick was dead, it still didn't feel like enough. I wanted everyone who knew and was involved gone.

"Aiden, please. You need to let this go. You have to. This is why we came here tonight. So you could get closure and we could end this once and for all. Please."

I let out a breath. Hearing her pleading with me broke me. It tore me to pieces. Because I knew she was right. I knew she was talking sense. That was why we came here. I needed to know the truth and now I did. Now I had the final piece of the puzzle.

I turned around in her arms and stared down at her.

"Okay," I said. "I'm trying."

The relief I saw in her eyes fractured me in two. On the one hand, I was angry with Tina for keeping the truth from me, but on the other hand, I understood it. She wanted to spare me that pain. And she had to think about how she could continue to afford to raise me and live. She relied on Rick for financial support. It was only after I started working for the Daniels that I set her up with a retirement fund. They paid me more than enough so it was something I could do for her. So she was no longer reliant on anyone else.

I couldn't allow this one thing to destroy my relationship with Tina, but I had to take some time to calm down about it before I talked to her. Besides, I didn't really have time to think too much on it. There were still things Rick had to tell us.

I looked over Avery's head at him.

"Why is she so important? What does Avery have to do with it all?"

"Why, everything," he replied, his expression grim.

Avery turned around in my arms to stare at him.

"What do you mean everything?" she asked.

"You're the final nail in the coffin, Avery. You own your father's company and you can either bring it crashing down or there is another option."

"And what would that be?"

He stood up and took a couple of steps towards us before he stopped and spread his hands.

"You can sell the company to The Harris Corporation for more than you could ever hope to get on the open market and wash your hands of it entirely."

TWENTY THREE

Avery

After everything I'd learnt in the past hour, this was the last thing I expected Rick to say to me. Sell Daniels Holdings to him? Was he crazy? After everything they'd done, how could I just wash my hands of it? That wasn't right, was it? I had too many thoughts running around my head and I had no fucking clue what to make of any of it.

Aiden hugged me to his chest, his arms tightening around me. I didn't know how he felt about this either. It's not like I could outright ask him in front of Rick. Or could I?

"Why would I do that?" I asked finally.

"You're a wealthy girl already, so I don't expect you want the money."

I shook my head.

"You dismantle the company; all those people lose their livelihoods. If you give it to me, I will ensure the ones who aren't dirty remain employed and taken care of. You and Aiden can do what you will with the proceeds of the sale."

I hadn't thought of that. Not once did it cross my mind how many people Daniels Holdings employed and if I exposed everything, the company would likely go down with me. All those people out of jobs. I couldn't do that to them. It wouldn't be fair. And yet, how could all the things the company had covered up go unpunished.

I turned my head to look up at Aiden. His expression was dark as if he was coming to the same conclusion as me.

"I don't know," I whispered.

His eyes told me he understood. His thumb circled my stomach, the action soothing my frayed nerves. I think if he let me go right now, I'd collapse on the floor.

This entire evening had been fucking crazy. Learning that my grandfather killed Aiden's mother was horrifying. I didn't need to ask how because Aiden already told me. I knew Nick wasn't a good man, but this was worse than I ever imagined. The fact that he would just kill a woman he saw as a threat to his family sickened me.

For all Rick's protestations at loving Lizzie and wanting to protect her, avenge her, he'd still been complicit in keeping her. Raping her. Abusing her. He'd allowed it all to continue when he could've stopped it. I might be glad he took revenge on Nick, but my grandfather was going to die anyway.

Everything else after that was just bullshit. He didn't have to sit back and watch Aiden destroy the empire my family built. He could've done it himself. Instead, he decided to keep his hands relatively clean and allow his own son to do his dirty work. I already knew that was the case from our last dinner together, but knowing the whole truth just made it so much worse.

Everything Rick had done was sick. How could I sell my company to him? But it wouldn't really be to him. It'd be to the Harris Corporation. Unlike Daniels Holdings, they were a public company with stock on the open market. That meant whilst Rick might be the CEO, he still had to answer to the shareholders and the board of directors.

Did that really make it okay?

Could I really rid myself of this mess?

"You don't have to make a decision just yet," Rick said.

I turned back to him.

"I still have things to show you."

"There's more?" Aiden interjected.

"I showed Avery the evidence I have for a reason. It's yours, but there's more. I have a gift for you."

Aiden stiffened behind me.

"A gift?"

"Yes, of sorts. Come."

He walked over to the door and opened it, stepping out into the hallway. I shifted out of Aiden's hold, turning to look at him.

"What more could he possibly have to show us?" I asked, my voice low.

"I don't know."

He took my hand and led me out of the room. We followed Rick down the hallway. I recognised it and its ornate wallpaper. He opened a door to the right and waited for us to enter. I looked up at Aiden. His eyes were narrowed and his body tense.

"What is in there?"

"Your gift," Rick replied.

I wasn't sure why Rick was being so cryptic and suspicious, but Aiden tugged on my hand and we walked in. The scene we were met with was not at all what I'd been expecting as Rick came in behind us, shutting the door.

I didn't recognise the room we were in, but the one I could see through the two-way mirror, I knew that one all too well. It was where Rick had put me when he'd had me tied up and forced me to watch the horrific video of my father and the other ones I'd rather not remember the content of.

That wasn't the worst part of all this. I realised exactly what this gift was that Rick had been alluding to when I saw who was seated in the chair I'd been in.

Uncle Charlie.

"What the fuck is this?" Aiden asked.

"I told you I would handle things. You have Ed and now you have Chuck."

Aiden let go of my hand and turned on Rick, eyes blazing.

"I didn't fucking ask you to kidnap Chuck for me."

"You haven't asked me for many things, but I'm giving them to you anyway."

I didn't understand why Rick had taken Uncle Charlie. His hands were tied behind his back and he was blindfolded. I could see the rapid rise and fall of his chest, but I wasn't entirely sure if he was conscious or not because his head lolled on his chest.

"Why?"

"I thought he would be top on your list of people to rid the world of."

Aiden's fists clenched at his sides. I looked up at him. His grey eyes were as hard as steel and he looked like he was holding back from completely ripping Rick a new one. I didn't know if I should touch him or not.

"He's going to prison. I'm not his fucking executioner."

Rick raised an eyebrow.

"No? Even after everything he's done?"

"Even after that."

Aiden told me no more bloodshed if we could avoid it. He'd not promised me it, but I could see he was trying to stick to his word for me. I couldn't stomach any more death no matter how much the need for vengeance pulsed in my veins. They needed punishing. We'd just wield the hand of justice by handing over everything we knew to the police.

"Then there's clearly things you don't know."

My stomach dropped. What else could he have hidden from us?

"What do you mean?"

Rick held up a hand before he walked over to a desk with a bank of monitors. He sat down and fiddled with the computer for a moment before he brought up a video on the screen. I immediately knew I didn't want to see this, but Rick pressed play.

I knew that room. What I didn't know is why the fuck there was a camera in it. There on the screen was me when I was a kid and my uncle entering the room. Why the hell had my dad put a fucking camera in my bedroom? Was it still there?

I felt sick.

"No," I whispered.

The entire scene I'd told Aiden about played out in front of us. From my uncle asking me about whether I'd kissed a boy to when he'd pushed me on the bed and held me there. It was the next moments which I'd left out. The ones I never wanted him or anyone else to know.

"You're so beautiful, Avery. I watch you. Your skin glows. Your body is heavenly. Do you know what I think when I look at you?" Uncle Charlie said.

"No," I whispered.

"A perfect little girl just ripe to be plucked and tasted."

I felt bile rise up the back of my throat. This part of our conversation disgusted me. Especially because I'd told Aiden I'd kicked him in the balls immediately, but that wasn't strictly true.

"What does that mean, Uncle Charlie?"

"It means that I want to love you in a special way. One which your parents can never know about."

"I don't understand."

"You will soon. I wish you'd stay like this forever. It would be my greatest joy."

I took a step back, putting a hand to my mouth. I couldn't look away even though I knew what was about to happen next.

"Turn it off," I said through my hand. "Please."

Rick either didn't hear me or he chose to ignore it because the video continued.

Uncle Charlie shifted his weight on top of me until my legs were ramrod straight beneath his. It was how I'd managed to kick him. My uncle ran his hand down my chest, stopping at where my breasts had started developing and fondled me there. I knew what I'd been thinking at the time. About how wrong this was but I was completely frozen in place.

"I don't like this," I whispered.

"You will, Avery. Soon."

"Please, don't."

"Shh, shh, you wouldn't want your daddy to come in right now."

"Stop."

He didn't. His hand continued lower until it reached the one place I never thought he'd ever touch me. That's when something inside me had snapped.

"Get off me," I shouted.

"Avery—"

Then I kicked up one of my legs in between his. I remembered the look on his face. The grimace of pain before he clutched his crotch. I'd scrambled out from under him and run.

The video went black.

No one said anything. The urge to be sick grew until I couldn't contain it any longer. I stumbled back into the wall, trying not to throw up all over myself. My movement caught Aiden's attention. He looked at me, his eyes were wide with shock, horror painting his features.

It was the last straw. I'd kept that from him all this time because I was so fucking ashamed that I hadn't pushed my uncle away sooner. How could I tell him that my own uncle had touched me like that?

I bolted, running for the door and ripping it open. I had no clue where the bathroom was, but I couldn't contain it any longer. Kurt was standing outside. When he saw me, he frowned for a moment as I made a slight noise of alarm before the heaving started.

"Second door on the left," he said, pointing down the hallway

I didn't thank him as I ran for the door he'd indicated. Shoving it open, I just about had enough time to fall to my knees in front of the loo before I was violently sick. A moment later, I felt hands on me, pulling my hair out of my face.

"Shh, it's okay, princess," came Aiden's hushed voice.

Everything inside me shattered. I kept hurling my guts up as Aiden held my hair and rubbed my back with his other hand. How the hell could he comfort me when he'd seen the evidence of my omission himself? And to me, it was a big fucking omission.

Tears streamed down my face as I gasped for air. Another wave of nausea drove through me. I wasn't sure anything else was in my stomach at this point, but more came up until it was just spit and bile.

I shifted away, lying on the floor, completely and utterly spent. I heard the toilet flush along with the lid being put down. I heard the tap running before Aiden knelt beside me and brushed my hair from my face. He cradled my head, turning it towards him as he wiped my mouth and face. I was pretty sure I looked like a state after all the crying I'd done and now being sick.

He carefully cleaned my face up completely before throwing the cloth back in the sink. He stared down at me, his grey eyes cautious.

"I'm sorry," I whispered.

"For what?"

"I didn't tell you everything."

He shook his head.

"I don't care about that, princess."

"You don't?"

"No, I care about you."

"I was ashamed he ever touched me like that. You were so angry that night I told you and I was scared."

He tugged me up off the floor into his arms and stroked my back.

"It's okay, princess."

There wasn't a hint of anger in his voice, just understanding. I relaxed into him, feeling the weight of everything that happened this evening seep from my limbs. Aiden was my safety. My home.

"Are you sure?"

"I'm not happy he did that to you, but I'm not angry with you. You're the last person who should be apologising. I know why you left it out."

I wanted to cry, but I wasn't going to succumb to tears again right now. I'd had enough of being a wreck. It was too exhausting and I already felt drained. Instead, I curled my arms around Aiden and buried my face deeper in his solid chest.

"I love you," I mumbled.

"I love you too, princess."

"You're always taking care of me."

I felt his chest rumble against my face with his chuckle.

"Only you. No one else gets special treatment."

"I should hope not."

"You're not getting jealous again, are you?"

I hit his back lightly.

"No, don't bring that up. It's embarrassing."

"It's cute."

Now he was just saying stuff to distract me from the real issue at hand. I appreciated it, but we also needed to go deal with my uncle and Rick. And I was in desperate need of a drink to wash the taste of sick out of my mouth.

I pulled away from Aiden's arms, staring at him. I ran a hand over his jaw, smiling. His eyes fell to my mouth. I shook my head, shifting away and getting to my feet. I didn't wait for him as I stepped over to the sink. The washcloth in it was caked in makeup.

I looked at my face in the mirror. A little worse for wear, but not as bad as I was expecting. I found mouthwash in the cabinet and gargled it before drinking some water from the tap. Next, I washed my face properly, getting rid of the last of the makeup.

Aiden was waiting patiently by the door when I finished. He took my hand and led me back into the room where Rick was. He gave us the once over.

"Are you okay darlin'?"

I let the fact that he said that slide because I wasn't in the mood to argue about it further.

"I'm fine."

It was a lie, but whatever. I needed this evening to be over. Enough revelations. All I wanted was for him to hand over the rest of the evidence so we could leave, but I knew that wasn't going to happen quite yet.

I wasn't sure how to deal with the fact that my father had cameras in my room and that they'd been there since I was young. It disgusted me as well as it being an invasion of privacy. What other videos did he have of me?

"How do you have this?" I asked.

"It was on Nick's computer. I don't think your father kept any other footage if that's what you're concerned about."

"I'm more disturbed by the fact he even installed a camera in my room in the first place."

"Your father was a very cautious man. I believe he and your granddaddy knew about your uncle's predilection. I imagine this footage was used to keep him in line."

I shuddered.

"Now, you two have some decisions to make. I have all the evidence you need on this hard drive here." He pointed to something on the desk. "I don't think you want to see any further videos of your uncle, but I assure you, there's more."

I tried not to think too hard on that. More videos meant he'd abused kids and I just couldn't go there. I was kind of grateful to Rick that he'd never shown me them that day he'd taken me.

"As I said, you can sign your company over to me or destroy everything. And you can take your uncle and your cousin or… you can end him here and now."

I knew exactly what 'end him' meant because my eyes fell on the table in the other room. Sitting in the middle of it was a handgun. I swallowed, looking over at Aiden. I couldn't read his expression but I knew he'd seen the same thing that I had.

"Aiden," I whispered.

His eyes met mine. I saw something in them I didn't want to. It was that cold, calculating look, but this time there was something else simmering below the surface. White hot rage. And it terrified me.

I took a step towards him.

"Don't, Aiden."

He shook his head slowly at me.

"Please, I hate him too, but this isn't the way and you know it."

His fists clenched at his sides.

"He's a sick fuck," Aiden said, his voice low and rough.

"I know, but please, no one else needs to die. Let the police arrest him, please."

We stared at each other for the longest time. My heart broke further with every second and I knew before he said it that he wasn't going to listen to me.

"I'm sorry, princess."

He strode out of the room. I tried to follow him. To stop him, but Rick held onto my arm.

"Let go of me."

"Let him go," Rick said.

"No, I can't let him do it."

I struggled in his grasp, but he tugged me against his chest and banded his arms around me, pulling me over to the two-way mirror. I watched in horror as Aiden walked into the room with my uncle.

"Who's there?" Uncle Charlie's voice came through the speakers in our room.

Aiden didn't say a word. He moved over to the table, picked up the gun and pointed it at my uncle's head.

"No, please, no. Please, let me go. Please, I have to stop him," I cried out, struggling against Rick's grip on me.

"Shh darlin', it's okay. He has to do this."

"No, he doesn't. He doesn't need to do it. My uncle doesn't need to die."

My heart was racing at a million miles an hour. I could hear it pounding in my ears. I had to stop Aiden if it was the last thing I did.

"Please."

Aiden just stood there holding the gun to my uncle's head without moving.

"Who's there?" Uncle Charlie asked again. "Don't be a coward, tell me who you are."

"Please, Rick, let me go. Let me stop this. Please," I begged. "Your son doesn't need any more blood on his hands. He's trying to heal. This will make it worse. Please. Please, let me go."

I don't know if my words were enough, but Rick's arms around me loosened and I ducked out of his grasp. I ran out of the room and threw open the door to where my uncle was.

Saying anything to Aiden wouldn't help so I walked up to him and wrapped my arms around his stomach, pressing myself into his back. I held him for the longest time as he stood there pointing a gun at my uncle's head, willing him to put it down. Willing him not to go through with this.

There was another way. We had the evidence we needed to send them to prison. All of them. Not just my uncle and my cousin, but all the men involved. We had to do it right this time. No more vigilante justice. It would only bring down more trouble on our heads. This time we had to do it cleanly.

I needed him to stop this. He had to put the gun down. He had to. He had to be the man I knew him to be inside. The one who didn't do shit like this anymore.

He had to be the Aiden I loved.

Because if he wasn't.

I wasn't sure if we could survive this.

I desperately wanted to.

We'd promised each other forever.

And I was going to make sure Aiden kept that promise.

Even if it was the last thing I ever did.

TWENTY FOUR

Aiden

"Further arrests have been made following the recent discovery of a long standing sex trafficking ring in London. Two weeks ago, Charles Daniels and Edward Daniels, who both worked for Daniels Holdings, were arrested following evidence coming to light showing they were the ringleaders in this sordid business. We also have confirmation that the deaths of Mitchell and Kathleen Daniels and Frazier and Tristan Shaw are also connected to this sex trafficking ring. The police believe their deaths were acts of revenge, but they do not have any suspects at this time."

I stroked Avery's hair as the broadcaster continued. She was fast asleep with her head in my lap. The past two weeks had been exhausting for her. The media circus following Chuck's arrest had been non-stop.

"A statement was released yesterday by Charles Daniels' niece, Avery Lockhart. Mrs Lockhart stated she was shocked and appalled by the allegations made against her uncle and cousins and that she would

personally donate to the fund set up to help the women who were trafficked by her family. Mrs Lockhart has also made front page news following the announcement this morning that Daniels Holdings is being sold to The Harris Corporation."

Avery stirred in my lap. She looked up at me, blinking. She'd woken up ridiculously early this morning because she was worried about the announcement, but by nine am, she'd rested her head in my lap and fallen asleep.

"What time is it?" she asked.

"Twelve."

"Oh, oh shit, I should be in the office."

She started to sit up but I stopped her.

"Shh, I told Saskia you're not coming in today. You're not needed. It's okay, princess, just relax."

The board was dealing with the sale of the company. It wasn't a decision she'd taken lightly. After what happened with Rick that night, I wasn't sure she'd go through with it. Avery ultimately decided she couldn't allow all of the employees to lose their jobs. We'd kept a copy of the evidence we had against the company which Rick didn't know about, but we were washing our hands of that mess. Avery just wanted it all to go away now we'd taken down their sex trafficking ring.

That night had been a shitstorm of emotional turmoil for both of us. If Rick hadn't let her go and if she hadn't come in the room and wrapped herself around me, I think I might have actually shot Chuck dead. It was her silently begging me not to do it as she held me which stayed my hand. Instead, I'd put the gun down and walked out of the room with her. We'd stood in the hallway for a long time, just holding each other until she spoke.

"Thank you," she whispered.

"He's going to rot in prison for what he's done."

"He will. We'll make sure of it. I don't want to do this anymore. I want to let it all go, Aiden. I want to take his offer. Take the money so I can help the girls and then I want to walk away."

"Okay, princess. That's what we'll do."

When she'd told Rick, he'd nodded and said he'd instruct his lawyers to draw up the official offer and the acquisition paperwork.

We'd gathered up the evidence from my flat as well as the hard drive Rick had given me before dropping both Chuck and Ed off outside a police station. We'd told them they were going to turn themselves in, providing the evidence necessary and plead guilty when their cases came to court. If not, then I'd find them and end their lives. Funnily enough, neither had objected at this point. Avery and I had watched them walk into the station with the hard drive. They didn't come back out and the news broke two days later.

Avery settled back down in my lap, staring up at me with those beautiful doe eyes of hers.

"It's almost over."

I nodded. It was. And I was fucking glad of it. All the women who'd been involved had been rescued and were now being cared for. Sophie and Cora had come forward and made themselves known to the police. Both were more than happy to give evidence against Robert Bassington and the other men they'd had to service.

"Have you spoken to Tina yet?"

I winced. I didn't really know what to say to her. She'd kept the fact that Nick Daniels had murdered my mother a secret from me. I wanted to forgive her and put this behind us, but that would take a conversation I wasn't sure I was ready to have.

"Aiden, you need to talk to her."

"I know. I know."

She looked over at the coffee table, spying my phone on it. Before I could stop her, she'd reached over and grabbed it. She knew my passcode by now so she unlocked it, pulled up the contacts and clicked on Tina's number. She held it out to me as it started ringing.

I took it from her, shaking my head. Even though she was interfering, I couldn't be annoyed about it. At the end of the day, Avery was my wife and I knew she was right.

"Aiden… I thought you'd never call," Tina said when she answered.

"I was going to…"

"You're angry with me. I get it."

The only reason she knew anything was because Avery spoke to her after the news broke. I wasn't ready and, in all honesty, I still hadn't entirely forgiven her for it.

"You could've told me."

"I wanted to protect you. You were so young when it happened and the longer I kept the truth from you, the harder it was to tell you. I'm so sorry. I really am. I should've told you when you came to me about Mitchell. I just hated him so much. Hated all of them. I wanted them gone just as much as you did. I'm so sorry, please believe me when I say that if I could go back, I would've told you the truth, but you know Rick told me he'd cut off the money. You really mean everything to me, Aiden. You know that, right? I love you like you're my own son."

I could hear her voice falter on the words. Something about it broke my heart. Tina would always be my parent even though we weren't related by blood. My only parent as far as I was concerned. Rick wasn't a fucking father nor would he ever be. He'd promised us that once the sale went through, we'd never have to see or speak to him again.

"I know. I love you too, Tina."

I heard her gasp of surprise followed by a sob. I'd never actually said those words to her before. She'd been in my life since I was five years old, but it was only now, at almost twenty nine, that I felt able to.

"Oh, Aiden. I…I…"

"Hey, don't get all fucking soppy on me. I'm just telling you the truth, okay?"

She was silent for a few moments. I suspected she was composing herself.

"That girl has changed you."

I looked down at Avery who was looking at the TV. I knew she was listening to my side of the conversation even if she was pretending not to.

"She has."

"I know I'm not your mother, but she is the perfect daughter in law. Don't mess it up ever again, you hear me?"

"I won't… She's the one."

That made Avery turn her head up towards me, her doe eyes wide. I stroked her hair, smiling.

"Are you talking about me?" Avery asked, her voice too low for it to carry to the phone.

I winked.

"I never thought I'd hear you say that about a girl," Tina said.

"I married her, didn't I?"

Tina chuckled and I saw a blush rise up Avery's neck and cheeks. Fuck. She was so cute when she got embarrassed. It wasn't that often I told anyone else how I felt about her and especially not in front of her face. She knew how I felt obviously, but that was different. I had no qualms about telling her just how much she meant to me.

I trailed my fingers down Avery's bare arm. She squirmed a little.

"And you know that was also an unexpected surprise. I'm glad you're happy. Do you think we can put all of this behind us now?"

I let out a long breath.

"We can try. Just give me time... How are the girls?"

"They're fine. They're still staying with me, but the police have interviewed them several times. I like having them here if I'm honest. I've told them they're welcome to stay with me permanently."

I smiled. I hoped Sophie and Cora would continue to live with Tina. They'd formed a kinship with her in the last few months. I might be her adopted son, but I was never really there for her in the way she needed. She'd constantly had to deal with me getting into trouble and when I'd left to join the army, she was alone. She'd never met anyone she wanted to spend her life with. I sometimes wondered if that had anything to do with me, but Tina had assured me it wasn't.

"Adopting more strays then?"

"You were not a stray and you asked me to take care of them."

I laughed.

"I've not heard that sound in a long time nor you making jokes."

"Another thing you can thank Avery for," I replied, still chuckling.

"It seems I have a lot of things to be grateful for when it comes to your wife."

I looked down at my girl. She was eying me warily because she could only hear my side of the conversation.

"Anyway, I should go. I said I'd make lunch for the girls."

"Okay, I'll speak to you soon."

I hung up, dropping the phone on the arm of the sofa before I leant down and stole a kiss from my wife who was about to open her mouth to speak.

"What were you saying about me?" she asked when I pulled back a little.

"Only nice things, princess."

"I take it from your smile that things are okay."

"Things will be fine… eventually."

I wasn't going to stay angry with her forever. It was time to let go of the past.

"Come on, there's something we need to do," I said, changing the subject.

"What?" she asked as she sat up.

"Something we should've done a long time ago, princess."

Both of us stood in the cemetery side by side. Avery hadn't really wanted to come, but we needed to.

"She was here this whole time," she said.

321

"Yeah… I guess she was."

The one thing Rick told us before he left was where they'd put Lizzie. In Avery's family's plot no less. Nick had told him before he died. Mitchell had been insistent about it. What better place to hide a body than in a fucking cemetery. They'd paid handsomely to keep it quiet.

"Are you okay?"

"Yeah… It's kind of a relief to know where she is, you know. Are you?"

We were going to have a gravestone put here for her at some point, but it wasn't urgent. Just knowing she was laid to rest made me feel better about saying goodbye. That was why I'd brought Avery here. So I could let go.

"Yeah… I never really said goodbye either."

She squatted down and placed a white rose on her parent's graves. She put a hand on the gravestone.

"Mum… Dad… There's a lot of things I want to say to you, but not a lot of them are good. I'll always love you because you're my parents, but that doesn't negate what you've done. If I come to visit again, it won't be to see you. I hope you understand that. I wish you'd lived so I could've said this to your faces. Told you how much trouble you brought, but it's okay. Your empire crumbled and that's good enough for me."

She rose to her feet and tucked herself under my arm and wrapped a hand around my waist, giving me a squeeze. I kissed the top of her head, knowing how hard it was for her to be here, but ultimately, she had to do this. For her own sake.

I stared down at the plot where my mother lay for the longest time.

"I wasn't sure what I'd say when I got here," I started. "And now I am here, I still don't know."

This was harder than I expected. There were so many things I wanted to say to her, but the words failed me. So I decided to tell her about the one thing I could talk about.

"I spent a long time being angry at the world, but not any longer. You always called me your angel, but I think perhaps I was destined to be someone else's angel instead. I think you'd like her. She's the kindest, most understanding and selfless person I know. I wish you could've met her. Just once. Then you'd know how much happiness she's brought into my life. How much she's healed me just by being her."

I felt Avery trembling next to me, but I didn't dare look at her because I was getting choked up with emotion too.

"It's over now. They can't hurt anyone else. I made sure of it. I did that for you even though you never asked me to. I did it for all the girls they'd hurt over the years. And I guess I did it for me too."

I heard Avery let out a little sob and it broke my heart. Fuck. This whole thing killed me. Saying goodbye was much harder than I ever expected.

"I love you, Mum. I always will. I promise I'm okay. I've got Avery and she's all I need in this world. We'll come see you again soon."

I let go of Avery so I could place the violets I'd brought with me on the place she was buried. When I straightened, I took my wife in my arms and let her cry on my chest as tears slipped down my face too. I wasn't sure how long we stayed like that, but when she looked up at me, she smiled.

"When I sign the papers, it'll be over," she whispered.

I reached up and dried her cheeks on my coat sleeve.

"It will be and we won't have to worry about any of this shit ever again."

She nodded, pulling away and taking my hand. We walked back to the car together, both of us having huge weights lifted off our shoulders.

We were almost there.

And very soon, our life together would truly begin.

Avery sat at her desk for the very last time. I leant up against it whilst two solicitors stood in the room watching her sign the papers along with one of The Harris Cooperation's lawyers. She shook out her hand before she signed the last document.

"There, the company is no longer mine," Avery said as she put the pen down.

"Very good, Mrs Lockhart," one of the solicitors said as he came forward to collect the papers.

She stood up, taking my hand.

"Do you need anything else from me?"

"No, no. Thank you for your time today."

She nodded at the assembled party before we walked out of her office together. She stopped off to say goodbye to Saskia and Clara before we got in the lift.

"How does it feel to be unemployed?" I asked.

She giggled.

"Weird, but good. Do I even need a job? I'm technically a billionaire."

"We're billionaires you mean."

She looked up at me, grinning.

"Well, yes, what's mine is yours."

"You're most definitely mine."

Her doe eyes glinted.

"Mmmhmm… I've belonged to you since the day we met."

And she knew very well I'd belonged to her since that day too.

The lift reached the ground floor and we walked out together, stopping off at reception to collect our helmets. I led her outside and we walked to where I'd parked my bike. She was wearing appropriate clothing for this, unlike last time she'd been on the back of my bike. She looked fucking hot in her jeans and leather jacket. That first date we'd shared felt like a lifetime ago and in a way it was. Over six months had passed.

"So, birthday boy, where to?" she asked, slipping her helmet on.

The fact that she'd signed over Daniels Holdings on my birthday was a bonus. It was the end of the year from hell and the start of something new. The start of our lives together.

"Home."

I straddled the bike and she got on behind me, wrapping her hands around my waist. I may have driven back faster than I should've, but she hadn't tightened her grip on me. When I parked, she jumped off the bike, pulling her helmet off. She had the hugest grin on her face.

"You look happy," I commented.

"You're going to say I told you so, but that was amazing. Can you take me out on the motorway so we can go faster?"

I laughed, wrapping an arm around her as we walked over to the lift.

"If you want to. Who'd have thought you'd turn into a little speed demon."

"I wouldn't go that far. Don't forget, I still can't drive."

She didn't need to when she had me. We got upstairs and into the flat. Avery took my hand and led me into the living room when we'd rid ourselves of our coats and shoes.

"Why do you have that mischievous smile on your face?" I asked, eying her warily.

"No reason."

"I don't believe you."

"Tada."

She put an arm out when we reached the room. Piled up on the sofa were several wrapped gifts. I looked down at her.

"When did you do this?"

"Well… it's hard to keep anything from you, but I uh, hid them in the cell."

I shook my head. That cell was going to disappear very soon. I'd hired the contractors to convert it and renovate the rest of the flat whilst they were at it.

"Sneaky girl."

"Come on, it's the first time I get to celebrate your birthday and you didn't let me do much at Christmas. Aren't I allowed to treat my husband?"

I leant down and gave her a kiss.

"I suppose you are."

She looked so fucking happy. It killed me. She dragged me over to the sofa and we both sat on the coffee table. She'd got me several items of clothing, including new trainers and t-shirts. She'd bought me a rather expensive watch which I'd pointed out when we'd been out a few weeks ago and a new set of boxing gloves.

"Thank you, princess."

I was about to give her a kiss when she jumped up.

"That's not everything."

I raised an eyebrow as she moved around the back of the sofa and picked something up. She held it up in front of her and I froze in place. It wasn't lost on me that I'd asked her to do this for me, but I hadn't expected her to have painted a finished piece quite yet.

There we were, arms wrapped around each other as we had our first dance as man and wife. She'd painted every last detail including the little beads on the bodice of her dress.

"Avery…"

"Do you like it? I can't see your face so you're going to have to tell me."

I stood up and walked around the sofa, taking the painting from her and placing it back down. She looked up at me, confusion in her eyes. I pulled her into me, cupping her face with both hands.

"I love it almost as much as I love you. When the fuck did you do this?"

"When you were busy… I wanted it to be a surprise. You really like it?"

"Yes, princess, it's perfect. You're fucking perfect. I'm a fucking lucky man."

She smiled, placing her hands on top of mine on her cheeks.

"And I'm a lucky woman."

I pulled her towards me and kissed her. When I pulled away, she was still smiling, her eyes wet with tears.

"Hey, why are you crying?"

"It's over, Aiden. It's all over. I can't believe it."

I smiled, wiping away her tears with my thumb.

"It is. You and I are together and that's all that matters."

327

She reached up, wrapping her arms around my neck and going up on her tiptoes. She pressed her forehead to mine.

"I love you so much. I'm so fucking happy. I don't even have words. I'm crying happy tears, I promise."

I held her close, revelling in the way she felt against me and knowing that she was fucking mine forever.

"I love you too, princess. Always."

EPILOGUE

Avery

I t wasn't often I was awake before Aiden. He looked
so peaceful as he slept, his hair ruffled and his face
clear of all worries and concerns. The sun streaming
in through the windows highlighted his tattoos. He'd thrown
the sheet off in the night. It was hot even though we had the
fan going. I'd forgotten to put the aircon on. I wasn't exactly
upset about it because Aiden looked so fucking sexy. I was
tempted to wake him up, but I couldn't. Not when he looked
so calm. I leant over and placed a kiss on his chest before
silently slipping from the bed.

I pulled on a robe and walked out into the open plan living
area. Marissa, our housekeeper, was in the kitchen.

"Morning," I said.

"Mrs Avery, you want a tea?"

I nodded, smiling. I leant against the dining table. A few
minutes later, she brought over a steaming cup for me.

"Is Mr Aiden not awake?" she asked, dark eyes glinting.

"No, he's still sleeping."

"I leave out breakfast for you both before I go."

"Thank you."

I strolled out onto the large deck, eying the pool and the sun loungers for a moment before I walked over towards where there were steps down to the beach. I sat down on the edge of the deck, letting my legs dangle down as I sipped my tea. It was stunningly beautiful here at this hour. The sun glinted across the clear blue water lapping up against the white sand.

I couldn't quite believe this little piece of paradise was ours. We'd been here for a month already and I didn't want to leave. It'd been good for us. Time to relax. Time to heal our emotional wounds. I wasn't sure I'd ever really be at peace with what I'd done, but the day I signed the company over to Rick was the day I decided I was done. The past couldn't be changed. I'd learn to live with it. I wasn't going to wallow in painful memories.

Perhaps we both deserved to be punished for what we'd done, but I felt like Aiden and I had suffered enough. And we'd done the right thing by turning in the rest of them. That was justice and it was being served without us needing to divulge our involvement.

Now we could move on. Now we could have a future. A quiet life together away from all the horrors and bullshit of our dark pasts. That was all that mattered.

I heard his footsteps across the deck, but I didn't look up until I felt his presence behind me. He was only dressed in a pair of swimming trunks, his bare chest still on display. I swallowed at the sight of him.

"You didn't wake me up."

"You looked peaceful, how could I?"

He smiled, settling himself down next to me with a mug of his own. I leant against him.

"I suppose I'll forgive you. I mean we are supposed to be on our honeymoon."

"This is a rather long, extended honeymoon. Gert and James keep asking when we're coming home."

"They can just fucking deal."

I grinned, sipping my tea. They did miss us, but they also knew we needed time away too. It'd been a few months since Aiden's birthday and in that time, we'd donated a lot of money to the fund set up to help the girls who'd been sex trafficked and bought this place in a secluded place on the island of Antigua in the Caribbean.

Whilst neither of us were particularly extravagant, Aiden had wanted to get away from everything and so did I. Rather than sinking money into an expensive hotel, we'd bought a little house instead. It was peaceful and we couldn't ask for more.

"We do have to go back at some point. Christmas is coming up and you know we promised to do another New Year's Eve get together at ours."

He took the mug out of my hand and stood, walking over to where the sun loungers were and placing them on a little table. He put his hand out to me. I got up, walking over to him with a smile on my face.

"We'll go home soon, I promise, but for now, you and I are going to enjoy the sun because I for one love this little tan you've got going on here."

His fingers went to the belt of my robe. I wasn't wearing anything underneath it, which made his grin turn wicked.

"Naughty girl," he growled, tugging me closer as his hand went to my breast.

"Marissa is making breakfast."

He sighed, rolling his eyes before he covered me up again.

"Okay, you're going to let me fuck you after we've eaten though."

"I promise."

We picked up our mugs and walked back into the house. As promised, Marissa was just putting out breakfast for us. She smiled.

"Do you need me this evening?" she asked.

"Is the kitchen stocked?"

"Yes, Mrs Avery."

"Then no. Aiden and I can manage."

She bobbed her head.

"I see you tomorrow."

I gave her a smile as we both sat down. Various fruits and fresh pastries were laid out for us. I shook my head. Marissa spoiled us. We paid her a good wage for cooking and cleaning for us and I think she was grateful. When we left, she would still have a job here, making sure the house was ready for when we returned. And Aiden and I agreed we wanted to come back often.

"So, when we do go home, what are we going to do?" I asked, spooning fruit into a bowl along with yoghurt.

"Hmm, you are going to keep painting and perhaps I'll buy you an art gallery."

I shook my head, snorting.

"I don't need you to do that. Be serious."

"I am. You can draw and paint at your leisure."

It is what I wanted to do. Be an artist. Not that I'd ever really amount to anything huge, but perhaps I could do portrait commissions. One thing that had come out of Aiden insisting I paint more was the realisation it was something I was actually pretty good at. The canvas I'd done of our wedding day would have pride of place in our living room. A reminder of the most perfect day of our lives.

"And you?"

"Well… I thought I'd go work with Ben, you know, run his business for him whilst he tattoos."

"You'd want to do that?"

He nodded, grinning as he dug into his own food.

"And have you spoken to him about it?"

"Skye is pregnant again."

I looked up at him.

"Again? But Josh isn't even that old. Also, when were you going to tell me?"

His grey eyes glinted and he shrugged.

"I'm telling you now. It wasn't planned, but I think he's happy. Anyway, he needs help, he asked me so I said yes."

"Good, I'm glad. You and him should spend more time together. Would give me a break from all the sex."

He rolled his eyes, giving me a sly smile.

"Hmm… are you complaining?"

"No, of course not. Don't forget, I'm the one who's not wearing anything under this robe because I was totally planning on stripping it off and giving you a little show after breakfast."

He raised an eyebrow.

"Is that so?"

"Yes, it is. So you better eat up."

And I'd never seen Aiden wolf down food so fast. Minutes later, he stood up and put his hand out to me.

"Now, you said you were going to give me a show."

Aiden

As soon as Avery said she wanted to give me a show, my cock got so hard, I could hardly think straight. Being out here in fucking paradise was the best thing for both of us. After all the shit we'd been through, we needed a break. Time to relax and decide on our next steps. And… fuck like rabbits.

Avery hadn't complained about the number of times I'd stripped her down and made love to her in the month we'd been on this island.

She put her hand in mine and I drew her outside onto the deck. I untied her robe again and tugged it off her shoulders. It fluttered to the ground. Fuck. She looked so damn sexy with that tan, her naked skin glowing in the sunlight.

Her wicked smile was the only indication I had she was up to something. She let go of my hand and dashed towards the pool before I could stop her. The splash she made was loud in the still and quiet air.

When she came up for air, she was still grinning. I shook my head as I tugged off my swimming trunks and jumped in with her. She tried to swim away from me, but I grabbed her and pushed her against the side, pinning her to the wall at the shallow end so we could keep our footing.

"Someone has been a very bad girl."

"Is that so?" she said with a glint in her doe eyes.

I didn't answer. I wrapped a hand around the back of her neck, holding her in place as my mouth descended on hers. She tasted like the dragon fruit she'd just consumed. My other hand fell between her legs, stroking her as she arched into me.

"You're mine, princess," I said as I pulled away and nipped her ear.

"Aiden," she moaned, pressing against my fingers.

"Are you going to do what I say?"

"Yes," she breathed.

Fuck. I needed inside her.

"Wrap your legs around my waist."

She shifted in the water, holding onto me as I helped her wrap her legs around me. My cock brushed up against her pussy. I moved away from the side of the pool towards the steps. Walking out of the pool with her wrapped around me, I kissed her again. I only pulled away when we reached the sun lounger. I sat down with her in my lap.

"I want you to sit on my cock, princess."

She shifted up on her knees and sunk down on my cock. Being inside her was fucking ecstasy. I pulled her against me, my fingers tangling in her wet hair. As I thrust upwards, she dug her nails into my shoulder and groaned.

"Mmm, that's it, princess. I'm going to fuck you long and hard until you're completely spent."

Her only response was to hold onto me tighter as I started to move inside her. Fuck, she was so beautiful. Inside and out. There was no one else in the world who could compare to her.

At least not for me. I worshipped this girl. This goddess. My wife.

It wasn't enough to have her sitting on top of me. I wanted more purchase so I could fuck her brutally. She'd run away from me and I wasn't going to allow her to get away with that.

"I want you on the bed, hands up against the headboard for me," I told her, my lips brushing against the shell of her ear.

She shivered at my words but got off me without hesitation. I watched her walk back into the house without a backwards glance. I rose slowly, snagging a towel from the side table and drying off. Then I stalked into the house and through to the bedroom.

She lay there, hands above her head exactly as I'd instructed. I walked over to the bedside table, her eyes tracking me the whole way. Pulling out a length of silk, I knelt on the bed and tied her hands to the headboard.

"Do you know why I'm tying you up?"

"I disobeyed you."

"That's right. You ran when you should've stayed. What happens to bad girls, princess?"

"They have to beg."

I smiled. She wanted to play that game, did she? It occurred to me she'd run away from me on purpose. My wife. Forever testing me and pushing the boundaries so I'd give her what she wanted. I couldn't complain. I loved the way she teased me to the point of madness so I'd tie her up and fuck her without mercy.

"Then you know what to do."

I shifted over her. We weren't quite touching. Already she was straining upward, desperate for contact.

"Beg."

It was one simple command, but it made her go still. She looked so fucking sexy lying there at my mercy. Her lips glistened as she ran her tongue across them.

"Please, please use me. I'm yours to command. I'll let you do what you want. Use me like your fuck toy. I want you. I need you. I crave you."

Her sweet voice was music to my fucking ears. I leant towards her, brushing my lips along her jaw. She whimpered at the contact.

"Please, you drive me crazy, please. I want you. I want your cock, please. I need it."

"How much do you need it?"

My lips trailed lower, down her neck and reaching her collarbone. She trembled below me, her skin a scattering of goosebumps.

"More than anything. I'm aching. Fuck me. Hard. Please."

"What part of you is aching?"

My lips met her breast, tongue flicking out across a nipple. She arched into it.

"My pussy. I want your cock filling me. Only you can give me what I need. Only you fuck me deep and hard like I crave."

Her pleas were almost my undoing. I was so fucking close to losing control. My cock throbbed. Lust, need, desire punctuated each word she spoke.

"Spread your legs."

She did it without a single moment of hesitation. I looked down at her. My beautiful wife tied to our bed in paradise begging for my cock. Never did I expect to find anything as close to heaven as this. Never had I expected to find any sort of happiness in my life. But Avery had given me more than I ever deserved. She gave me everything I needed. And I gave her everything in return.

I sat up, pressing my palms against the backs of her thighs and slid inside her slick, deliciously tight heat. I shifted, moving my hands up to rest on the bed beside her head as I fucked her with long, hard strokes. She moaned and writhed beneath me, crying out when I thrust deeper.

"Aiden, please don't stop. Fuck. More, I need more."

"You want it harder. You want me to prove no one else can give it to you this good, don't you? Who do you belong to?"

Her eyes flew open and she stared up at me.

"You. Always you. Only you."

She looked so open and vulnerable. Her expression spoke volumes. Avery was mine. Heart, body and soul. I almost faltered in my thrusts. Fuck. She was everything. All I could ever need. All I could ever want.

I leant down, my breath dusting across her ear.

"And I'm yours, princess. I belong to you. Only you. Forever."

I kissed up her jaw and captured her mouth, tasting her, devouring her, claiming her as mine. I fucked her harder until she cried out in my mouth, trembling and shaking beneath me as her pussy clamped down on my cock. Fuck. She was so tight and wet and it was fucking amazing.

I shuddered above her, grunting as I came too, unable to hold back against the onslaught of her climax. My cock spurted deep inside her. The release was the sweetest damn fucking thing.

I tried not to collapse on top of her and squish her into the bed. Panting, I reached up and untied her hands, letting her wrap her arms around me and hold me. She kissed my cheek, murmuring how much she loved me in my ear.

Contentment washed over me. For the very first time, I felt free. Nothing holding me back or pulling me down. And it was all down to this girl clinging to me.

Fuck did I love her.

And fuck did she love me too.

Did I ever think I'd be walking along an empty beach with the sun setting on the horizon with the girl of my dreams?

Not once.

Avery's raven hair glittered in the dying light. She wore a black kaftan over her bikini. We were both barefoot as we strolled along, just enjoying the peace and listening to the waves lapping against the shore.

"Did you think we'd end up like this?" Avery asked, breaking the silence.

"Like what?"

"Together with everything behind us and only the future to look forward to."

I shook my head. I never considered what it'd be like when the empire was finally destroyed and the people responsible either dead or awaiting trial. As much as I hated my father still, he'd avenged my mother. I'd let go because it wouldn't make me happy to continue to want him gone. My destructive path of revenge was over. I no longer felt the urge to destroy everything. I wanted to build things instead. Build a life with the girl next to me most of all.

339

And a part of building that life was creating a home with her. When we returned to the UK, our home would be renovated completely. It was the very last thing John was doing for me before he left the country for good. Supervising the contractors. He was ready to retire and I couldn't blame him. The man was a fucking lifesaver and I'd never forget what he'd done for Avery and me.

"But you're happy, right? That it's all over."

I stopped, looking down at her as she came to a standstill too. I drew her closer to me, cupping her face.

"Avery, princess, I'm happy because I'm with you."

She bit her lip.

"Aiden…"

"Don't start getting all shy on me now. You're the reason for all of this, princess. You made it possible."

Her cheeks stained red.

"Quit being so… damn sweet."

I raised an eyebrow.

"Is this me being sweet? I just thought I was being honest."

"Damn it, Aiden. When you say stuff like that it makes me want to cry happy tears."

I grinned, stroking her cheek.

"No crying now. Not allowed tears in paradise."

I leant down, kissing her forehead.

"No? If I start crying, will you punish me?"

"No… I'll kiss away your tears."

"I'm warning you, any more of this and I will be sobbing on your chest."

Her doe eyes were bright with amusement, love shining in them too.

"No crying, princess. Not when we have so much to look forward to."

"We do?"

I nodded, leaning down towards her again.

"Yes, we're going home soon and we're going to start a new life together. Just you and me… and perhaps one day soon, we might add to that number too."

I'd thought about it long and fucking hard. The crazy thing about having a nephew, even if he wasn't a blood relation, and seeing how happy it made Ben and Skye was it made me crave that with Avery.

"Are you serious?" she whispered, reaching up and wrapping her hands around my neck.

"Very."

"Fuck… Fuck, I love you."

I smiled.

"I fucking love you too, princess."

I pulled her closer and kissed her under the light of the dying sun.

And nothing and no one could take that moment away from us.

I was hers.

And she was mine.

ACKNOWLEDGEMENTS

Thank you so much for taking the time to read this book. Where do I begin with this one? Writing the end of Aiden and Avery's story has been an emotional one. There were moments where I thought I'd never get through this book because I didn't want to say goodbye to them. Ultimately, they got their happy ending and I really hope that it was worth the wait.

I felt it was important to tell the story of what happened before Avery's birthday event and give an account of their wedding. This felt like a pivotal moment in their journey together. And they went through a hell of a lot of ups and downs after that along with heartache and turmoil. Aiden finally got his closure and Avery put her demons to rest.

As hard as saying goodbye is, I'm honoured I got to tell their story and be a part of their journey. I can only hope that you've all enjoyed it too.

A huge thank you to all my readers for sticking with Avery and Aiden. Especially my ARC readers! Knowing you've loved these two as much as I have gives me the utmost joy. As an author, knowing that my stories are enjoyed and loved is what keeps me going.

Thank you to my amazing Twitter Gang and everyone who's supported me on this journey. I really couldn't do any of this without you. Your support is invaluable and gives me the strength to carry on even when things get tough.

Another big thank you goes to my two writer besties – Sean and Sabrina. You two are my biggest inspirations. You give me hope. You give me strength. And you certainly give me all the best laughs too. I love you guys so much!

Sean – you always manage to cheer me up when I'm feeling down and are an amazing cheerleader. We celebrate each other's successes and I'm so lucky to call you my best friend.

Sab – you're simply one of the most amazing people I've ever met. You're my twin. My soulmate. My Savage Slytherin Sister. I honestly don't know what I'd do without you. Never stop believing in yourself. I'm so proud of you.

Thank you to my mum for reading all these stories and helping me proofread. You're an absolute star and I couldn't do this without you. Even if you do like to make crude jokes about it all!

And lastly, as always, my biggest thank you is to my husband. I genuinely have no way to tell you how much I appreciate your support. You've made it possible for me to achieve my dream to be a writer. I love you to the stars and back.

About The Author

Sarah writes dark, contemporary, erotic and paranormal romances. They adore all forms of steamy romance and can always be found with a book or ten on their Kindle. They love anti-heroes, alpha males and flawed characters with a little bit of darkness lurking within. Their writing buddies nicknamed Sarah: 'The Queen of Steam' for their pulse racing sex scenes which will leave you a little hot under the collar.

Born and raised in Sussex, UK near the Ashdown Forest, they grew up climbing trees and building Lego towns with their younger brother. Sarah fell in love with novels as teenager reading their aunt's historical regency romances. They have always loved the supernatural and exploring the darker side of romance and fantasy novels.

Sarah currently resides in the Scottish Highlands with their husband. Music is one of their biggest inspirations and they always have something on in the background whilst writing. They are an avid gamer and are often found hogging their husband's Xbox.

Made in United States
Troutdale, OR
09/28/2023

13266387R00212